P9-CNI-377

## Also by Ilyasah Shabazz

*Betty Before X*, with Newbery Honoree Renée Watson

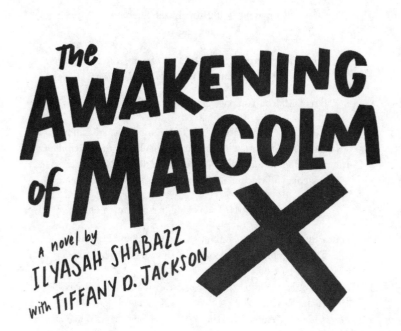

THE
AWAKENING
of MALCOLM
X

A novel by
ILYASAH SHABAZZ
with TIFFANY D. JACKSON

FARRAR STRAUS GIROUX
NEW YORK

Farrar Straus Giroux Books for Young Readers
An imprint of Macmillan Publishing Group, LLC
120 Broadway, New York, NY 10271
fiercereads.com

Copyright © 2021 by Ilyasah Shabazz
All rights reserved.

Word definitions transcribed by Malcolm are quoted from
*Merriam-Webster* and *The Oxford English Dictionary*.

Photo of Malcolm on page 306 courtesy of Ilyasah Shabazz.

Our books may be purchased in bulk for promotional, educational, or
business use. Please contact your local bookseller or the Macmillan
Corporate and Premium Sales Department at (800) 221-7945 ext. 5442
or by email at MacmillanSpecialMarkets@macmillan.com.

Library of Congress Cataloging-in-Publication Data

Names: Shabazz, Ilyasah, author. | Jackson, Tiffany D., author.
Title: The awakening of Malcolm X / Ilyasah Shabazz and
   Tiffany D. Jackson.
Description: First edition. | New York: Farrar Straus Giroux Books
   for Young Readers, 2021. | Sequel to X : a novel. | Audience:
   Ages 12–18. | Audience: Grades 10–12. | Summary: While in
   Charlestown Prison in the 1940s, young Malcolm Little reads
   all the books in the library, joins the debate team and the
   Nation of Islam, and emerges as Malcolm X.
Identifiers: LCCN 2020009789 | ISBN 9780374313296 (hardcover)
Subjects: LCSH: X, Malcolm, 1925–1965—Childhood and youth—
   Juvenile fiction. | CYAC: X, Malcolm, 1925–1965—
   Childhood and youth—Fiction. | Prisoners—Fiction. |
   Reformers—Fiction. | Racism—Fiction. | Civil rights—
   Fiction. | Black Muslims—Fiction. | African Americans—Fiction.
Classification: LCC PZ7.1.S47 Aw 2020 | DDC [Fic]—dc23
LC record available at https://lccn.loc.gov/2020009789

First edition, 2021
Book design by Cassie Gonzales
Printed in the United States of America

ISBN 978-0-374-31329-6 (hardcover)
1   3   5   7   9   10   8   6   4   2

This book is dedicated to my father, El-Hajj Malik El-Shabazz, Malcolm X. You marched to the beat of a different drummer in a lifelong quest for knowledge, truth, and justice. What a wonderful and exemplary teacher and leader you were and still are in our hearts, minds, and spirits! You continue to blaze a promising new trail for our people—and for all people. I am forever proud to be your daughter!

To my beloved mother, Dr. Betty Shabazz, who stood by her husband shoulder to shoulder, hand in hand—his muse, partner, and eternal friend. Together and apart, you taught us well and never dropped the baton of love and the pursuit of equality. You are forever etched in my heart.

And to the brave and bright young people of every race, creed, and color who have taken the baton firmly in hand, who will keep alive the work and spirit of Malcolm, Betty, and selfless teachers everywhere—past and present. It is you upon whom we rely to cross the finish line in the race for world peace and universal human rights.

And lastly—to the incarcerated. May God continue to bless each one of you with an abundance of love, faith, and determination.

—ILYASAH SHABAZZ

# The AWAKENING of MALCOLM X

# PART 1

# FEBRUARY 1946

"Are you sure about this, Red?"

Shorty paces, still in the same clothes they arrested us in five weeks ago, the cramped quarters of this cell making us feel like we're living inside an icebox.

"Man, you know I can't go to jail. I'm a musician. I got plans!"

"Don't sweat it, homeboy, it's cool," I reassure him. "We went over this. Just tell the judge and that jury it was my idea. Those cats will take it easy on you, for sure."

"But it *wasn't* your idea," Shorty counters, his voice sharp. "It was them girls! We're in here and they're out there jivin' us, man."

I shrug. "They ain't putting pretty girls like them in here. It's all a part of the play, you see? Sophia is just gonna tell them that we're not real robbers. Got it?"

And it's true. Sophia's idea to snatch loot from those empty homes was brilliant, but we're not hard criminals. We could barely break open a back door. Only reason we got caught was because I took that watch and tried to get it fixed.

Should've just walked myself right into the police station. It would've been faster.

"We're not going to get any real time. We're too young," I say. "They'll see neither of us have ever been to jail a day in our lives. Hell, we'll probably be out by the holidays, maybe even fall. I guarantee you, homeboy, they'll see we ain't no real criminals and let us go."

Plus, with Sophia sticking up for us, I have the ace of spades in my back pocket. We just have to play it cool.

Shorty rubs the back of his head. "You sure you trust her?"

"She don't want to lose me. She loves me, man. And maybe, maybe when this is all over, we'll be together for real, you know."

Shorty's lips press into a hard line.

"Don't know about this, Red. Something don't feel right. Those girls haven't even checked on us. It's been *five weeks*! They got us in here trapped like some slaves!"

Shorty shakes his head, chewing on his nails, eyes wide and jittery. It's strange to see him this way. He's cooler than a cucumber any other time. With so many days since my last high, it's hard to keep my composure. But I have to, for Shorty's sake. He's been there for me when I needed him the most. Only right to return the favor.

"Remember that day you told me you got cleared from the draft?" I ask. "And I caught the first thing smoking out of Harlem. Had to celebrate with you, man! We had on our clean threads, all them pretty girls eyeing us. And you and your band up on that stage at the Crow? Boy, you were something else. I had no idea you could blow like that!"

He chuckles. "Yeah. I remember. That night was something."

"Well, today is gonna be just as smooth, homeboy. Then . . . you'll be back with your band, playing that sax in supper clubs and ballrooms all over this city. Maybe even on tour. And I'll be your road manager."

"Hey! Who said I was hiring?"

"You know you gonna want your main man with you!"

He nods. "You brilliant, you got that gift, Red. Can't take credit for that. Aight, sounds good!"

We slap skins, a small smile returning to Shorty's face.

"We'll be back in Roxbury before you know it," I say.

Even if my heart is in Harlem.


Shorty and I enter the courtroom together. The charges:

- Breaking and entering
- Possession of stolen property
- Grand larceny
- Carrying a firearm

The words sound heavy and full of time.

On the stand, Sophia sniffles, her blond hair pinned back

off her face. I've never seen her dressed this way before. Not a slice of skin to be seen. She even has on eyeglasses. They make her look real sophisticated . . . and innocent. Something doesn't sit right in my gut. Maybe it's her getup, maybe it's because she won't look at me. I've tried for the last twenty minutes to smile at her so she knows I'm all right.

But why won't she look at me?

Head bent low, holding one of those little embroidered hankies, Sophia begins to whimper and the jury hangs on her every word. She licks her pink lips a few times. Something I've seen her do before . . . when she's about to lie.

"They're just so big," Sophia says. "I was scared to say no."

I sit up straight as my heart starts to race, my mouth going dry. Shorty's face crumples and pales as he turns to spot his mother in the audience. I don't move, can't look at Ella's face. It'll break me.

I turn to our lawyer, who seems uninterested in the proceedings.

"Aren't you gonna ask her questions or something? She's supposed to be on our side!"

"Nothing to say. She's not my witness. Prosecution brought her in." He rests his hands on the table. "She's their witness, not ours."

"They said if I didn't help them," Sophia cries, "they would . . . they . . . I was just trying to protect my little sister. She's only a kid, you know."

But *I'm* only a kid, I thought. And I was a kid when I met her.

"So this wasn't your idea?" the lawyer demands. "You had nothing to do with this plan."

"No. It was them. They took advantage of us. The tall one."

"What?" I mumble.

"They tricked us. I didn't know what I was doing," she says.

"But you drew the map!" I burst out. "You picked all the houses!"

The judge slams down his gavel three times. "ORDER! Counselor, control your client!"

My lawyer shushes me as Sophia's guilt-filled blue eyes finally meet mine.

"She's lying," I whisper, insides burning, as I watch her sit up there sniveling while we're down here in handcuffs.

"Be quiet. You shouldn't have been with a white woman anyway."

The jury leaves the courtroom to deliberate, a few of them staring me down on the way out, like they've already made up their minds.

Shorty palms the side of his head, and any confidence I had quickly dissolves into fear.

Eight to ten years.

The moment after our sentences are read, I look at Ella.

"I'm sorry," I cough out, just as Shorty faints, slumping to the floor.

The officers kick him a few times, yank him to his feet, and usher both of us out of the courtroom. I try to take one last look at Sophia, but she's gone.

Shorty and I are put on separate buses. I have no idea where he's going, they won't say. Fear spreads through my bones, pulsing.

The men on my bus are the kind of men I've met a hundred times before. Their faces stoic, eyes hard, staring straight ahead as we're driven over to Charlestown. The state prison on Lynde's Point. We are unloaded at the gate, ushered through a long dark corridor to frigid, windowless cement rooms. In an instant, I gag at the revolting, suffocating smell. Boots and screams echo all around us. Something squeaks under my shoe and I stumble.

"R-rats," I stammer, but none of the guards seem concerned.

"Line up!" a guard shouts.

"What's happening?" I whisper to the older brother beside me, heart pounding so loud I can barely hear myself think. "Where are we?"

But he says nothing as we're surrounded by guards, weapons drawn like a firing squad. My heart drops.

Oh, God, no . . .

"Niggers, strip!" a guard orders, and I watch the others begin to take off their clothes.

"Faster! Move it!" he screams, and I fumble with my belt, buttons, and laces, fingers trembling.

Even though I'm from Michigan, and have lived in Grand Rapids and East Lansing, I have never experienced any place colder than here. The kind of brutal cold that pinches the tip of your earlobes and won't let go. The cement floor is wet, my bare feet standing in a puddle of ice, as if it rained inside and froze solid. Is there a leak somewhere? But then I see it, the water hose. It comes alive with a shriek, and the water hits our bodies, slamming us into the cold cement wall with all its pressure. I huddle, letting it beat me.

God, please help me.

Water off. More shouting. Screaming. A hot, loud breath in my face. The brother next to me begins to cry. The guards inspect and shepherd us like cattle, pushing and kicking the ones who move too slow. Afraid the guards will shoot, I work fast to follow their orders. They give us dark blue uniforms and a few small items. Something jabs at my back. A baton.

"I SAID MOVE!" a guard barks in my face. My fists clench close to my body. We're lined up, heading down the tunnel, toward light. At the end is a counter, another guard working behind it. He hands me a piece of paper with the numbers 22843 scribbled on it.

"What's this for?" I ask.

He doesn't look up at me as he checks off something on his clipboard.

"Your new name, boy."

The guard shoves me forward into a massive hall. So many eyes and hard faces stare at us through thick iron bars. I try to get my bearings. The rancid smell, rodents scurrying across the floor, keys jangling in the guard's hands. He stops short in front of a cell the size of a closet and shoves me inside. No windows. The cement walls littered with scratches, closing in on me. My chest tightens with a pent-up scream as the door squeaks then slams shut behind me.

# CHAPTER 1

*If you stick a knife in my back nine inches and pull it out six inches,*
*there's no progress. If you pull it all the way out, that's not progress.*
*The progress is healing the wound that the blow made.*

—MALCOLM X

My mother's dress was sky blue with tiny white polka dots
sprinkled like snowflakes. She wore it with her pearls when
she went into town. She walked tall, head high, with a beautiful smile and skin bursting with pride so thick people felt
her before they saw her, wondering what this white woman
was doing with all these Negro children. All seven of us lined
up like ducklings behind her. Even when we were home, we
orbited her like the planets. We couldn't get enough of her.

I lay my head on her shoulder as she cradled Wesley in her
arms, singing to us in English, French, Creole, Yoruba. Eyes
closed, voice like a hummingbird. Mother soon fell asleep.
She must have been tired from staying up late the night
before, working on an article she was writing for the *Negro*

*World* newspaper. She was by far the most beautiful woman I'd ever seen. It was probably why Papa always brought something home for her after his travels—nutmeg, mint candies, new books.

In the living room, some of my brothers and sisters were hunched over their encyclopedias as news hissed from the radio. Outside, the sky was pinkish peach and orange as the Midwestern sun slowly set on Lansing, Michigan. I could smell Hilda's cinnamon hot cross buns rising in the oven and Mom's West Indian stewed chicken simmering on the stove next to a pot of greens seasoned with her own garden spices.

We were all together: Papa, Mom, Wilfred, Hilda, Philbert, me, Reginald, Wesley, Yvonne—even Robert. Though he wasn't born yet, he was there, and everything was perfect. Warm, cozy, safe. No one could harm us. No one could break us. Papa wouldn't let them. We were family.

But in a blink, it all changed.

Mom startled awake with a gasp that shot up from her toes.

"Mommy?" Hilda said from the stove, tending to the pot. "Mommy, are you okay?"

Mom placed a trembling palm on the table to balance herself, eyes searching, taking each of us in. Wilfred, the eldest, entered the kitchen, book still in hand, followed by the others.

"Where's your father?" she whispered.

"I think . . . he's in his room," Wilfred said.

"You think?" she snapped, passing the baby to Hilda. I scrambled out of her way as she rushed into the hall.

"Earl!" she called. "Earl! Where are you?"

There was a frantic desperation in her cries that we hadn't heard since the night the KKK set our first house on fire in Omaha. I remembered the way we had burst out into the night, her screams urging us to run. Philbert stood behind me, holding my shoulders, Reginald squeezing against my side.

Now we listened to my father's heavy footsteps slowly walk down the hall before he appeared at the kitchen doorway, dressed in his clay-brown tweed suit, hat in hand.

"Well, good morning, sleepyhead," Papa said to her with a grin. "You dozed off there real good."

She took in his tall, stocky frame and smooth black skin but didn't seem comforted by his presence. "Where are you going?"

Papa chuckled, fixing the brim of his hat. "Going into town to collect rent and money for the chickens."

Mom bit her bottom lip and shook her head real slowly. "No. Earl. Don't go."

"Woman, I am not afraid of those—"

"Earl, don't!" she snapped. "Just listen to me, now."

"Louise, don't start this funny business again. Now you know—"

Mom's voice became real soft, at the edge of tears. "Earl, if you go, you won't come back, ever!"

The room fell silent, even the radio lost signal. My heart started to race wildly. What did she mean, Papa wouldn't come back? Of course, he'd be back. He'd be back in time for supper. Then there would be work to do, meetings to attend, time to spend ministering to people and spreading Mr. Garvey's teachings. Papa said I could go with him again to the next meeting. It was good for my training, my organizing, my destiny. Papa said I was going to make a great leader someday.

My brothers and sisters huddled together by the table as if to keep warm, trying to make sense of Mom's words. Mom's words were always soft yet firm and true. She was never ever wrong. But these words, they frightened us, more than anything. I needed her to be wrong.

Papa touched the top of Mom's head, cradling her cheek with a smile. Papa, with a body as strong as the finest steel, could be tough on us kids, but he held a sweet spot for Mom. We could see it in his eyes, the way he looked at her, endearing and proud.

"Louise, don't fret, okay? I'll be back before supper. Nothing will ever take me away from our family. Nothing will ever take me away from you."

"Papa?" Wilfred started. He wasn't a man yet and he wouldn't dare question Papa's decisions, but the way Mom clutched herself, he at least had to try. "Uh, can I come with you?"

"No, son. I'll be back before you know it. You check on them chickens?"

"Yes, sir."

"Good," he mumbled. "Finish your studies and watch after your mother, you hear?"

"Yes, sir."

Papa nodded at the rest of us, put on his round spectacles, and headed down the hall. The front door creaked and slammed shut behind him. Mom stood there, staring at the door as if she hoped he'd change his mind. The door didn't open. A darkness fell over the house within seconds.

"Mommy?" Hilda asked gently. "Is it . . . is it one of your premonitions?"

Mom glanced down at me, her forehead creased with worry. She slid a hand down my cheek and said, "Malcolm. Malcolm? It's time for you to wake up, sweetheart."

Wake up? But I wasn't asleep.

"Huh, Mom? What are you talking about?"

"Malcolm, it's time."

Her voice sounded distant, far away, like an echo underwater. My arms and legs went numb. Felt like I was falling.

"Malcolm. Malcolm! It's time. Wake up!" she shrieked, her scream like a stuck piano key thumping through my head. I closed my eyes and pressed my ears into my skull.

*"Wake up, Malcolm! Wake up! Wake up! Malcolm, wake up!"*

"Wake up, nigger! Move your ass! Now!"

The wooden baton clacking against the bars of my prison cell rang like harsh chimes.

My eyes pop open wide at the wrinkled white face screaming inches from mine.

"Lazy nigger! Move it!"

The guard backs out the cell as a commotion stirs in the hall. I set a palm down on the rough sheets, staring up at the ceiling to ground myself. Every time I open my eyes, I remember where I am. I'm in hell and there's nowhere to run.

"Line up, convicts! Now! Eyes forward. Stand straight!"

I splash some cold brown water on my face and slip on my blue uniform.

Out of my cell, I fall into position as the guards take count. My legs are wobbly, eyes still adjusting, heart pounding like a mallet against my rib cage.

I was there. I was home. With my family. I could almost smell the wild honeysuckles outside our window.

I remember the day my mother predicted my father's death. I remember how he didn't come home in time for supper like he promised, and we went to bed empty, deprived of his presence. I remember drifting off to sleep next to Reginald and awaking to screams. Mom's screams. There's no scream more gutting than your mother's. It's the first sound we hear at birth, delivering us into this world.

*Time to wake up, Malcolm.*

"Cellblock Double A, sound off!"

One by one, each prisoner yells out his number. Who we were before ceased to exist the moment we entered this place. I'm no longer Malcolm Little nor Detroit Red. I'm 22843. They had us memorize it. They stripped us of our names, preventing us from being men, reducing us down to a bunch of numbers.

"Rough night?" a voice whispers behind me.

I look quick to my right, at my cell neighbor, Norm.

"You were talking in your sleep again—full-blown conversation. You be killing those dreams, youngin."

A dream. Yes, that's what it was. But how could a dream like that feel so real? The cold on the back of my neck is real, so are the lungs that can't seem to suck in enough air. I tighten my fists to keep cool around the guards.

"My old boss man, he used to say, 'Don't drink that stuff past midnight or you'll end up having some wild dreams about—'"

"Hey! You wanna go to the hole, convict?" a guard snaps.

Norm straightens his back, staring straight ahead. In the wet cold, I see his breath billowing around his dark skin.

*Time to wake up, Malcolm.*

I don't consider myself a superstitious man in no kind of way, but my mother's dreams were vivid snapshots that could foretell the future, sweeping any doubting words right out your mouth. Did she dream I'd get locked up in this hellhole?

With lineup complete, they send us out single file, barking orders and threats as we march on cue like marionettes. In the mess hall, I make eye contact with one of the cooks, Jimmy. We can communicate without words.

"How's it going, homeboy?" He winks.

"Can't complain but I do." I nod, leaning in. "Just another day in paradise."

He chuckles. "Keep on dreaming, homeboy. You'll be there soon enough."

He nods and sneaks a matchbook next to my bowl of hard oatmeal. Good ole Jimmy, always dishing out encouragement with a side of nutmeg. I slip the nutmeg into my cup of water, and take it back like a shot. It's not reefer but it's enough to take the edge off that dream. I can still hear Mom's voice in my head. I don't want her voice with me in here. I don't want the reminder that I've failed the only people who truly love me. I don't want to wake up. I don't want to be here—

"Hey, Little," Walter from the shop says. "You see this? There's gonna be a fight in a few weeks."

He slides a newspaper my way. A fight would do me solid

right about now. Could set up some bets with a few of the cats I've made good with in here. I scan the headline, noticing the date underneath. May 19.

Today is my birthday. I'm twenty-one years old.

I fold up the paper as if it never touched my hand.


Charlestown State Prison is about seven miles from Roxbury. Seven miles from the second place I called "home." That's what drives me to madness. So close yet too far to comprehend. I wonder if Fat Frankie is still hustling folks with his card tricks and who might be singing at Roseland tonight and what Ella has cooking on the stove. Stuff that no longer matters as long as I'm locked up in this hellhole.

Here in Charlestown, every day is the same day:

> **6:00 a.m.** Alarm
>
> **6:30 a.m.** Shower/handle your personal business
>
> **7:00 a.m.** 30 minutes for breakfast
>
> **8:00 a.m.** Slave/Work detail
>
> **11:00 a.m.** 30 minutes for lunch
>
> **12:00 p.m.** Slave/Work detail
>
> **3:00 p.m.** Quitting time
>
> **4:00 p.m.** The yard
>
> **5:00 p.m.** 30 minutes for supper

**6:00 p.m.** Remain in cellblock housing area

**8:00 p.m.** Return to cell

**10:00 p.m.** Lights-out

Seems real simple, but the seconds pass like hours, days like months. This place is an old barracks dump designed by someone who has no regard for human life. So old it should be condemned. Wouldn't wish this on my worst enemy. I've been locked up for the past three months. Could probably tell you the time down to the second even without a watch.

But . . . a watch is how I ended up here in the first place. A watch I stole and took to the pawnshop for repairs instead of selling it to the highest bidder. When I went to pick it up, that's when the cops got me.

I'm six foot four, size fourteen shoe. My iron cage is no wider than the length of my stretched-out arms, palms up. I call it a cage because that's exactly what it is. A place where they put stray animals, as if to tame them into submission. But they can't tame me, they can never tame me. Something's churning fast inside my chest, making it hard to sit still. I pace up and down, around and around. Each turn makes me question all the other turns I could've made in my life. How did I get here?

*4KD-589. 4KD-590. 4KD-591. 4KD-592.*

My work detail is in the license-plate shop. I'm stationed

at the conveyor belt, painting freshly pressed Massachusetts license plates dark hunter green. When my mind is not in a fog, I can still memorize numbers like West Indian Archie showed me. He was the biggest player in the Harlem numbers game. Taught me everything there was to know about the hustle . . . until he tried to kill me for it.

By now, I know the license-plate numbers of at least a thousand cars out on the road . . . driving.

Free.

"Hey now, young brother, steady on those strokes!"

That's Bembry. Works on the conveyor line, too. He's one of the older prisoners. There's a bunch of them down here, from all different walks of life, cracking jokes about everything under the sun as if this place is a country club. Not me, though, I keep to myself. There's nothing funny about being in here.

"You know, I wouldn't mind doing this type of work on the outside," Bembry says. He's a tall, fair-skinned man with a heap of freckles scattered on his face. "Making a good living."

"Can't see it making no real money, tho," says Leefoy, a burly, brown-skinned man with a bald head. Everyone calls him Big Lee. He lays the big sheets of tin down to be pressed with numbers. He's always hollering about Jesus, and today I hope he keeps his comments to himself. Especially when Mom's words are still floating in my head.

*Wake up, Malcolm.*

"This is still good work at the end of the day," Bembry says. "Come in here, do what needs to be done, break for lunch, finish for the day, go home to the wife and kids."

There's a sadness in his voice. Not sure if he has a wife and kids, or maybe he's just thinking of a life he wishes he could have. This place will do that to you.

"Probably get myself a nice house. No apartment, a house! Pay for it with my own money, with a big kitchen for the wife, you know, since she likes to cook and all. Maybe one of them nice, clean Ford cars for one of these plates and—Hey, hey now! Watch out with that, young brother." Bembry glares at me over the presser. "You'll get paint over everything, then we'll all be scrubbing this machine down!"

All the men chuckle.

"Car, house, and family? Sounds like you trying to live that American dream, Bembry!" Big Lee says.

American dream. Papa used to talk about that. How, whenever they came up with that talk, it wasn't meant for us Negroes. In this cage or on the outside, it's all a nightmare at the end of the day. This world doesn't give a damn about our dreams.

Bembry shrugs. "Or just a dream. We all need to have them. Life ain't worth living without it and—Hold on now, young brother. You gotta be careful with her. You know, it's not always about getting it done, but getting it *right*."

Bembry's voice is calming, like the cup of tea Mom used to fix when we had colds. No one even minds his chastising.

"Well, God willing," Big Lee says, "you'll be blessed with that house one day."

Bembry and I catch eyes.

God willing. That's another phrase that wasn't meant for Negroes. Did God will this for us? I look around the room, at all these different faces. Hundreds of weary Negroes living behind these bars, pressing plates for cars we'll never drive or pay we'll never get. What type of God would let this happen?

"Indeed you will, my brother," a Muslim guy says. That's Walter, or Kabir Muhammad, but everyone still calls him Walter. He operates the roller that turns the raised letters white after the plates dry.

"The *Honorable* Elijah Muhammad says, 'What we long for, will finally appear.'"

But I didn't want to talk about the Lord, Jesus, or any of those deities. Who cares what they say or will? They mean nothing to me.

I clutch a plate in my hand, ready to snap it in two.

"You all right there, young brother?" Bembry says to me, eyeing my white knuckles.

I don't answer. Afraid to say one word while the fire sizzling inside me is ready to boil over.

After dinner, I sit on my creaking wiry mattress, wondering how many other Negroes slept right here in this space. Hundreds? Thousands?

But the worst part is the smell. One hundred and forty years of cumulative funk.

A mixed batch of sweaty bodies, vomit, and hundreds of shit buckets baked into the granite walls, our clothes, our skin. We eat with the stench. We brush our teeth with the stench. We clean our bodies with the stench.

How can Walter and Big Lee talk of salvation when they are surrounded by hell?

Still, the strength in their voices, their plans for the future remind me of Mom. The way she used to speak of our past, our history.

Outside the screen door, royal-blue butterflies fluttered and danced as wind whispered through the cracks in our home.

"Malcolm. Malcolm?"

Mom.

She gently turned my chin in her direction. Her face could look so pale at times, like the cream you put in your coffee. Pearls shined like white marbles around her neck, her long hair tucked into a neat bun. But her smile—the way her teeth sparkled—always reminded me of sunny days, no matter the cold digging holes into my bones.

"Now, what did I just say?"

The sweet smell of simmering greens filled my nose. At the table in our kitchen, I was surrounded by Wilfred, Hilda, Philbert, Wesley, and Yvonne. Vegetables hung out of a boiling pot of stew, and a *Negro World* newspaper was in Mom's hands as she tapped her foot.

"Um, I don't know," I admitted.

Mom sighed and folded her paper.

"You have to listen, Malcolm. You will not learn anything if you don't listen. Your life will be meaningless if you don't learn." She stopped to give us all a hard look. "Do you hear me, children?"

"Yes, ma'am," we said in unison.

She didn't look satisfied.

"What are the principles that define us?"

"Self-love. Self-reliance. Unity," Wilfred said.

"See, Malcolm," Philbert teased, punching me in the shoulder. "Pay attention and stop being a stupid nigger."

"You watch your mouth, young man!" Mom snapped, slamming the paper on the table and rattling the dishes. "We don't use that word around here, not in this house. You hear me?"

"But . . . aren't we niggers, Mom?" Philbert said. "That's what white folks call us."

Mom's eyes grew hard as she stared through him. "Who defines this word *nigger*?"

"The white bigot," we said in unison.

"And for what purpose?"

"I don't know," I said.

Wilfred turned to me and said, "White bigots made up names to keep 'Blacks' feeling bad about ourselves. To keep us thinking that we're worthless. Blaming it on the color of our skin."

"You are Black, like your papa," Mom said, shaking her head. "Proud, smart, and Black. Beautifully Black, Scholarly Black, Lovingly Black. You hear me? You are a child of God, strong and protected by the universe. Now, Malcolm, answer my question—where do you come from?"

"Um, from Omaha, Nebraska, and Lansing, Michigan."

My sisters and brothers snickered at me. Mom slowly shook her head.

"No, Malcolm. Where are your roots from, your heritage, my love?"

"Oh," I said. "My heritage is from Africa. The kingdom of Benin, which once encompassed all the land of West Africa before the Europeans colonized it. We were known for the riches and craftsmanship of precious metals—like gold— iron, brass, and even wood and ivory. We are also known for our wisdom, intellect, and democracy."

"Correct. You have rich African blood in your veins. Don't

you, young man?" Mom's voice calmed. "The blood of kings and queens, inventors, farmers, and scholars. My grandparents and your great-grandparents are Yoruba from what is presently Nigeria. They sailed to the Caribbean island of Grenada as emigrants. Your great-grandparents' daughter is my mother. My father was a Scottish man who . . . was wicked to my mum. Hilda, tell me about your father's great-grandfather."

"Papa said his name is Hajja and he was from Mali, where the Dogon tribe is from," she said proudly. "The Dogon tribe dates back thousands of years and they are also known for their knowledge of astronomy and their superior intellect. Papa said that's why we're so smart."

Mom smiled and talked more about the different countries in Africa and why it's important to know your roots. She said that the Dogon were some of the smartest people in all humanity. Europeans were intrigued by the Dogon people because of their knowledge of the companion Sirius B star, which orbits Sirius A.

"So you see, we came from somewhere. We have an identity, a culture, a history, long before the European colonizers invaded the continent, and long before Christopher Columbus stumbled upon the Americas. Long before slavery existed. Do you understand me, children? Black people were compassionate and built thriving civilizations."

She passed me one of my favorite books to look at. It had

pictures of far-off places. Pictures of pyramids, people, lions, zebras, and turquoise oceans. Even pictures of Mansa Musa, the wealthiest man in the whole wide world, who lived in Mali and looked so much like Papa. Except he wore a turban, and Papa wore a top hat.

"Maybe I'll go there sometime," I said. "To Africa."

My brothers and sisters laughed.

"How are you going to do that, silly?" Yvonne giggled.

Mom's lips turned into a curved smile. A proud smile. "I hope you do. I hope we all do, one day."

Hilda tended to the pot of dandelion stew on the stove. The stew was never filling but my mouth watered for it nonetheless. Mom said it had all the nutrients we needed.

Outside, the royal-blue butterflies danced among the sunflowers. I wanted to run outside, barefoot on the thick green grass, and chase after them. Add them to my collection next to our library. Then, run farther and farther. Run straight to Africa, Asia, South and Central America, and then Europe. I wanted to see the world before returning back home to America, to Michigan, to Lansing.

The front door slammed. Reginald, all wobbly legs, skin and bones, rushed into the kitchen, a knit sack hanging over his shoulder.

"Sorry I'm late!"

"I've been wondering what happened to you, dear," Mom said, crossing her arms. "What do you have there?"

Reginald dumped the bag on the counter, the contents falling like bricks.

"Bread."

Hilda took a loaf and banged it against the counter.

"You mean *rocks*."

"It'll go nice with the stew," Mom corrected her. "Come now, let's eat."

Mom removed her shoes, massaging the balls of her feet while Yvonne sawed through the bread and Hilda ladled stew into our bowls.

Mom rinsed her hands before joining us as we bowed our heads in unison for prayer.

I dipped a piece of bread into the stew to soften it, and everyone else did the same.

"While you all are eating supper," Mom said, laying her spoon on the table, "I'll read one of these old letters from Papa."

The table stilled, the mention of Papa casting some type of spell on us. Mom pretended not to notice as she unfolded the letter, reading it aloud:

My Dearest Wife,

I trust that all is well and prosperous at home. It is good to hear the children are doing well and learning about truth and justice for Black people of the world. It is important that they see themselves

31

*outside of the four-square-mile radius in which they live. They must see themselves as global citizens, not as minorities, and have a healthy and positive sense of who they are and of those around them.*

Papa wrote about his travels to different towns where he preached about the injustices of the world. He ministered to Black folk, encouraging them to be self-sufficient and to not rely on the government, which historically had not been a friend to them. Papa was the chapter president of Marcus Garvey's Universal Negro Improvement Association, an organization that commanded millions of followers worldwide. And folks looked up to Papa. I looked up to him most of all. Mom was right—listening to Papa's letter brought us some comfort, reminded us to be proud of all the great work Papa had done.

"Mom," Wesley asked in a small voice. "Why did Papa die?"

The question whipped like an ice storm around the room, freezing us solid with our spoons raised in midair.

Mom took a steady breath.

"Papa didn't die. Papa was killed," she said, her eyes hardening. "He was killed for his kindness. He was killed for trying to invoke change in our people, to wake them up. He was killed by ignorant men. You see, Black people all around the world endured hundreds of years of chattel slavery—they were hunted, stolen, tortured, separated from families, forbidden to read and write. There were no laws to protect us from these criminal acts, you see. And your father, he served a mighty God. He challenged us to stand up and to restore our own humanity. You must never forget that. You hear me?"

Reginald looked across the table at me, his eyes softening.

Wesley eyed the floor. "Will they . . . kill everyone like that?"

My veins felt heavy, weighing me down into the seat. I wanted to reach across the table, zip Wesley's mouth shut.

Mom softly cupped the side of Wesley's cheek, and her words came out like a soothing song.

"No, baby. They won't kill everyone. But they will try to kill the ones who they fear will bring unity to the masses. The ones who will challenge the unlawful crimes against humanity."

"Why does God let this happen to us?" Reginald asked.

But Mom looked directly at me. "To make us strong. To remind us of the fire within. Your papa, he was like a match, ready to set the world on fire with his light, when some just wanted to stay in the dark. He said you're either part of the problem or part of the solution. No middle ground, one or the other. So are you going to be a light or are you going to dim your light?"

"But," I said, "why did Papa have to be the one to die?"

Mom smiled at me. "Sometimes change requires the biggest sacrifice, my love. Your father, he lives on forever. He lives in each one of you. You can call on him whenever you need him. He is always with you."

By lights-out, they finally come around to empty our dump pails. I gag as the cart squeaks by, wondering how Shorty's faring, wondering if he's as lonely as me.

Wherever he is.

# CHAPTER 2

*You can't separate peace from freedom because no one can be at peace
unless he has his freedom.*

— MALCOLM X

My half sister, Ella, sits across from me. A spot of light in the
darkness.

"Did you hear me?" she asks, her voice hard.

The room spins and I place a shaky hand on the table to
steady myself. For a moment, I forgot where I was. Then it
comes back, hitting me like a train until my chest caves in.

I remember the courtroom, the way Sophia sobbed on the
stand, tears streaming down her white cheeks, her fire-red
husband angry enough to spit glass. I remember the judge
slamming down charges—fourteen counts, each one with
eight to ten years, to be served concurrently, luckily. Lawyer
said he went "easy" on me because I'm still just a kid. But I
know white people who've done worse and haven't spent a
minute in a place like this.

"Yeah. Yes," I whisper, and clear my throat, folding my hands together.

Ella watches my every move, studying me. She was the first to visit me, though I told her to stay home. I didn't want anyone seeing me in *this* dump. But Ella has never been good at taking orders.

The visitors' center is much like the mess hall but a little nicer, if that's possible. Long wooden tables in rows of three and high barred windows. Visitors sit on one side and prisoners on the other. Hours vary by the day. Sometimes folks travel half a day or more to see their loved ones only for the warden to shut down visits for the week. So families make a long trek for nothing. Guards canvass the perimeter of the room, gripping their holsters, slapping batons in their palms. Exerting a false superiority.

Wonder if she can smell it. The funk hovering around us like a fog. Do I smell of it? Will she tell my brothers and sisters that I have hit rock bottom and reek of desperation?

Ella shakes her head and starts talking. Telling me all the gossip on the Hill, which isn't much of anything I am interested in. I don't want to hear about her uppity friends' progress. I want to know what jive is happening in Roxbury. What's the latest tune everyone is hopping to? What's happening in Harlem? What number hit? What's going on in the real world? But how can I ask her about what she's never tasted?

There are a few families in the room with us: A mother visiting her son. Two women—one young, one old—visiting their brother. Another mother with five children visiting their father—I recognize him from the license-plate shop. He's been in Charlestown for at least a decade. Some of those children don't even look that old. Two tables over, a little boy squeezing a teddy bear sits next to his mother, visiting a cat from my unit named Lightning. The woman is a piece of melted caramel with them pretty red lips and eyes that make you feel that everything will be all right. The little boy could be Lightning's twin. She reaches across the table and tries to take Lightning's hand.

"NO TOUCHING!" the guard barks, spit flying out his skinny lips. Veins bulging on the sides of his temples. He slams his baton on the table. Everyone jumps, gasping. The little boy drops his bear, crying.

"Didn't I say no touching?!"

"Sss-sorry," Ms. Caramel whimpers at the guard.

He smirks, peering down at her, as if he could see down her dress.

The walls squeeze real tight around us. Cats look at one another. If someone makes a wrong move, they can shut visitation down, throw us all in the hole.

"Hey, man. Uh . . . she didn't mean it, she didn't know," Lightning begs, holding his hands up, then glances at her. "It's all right, baby. It's all right."

The little boy stares at the guard from within his mother's embrace, eyes wide and filled with tears. Makes me almost glad I don't have children. I would never want them to feel helpless and unprotected, or to see their father in here.

The guard walks off, swinging his baton. I scratch the back of my neck. Ella, her face almost pale from watching it all unfold, swallows hard.

"Why would you give your power to these monsters? Are you eating?" she asks, worry in her eyes. "You're all skin and bones."

Ella looks older in the face than I remember. The darkness of this dungeon makes anyone who enters appear meek and helpless. Mind games, prisons are all about mind games. First, they make you believe you're an animal, then they make you believe you're easy prey to kill.

"Yup. Serving me the finest chicken fried steak in here," I chuckle, and pat my empty stomach. It aches just from the sound of her voice, remembering the good meals she used to cook. Her oven-roasted chicken, her okra, her mac and cheese, and her warm apple cobbler with a scoop of my favorite strawberry ice cream. I could sure use a plate of that right now.

"How do you find a way to make a joke at a time like this?" Ella huffs.

My sister, always stuck on what I *should* be doing rather than what's real. Here I am in prison and she's still trying to give me orders.

She rubs her hands as if starting a fire, then blows into her cupped palms.

"It's freezing, Malcolm. Can I send you a proper sweater? My heavens. Will they let you have that, at least?"

I'm so numb I barely notice the cold anymore.

"No. They make us wear these stupid thin jackets," I mumble. "Hey, I heard there's a big fight coming up in a few weeks. Please lay a bet for me, will you?"

Ella's gaze drops to the table. "Oh, Malcolm."

Disappointment. That's why I didn't want her to come. I don't want to see myself in her eyes. In our father's eyes. I don't want to see the disappointment.

"Well, I just hope you see the good in this lesson," she says.

"Lesson?"

"Yes. Everything we go through in this life is meant to teach us something, one way or another."

I squeeze my fist under the table. "Well, that's real easy for you to say when you're not the one in here."

"You're right, I'm not. You are. This is *your* journey. Everyone has their own."

"So you think I was meant for this?"

She shakes her head. "You never had to sleep anywhere but

in your own bed. And you've been sleeping for a while. You've been spoiled, pampered, living . . . that life. Now you're in a place like this, with no power, and you still don't know how to wake up."

*Wake up, Malcolm.*

I shake the noise out of my ear.

"Are you okay?"

"Um . . . I'm . . . yeah."

She frowns. "Hilda sent a letter. Family's asking about you. They want to come see you."

"Tell them I'm fine."

"But you're not fine, are you? You need your family. Now more than ever."

"I don't need nobody, you understand?"

Ella leans away from me.

"What's . . . gotten into you, Malcolm? When you first came to Boston . . ." She puts her head in her hands for what feels like forever. "Hilda blames me. All your brothers and sisters think this is my fault. That I encouraged you to run wild, hanging out with them hoodlums, and that I knew, just knew, you'd end up in a place like this. Because Papa left my mama to be with yours. But we are blood, Malcolm. I didn't wish this for you."

I want to tell her how she has so much of our father in her face, but I don't.

"I pray for you, Malcolm. Every night, I'm on my knees

praying hard to the Lord to protect you from these animals and restore your mind. I pray to God."

The word *God* made me want to spit. Is God gonna get me out of here? Where was God when Papa was killed? When they took away Mom and locked her up in an institution? Where was *He* then?

"Don't waste your breath." I shove my seat back and stand. "Don't pray for me. I don't want nobody praying for me for nothing. God? *He* ain't been there for me before, and *He* sure ain't here now."

The guards flinch. "Little! Back in your chair."

"We done here," I bark back.

"Little, I said get in your seat."

Ella reaches for my hand. "Malcolm, I'm just trying to—"

"NO TOUCHING!"

Ella reels back, her arms up as if to block a hit.

"Okay, visitation is over. Everybody up!" Ella doesn't like anybody telling her what to do, especially no white man, so she stays there.

The guards descend, yanking each prisoner by the arm without a moment to say goodbye, slapping on cuffs, hauling us away, leaving women and children in tears as they see their men, their so-called protectors, powerless this way.

This is the picture they paint of us, this is the nightmare they give our children. Makes me want to punch the guard in his face and shove a knee in his stomach.

My Dear Brother,

How are you? I pray this letter finds you well. Ella said she is working on getting you moved from that dreadful place. Said last time she visited, you were as thin as a twig. You can't be tall like Papa and thin as a rail. Are you eating? Why haven't you written back to my last letter? I know I wrote to the right address. Your family is very concerned about you.

Things are fine here in Lansing. Been looking through some of Papa's old books I had stored. Do you remember how well Mom used to take care of them? The way she made us read them over and over again, and then we had to wipe them clean before putting them back in the cupboard? I finally understand why reading was so important to Mother. It was also important to Papa and to Mr. Garvey. Reading helps you find new ways of looking at the world in which we live. We discover new skills and ideas toward becoming better people and how to improve our situations. That must be what drove Papa to strive for perfection in all he did. I'm sure I'm not telling you anything new. Remember how you would write your own books and then read them to us? *You are a perfectionist, too. You loved to read. I hope you're keeping it up. "Reading maketh the full man."*

*Daddy always said you were just like him. Remember who you are, Malcolm. That's the only way you'll find solace in your time of need.*

*Your Big Sister,*

*Hilda*

There is a small fire burning in my fingertips. Every morning, I wake up and feel it there first. Under my nails, crawling up to my knuckles, covering my hands. Gloves of flames spread. Then arms, chest, and legs blaze until my whole body is covered.

Big Lee has a deep bass voice, like a blues singer who lost his guitar. Used to hear men like him singing on the road all the time, in juke joints and speakeasies, where cats just kicked it with one another and danced freely. Drinking homemade moonshine without a worry in the world.

I sit in the back row of the chapel now, listening to him sing. Reminds me of Paul Robeson's bass-baritone.

*"Mary had a golden chaaaaaiiiiiin, ev'ry link waaaaas my Jeeeesus' naaaaaaaame . . ."*

Big Lee stands at the front of the chapel, eyes closed, mouth grinning. He sings all the time in the shop or in the mess hall, trying to ease spirits. Those old-timey Negro songs don't do nothing but make me angrier, that God would give a man such a gift and let him rot.

The chaplain runs Bible study on Mondays and Wednesdays. The chapel is nothing but a room with a wooden cross hanging on the wall behind the pulpit and a picture of a white Jesus. Papa said Jesus was Black, with woolly hair and feet of bronze.

You can still smell the stench in this so-called sanctuary, feel the draft through our paper jackets. There are more of us here today. Yesterday, another prisoner hanged himself with his bedsheets. That's the seventh suicide this month. Your mind plays tricks on you. The escape route seems easier than living, I guess.

Maybe some of us are here trying to find meaning in our existence. Maybe not. I only go to chapel to keep from having to stay in my iron cage longer than I have to. Helps pass the time. But after Ella's visit, the fire burning inside me feels more urgent. I thought the two extra matchbooks of nutmeg I had at breakfast would curb an explosion, but I feel nothing. The fire swallows anything I put inside my body, trying to keep the flames at bay. No way out.

Jimmy sits next to me, humming along with Big Lee as he ends his hymn. Everyone in the room applauds like they were watching a performance of Duke Ellington and his big band. Jimmy claps the loudest.

The chaplain looks like most white men do, pale and lanky, spitting words of authority from a book not made to inspire or rehabilitate. A book not made for us. Jimmy hangs on to every word like a helpless child, grunting along with the flat sermon.

"Homeboy, you really into all that?" I whisper to him. "You don't believe this shit, do you?"

He cuts me a surprised glare. "The question is, why ain't YOU a believer, homeboy?"

He can't be serious. I could think of a dozen reasons.

"As it says in John 3:16," the chaplain shouts. "'For God so loved the world that *He* gave His one and only Son, that who shall ever believe in Him shall not perish but have eternal life.'"

*Ha!* I chuckle. Loud.

"Excuse me?" the chaplain squeaks.

The entire room turns to stare. Big Lee raises an eyebrow.

"Yes, sir?" I say with a hint of amusement.

"Is there something . . . funny?"

"Nothing really, it's just brainwash. I think it's wrong for you, as a man of God, to be lying to us like this. Like you really care about us."

The room stirs. Panicked, Jimmy jumps to his feet, cap in his hands.

"Uhhhh, s-sorry sir," he stutters. "Young brother's not feeling too well."

"I can speak for myself," I say, still seated, crossing my arms.

Jimmy plops back into his seat, muttering under his breath, "Cool it, homeboy. You trying to get yourself buried? What's going on?"

The chaplain collects himself. "And what part do you not believe?"

"He loved His Son so much that He sacrificed Him to bloodthirsty men? That sounds like love to you? Sacrificing His only child! Would you do that? Would any of you?"

The chaplain's face turns red. "God's love is greater than our understanding."

I laugh. "Where are you getting this stuff from?"

"It's good to have questions, Malcolm. But about your faith, lean not on your own understanding . . ."

Something about him saying my name, as if he knows me, makes my skin crawl. He doesn't have the right to speak my name.

"Oh, you're very mistaken. I don't have questions. I have answers. And the answer is God's words ain't in that book and it damn sure ain't in here."

In my whole life, I ain't ever heard grown men gasp like that before. Stunned, Big Lee can only shake his head and turn away.

The chaplain swallows, now sweating. "Malcolm . . . are you saying—"

"Yes, I'm saying it! God ain't here! He ain't with you! If He was, then wouldn't you and Him try to help us? I mean, really help us. You think God allows families to be ripped apart? You think God would allow Negroes to suffer like this? In this pigpen? I don't need some kinda God that exists one way for you and another way for me! What kind of God is that? Huh?"

The chaplain stands frozen for a few moments until he finally gives the two guards in the back a small nod. Jimmy whips in my direction and taps my leg. "You gotta cool it or you'll—"

"All right you, up! Let's go."

The guard's voice makes Jimmy jerk upright, eyes forward.

"Why? This is Bible study and I'm studying," I snap.

"Not anymore," the guard says. "Let's go!"

I don't know how it happens. I think the thought of their filthy hands touching me sets the fire ablaze and I slap one white hand away, then another, and another, until we're all on the ground, wrestling. I spot Jimmy's face, the look of terror in his eyes. I see that helplessness and I start fighting harder.

"That's it! Back to the hole."

The word *hole* sends a chill up my spine that extinguishes the fire, but I'm still swinging and slapping the hands trying to grab me, not so much in rage now but in fear.

"No! No!" I gurgle out. I can't, I can't be there again. I try to stay tough but I can't anymore. "Please, please," I cry. "Please don't send me back. Please!"

Six guards with their six batons, with their knees, elbows, and fists, knock me out cold.

The type of cold in the hole can match the Upper Peninsula of Michigan's worst winters. Teeth chattering, I awaken— senses skewed, eye swollen, lip busted, my jaw and back sore. My one eye is barely open and I see nothing but darkness. The type of darkness that makes me remember the first time I was in the hole. How the isolation swallowed me, ripping apart any dignity I had left. How I begged, devoured stale bread, and wept for Mom.

"No," I murmur and stumble to my feet. I can't go back to that place.

The hole is so dark that I can't see my hands in front of my very own eyes. Fumbling, I pat the walls, fall over the cot low on the ground, and hit the door.

The hole feels tighter this time. It's not just a box, but a coffin, shrunk airtight. Breathe. I'm desperate for fresh air. My family. I need my family.

"Let me out! Let me out!" I scream, but it comes out as a whimper until I'm weeping on the cold, damp ground. The steel door has deep, hectic grooves. Dents. From another poor soul thrown in here. This place is for no man.

And I demand again, *Where is God?*

What little light there is in Charlestown hurts like a thousand pieces of glass thrown in my face when they finally open the door. I block the glare with my hand, squinting up from my sunken place on the cold ground.

"All right, Little. You're out."

My eyes try to adjust to the figure standing at the door. "What . . . day is it?" My throat is scratchy, maybe from sobbing.

"You wanna stay in here? Move it, prisoner!"

I'm led back to my cell, the stench of the halls waking me up. There's no sense of time in the hole. You are only aware of your breath, your thoughts, and the darkness. My cell hasn't changed. Still the same way I left it. The wooden bucket hadn't been dumped, the smell now baked into the slabs of cement and cast-iron bars. I change my uniform, noticing it fits looser than before, and glide a trembling hand down my side, ribs pushing through my skin.

They can do it again, I thought. They can put me in the hole whenever they want, for however long they want. They could destroy me, kill me . . . if I let them.

First things first, I need to stop by the kitchen for a fix. The fight gotta be coming up, and I need to make my rounds and collect bets. I need to be ready before someone steals my coins. It's not like it's real money but it's all we got in here: a few pennies, nickels, and maybe some loosies. Heck, keeping busy is the only way to stay sane in this hellhole.

Haven't written any letters in . . . who knows how long. Long before they dropped me in the hole. My family must be looking for me. Thinking of them keeps me sane, gives me something to live for.

It's late so I head straight for the mess hall, last in line to grab a tray. A hush takes over the room. Eyes tracking my every move. Everyone is staring. Hard. Even the cooks look at me funny. Don't know if everyone's surprised to see me so soon or if it's been longer than I thought.

I take my tray to an empty table, facing the crowd, the tallest cat here, scanning the room for a newspaper. What's the date?

"Hey, they let you out. Glad you still alive, man." Norm stands at the head of the table, looking to join me, and I don't stop him.

"Alive?"

"You talked back to the chaplain and the guards."

Norm pauses to bow his head, praying over his lunch slop. With a greedy smile, he dives into his food like it's a feast, the best thing he's ever eaten. Norm ain't that much older than me. Maybe he's twenty-two. Reminds me of Wilfred with his broad shoulders and height, but still not taller than I am. Not sure where he's from, but wouldn't be surprised if we were distant cousins.

"You know," he starts, using a fork to mix his hard rice. "Folks around here been calling you Satan."

I stare at him for a moment, waiting for the punch line. He just eats his food.

"Satan? What for?" I snap. "And say, what day is it?"

"Man, it's Tuesday. Anyway, it's because you questioning God and you talking to the white folk like they Negroes. Like you not scared of nobody."

So that's why everyone's staring. They think I'm Satan in the flesh. Ha, if I'm Satan, then who are they? Who are the guards that throw us in the hole and gang up on us? Six of them beating one defenseless man. We ain't got no guns. They don't know a damn thing!

I snarl, taking a giant sip of water. "Don't care what anyone thinks of me. Doesn't make me anymore free than the rest of you. We all locked up. We all in this nightmare together."

Big Lee stops at our table with his empty tray, his face expressionless.

"Three," he says, slow.

Norm and I glance at each other, waiting for more.

"Three what?" I say to him.

"Three weeks. That's how long you were in the hole. No one ever knows when they first come out."

My chest caves in. Three weeks. That's it? It felt like three years.

"Yeah, um . . . thanks," I say.

Big Lee lifts his chin. "Mmm-hmmm. It's the Christian thing to do."

He walks off as slow as he came. *Christian thing?* Doesn't he mean the right thing? The decent thing? The *human* thing?

Norm shakes his head, working on his plate as he glances around the room.

"You know, you ever stop to think they just so many!"

"So many what?"

"Of us! Negroes," he says, nodding at the full mess hall. "Ain't never seen so many in one place in all my life, and this ain't even all of us. Probably could fit my whole town up in here."

For the first time, I notice what Norm is really seeing. There is an endless field of us in here. So many strong Black men who could lead our kind right out of this place. There's strength in unity.

*Up, up, you mighty race!*

The thought of Papa's teachings comes back to me in a hot flash. But I push those thoughts away. Hell, if he was alive today and saw me in here . . . oh man. I don't even want to imagine it.

"This ain't nothing like it is in Roxbury," I say, clearing the sadness from my throat. "I've seen thousands of Negroes, drinking and Lindy Hopping . . . those pretty dames having a sweet time."

I think of my nights at the ballroom, the girls I used to spin around the dance hall, hitting a bottle with Shorty till sunrise . . . and I grow hungry for home again.

Norm waves me off with a grin. "Oh, that city life ain't for me. Too many violent criminals, them bad-ass Negroes, living on top of one another."

"Have you ever been to a city before?"

"No. But my boss man told me what it's like."

"And you just believed him?"

He frowns. "He ain't got no reason to lie. Look, he's been good to me. Not all white folk are bad. Anyway, you missed it while you were . . . uh . . . gone, I guess. We got like fifty more coons up in here, coming from all over. Bunch of thieving, murdering, raping, and drug-dealing coons. All of them."

What's he talking about? Doesn't he know half of us up in here didn't do nothing but be Black?

"How you end up in here?" I ask.

He winces a nervous smile. "Oh, that was nothing but a big ole misunderstanding."

I laugh. "You ever think that the rest of us are a bunch of 'misunderstandings'?"

He looks at me straight. "No. Not me. I've been writing to my old boss man. He's gonna help me get out of here. That's what he says. Mmm-hmm, of course he would. He can't run no store without me there! Said I was the best nigger he got. Just was lost in a . . . uh . . . mix-up."

"Yeah? Tell it."

He sighs. "Some Negro grabbed a loaf of bread from a store down the street. My boss saw me on the stairs and mixed me up with him. Next thing I know, police at my front door. I told them I was working, that my boss man can vouch for me, but they didn't have the chance to ask him yet, that's all."

Norm was the type Shorty told me to watch out for. The type that is so brainwashed he'd bend over backward for a white man who would sell his whole family to the lowest bidder. Shorty gave me a lot of lessons, but that one stuck like glue. Yet Papa would say that he's our brother. We should keep one eye open but never leave him behind.

"You ever wonder what them white prisons are like?" I ask Norm.

He laughs. "Probably empty. They ain't criminals like us."

"And you don't find it . . . strange . . . that we are the only ones doing all these crimes? And if we are the criminals, then why are we afraid of white folks? You ever think about that?"

"We don't know no better, that's all. Look, we've had some hard breaks. But if you keep your head down and do what you told, you'll survive better than you think."

The word *survive* hits me heavy. That's all any of us have been doing, inside and out of this shithole—just trying to survive. But just exactly what are we trying to survive? And at what cost?

There are only a few things in prison that bring all of us together—food and sports. Tonight, we crowd into the mess hall, hundreds of voices drowning out one single radio the size of a lunch tin.

"I can't hear nothing," Jimmy groans. "Thought y'all fixed it last time."

"This is why we need Big Lee," Walter says, fussing with the dial on the old radio. "He's good at this kind of thing. Where he at?"

Walter is real serious when it comes to fights and baseball games. Never met a more competitive person. Nor someone with such an itch to place a bet. Double or nothing, he's down to risk it all and always squares up, no matter the cost.

He curses over the box. "Fight probably already started and we gonna miss the whole damn thang!"

A man named Mack hobbles out of the kitchen, his left eye sewn shut and caved in. He goes over to the radio and hits the top hard. It makes a loud screech before the announcer from the Joe Louis vs. Tami Mauriello fight pops on.

"Shhhh," Mack tells us, and hobbles back into the kitchen.

There's a small cheer as cats tune in to the fight. Listening to the Brown Bomber's fight makes me think of all the times

I listened to the fights back home with Philbert. It brings me a small slice of relief. Wonder if he's listening, too. Yeah, I bet he is.

"Don't mess with it again," Mack says. Mack has a loud, raspy voice with an aggressive tongue to match. Bet if he ever pays you a compliment it would sound like an insult. Not that he's ever said more than a word to me.

"What you doing, Mack?" Jimmy asks. "Come hear the fight!" Jimmy always wants everyone to listen to the fight together. Like we're one big family, gathering around the fireplace.

Mack shakes his head. "Can't see how anyone could enjoy themselves when men are down in them holes."

*"Louis hit Mauriello with the left!"*

Mack is the type that says little but a whole lot at the same time. Keeps to himself for the most part. Lives in our unit but works kitchen duty. Practically glued to the sink, he's always scrubbing pots and pans.

*"Louis puts Mauriello down for the count!"*

Walter is on his feet.

"What?? NO! That's it! One round?!"

"What? I missed it already?" I ask. "Who won?"

"Louis." Walter pouts. "Damn. That's gotta be the shortest fight in history."

# CHAPTER 3

*There is no better than adversity. Every defeat, every heartbreak,*
*every loss, contains its own seed, its own lesson on how to improve*
*your performance next time.*

—MALCOLM X

Only way to keep afloat is to stay away from what weighs you down. That's how I've been surviving. Pretend I'm not here. Keep my head above water and keep busy. Back in Harlem I learned that you can run a hustle anywhere you're planted, and that's what I have to do here. Just work through it all.

"Red, when I get outa here, man, first thing I'ma do is get on my knees and pray," Lightning says from his cell two doors down. "I'ma pray to the Lord that I made it through this hell. Lord knows I didn't kill nobody. I ain't never hurt a fly. Then, I'ma go get me a bath and put on my church suit, sit at the table with my mama, and eat me a good meal, a nice home-cooked meal, Red. Yes, sir. I'ma just sit an' look at my mama and eat till the sun rises again. Then, we gonna go to church."

Lightning's always talking about what he's gonna do when he gets out. About food, the Lord, and his mama.

"Yeah, I hear you, boss," I say, folding my blankets. "What your mama making today?"

"We got some corn bread, pot roast, and gravy, and we got . . . wait. Guard coming!"

The unit goes quiet as boots stomp in our direction.

"I need the showers," I say as the guard opens my cell. I've sweat through my clothes, soaking the mattress from another night terror. Need to freshen up, pretend this is just another day in Roxbury.

"Not today," the guard grumbles.

"But it's my day."

The guard turns to glare up at me, his face in a tight knot. When I first entered Charlestown, I tried to remember each of the guards' faces and names. Memorize them like I memorize numbers. But, as the months went by, all the guards began to look the same. Their eyes soaked in pure hatred, faces molded into permanent scowls.

He points his baton in my face and snarls.

"Listen, nigger," he shouts. "I'll tell you when it's your day and when it's not, you understand. Now fall in line! All of you stink whether you shower or not."

My family and I, we come from a clean household. Wash our hands and bodies daily. We make our beds every morning, then scrub, dust, and wash down every nook and cranny of our home. Our clothes are clean and neat, mended with love.

Maybe that's why the memories of home wander in my mind, why I can't sit still. The filth surrounding me, on me, on everyone, makes me long for the smell of my mother's hair, the taste of her food, the warmth and stimulating conversations of my siblings sitting beside me with the Michigan sun shining through the windows of home.

Safety. Laughter. Love.

I slide my uniform over my sticky skin, feel the grime on my teeth, and walk out of my cell into the funk.


I'm like a shark when I enter the mess hall, looking for my next meal. Time to collect. During the week, I've been chatting up the cooks in the kitchen and the porters at night, taking bets. We're all grimy. They make sure of it. Grimy or not, I'm easy to talk to, easy for people to trust.

"So what'll it be?" I ask Jimmy.

He winces, checking over his shoulder.

"Um, man, I'm dry," he says in a hush. "Hoping my old lady will put something on the books for me. Got three mouths to feed and with me being away, she ain't got it to spare."

I've learned to be sharp with folks here.

"I'm sure you got a little something," I push. "You in or not?"

He rolls his eyes with a chuckle. "All right, kid, put me down for two and no more."

This ain't nothing but a cakewalk, I think, as we slap skins before he dumps a lump of gray oatmeal, cold like a scoop of flavorless ice cream, into my bowl with a half slice of dried-up bread.

"22801, it's time!" a guard shouts from the other side of the mess hall.

I glance over my shoulder at the commotion, seeing it's my man Lightning, and that same guard who barked at us during Ella's last visit.

"N-noo, sir," Lightning stammers, his eyes wide. "They said they were waiting for my papers. They said I could appeal again."

Without warning, the guard shoves him in the face with his baton. Blood shoots out his nose.

"What did I say!" the guard barks.

"Please, sir, I ain't ready. I just need more time. Please!"

"Hey, man, what's going on?" I whisper to Jimmy.

He shakes his head. "Lost his appeal. They taking him down to death row."

"What?"

A herd of guards descend on him, their batons whacking against his head, his body with loud thuds that echo through the mess hall. Lightning is surrounded. He tucks himself into a ball, covering his head. The mess hall falls silent, food left untouched.

"Wait, please," he gargles out, drowning in blood. "Ain't . . . do . . . ah . . . please, no!"

A dozen or more drag him by the ankles through the doors.

Heart pounding, I realize I'm following them, like a reflex, ready to help him. We should all do something to help him. Everyone in this prison should rise up!

But no one moves. After all, we can barely help ourselves. I stop at the door and watch them drag his body down the hall, still fighting for his life.

Dear Malcolm,

Your letter arrived today. It caught me by surprise. It's good to hear from you. You know the way Hilda worries over you, she's always the mother hen. You may have been knocked out a few times like Joe Louis, but you still have some good sense.

Things are fine here at home. Yes, I check in on Reginald almost every day. We've all converted to the Muslim faith and are following the teachings of the Honorable Elijah Muhammad. He is a minister like Papa, but also a messenger of God in the flesh. He is smart. He ministers on the history of the Black, which reminds me of the old days when Mr. Garvey used to visit our house. Remember they said that the Black man was the chosen one? It's true. He is doing work similar to Papa's. It's like the old days, Malcolm. We are planning to come and see you soon. Just wait, we will uplift your spirit. Please keep strong and safe.

Your Brother,
Philbert

That night, I lie awake, arguing with God.

*Is this it? Is this the life you have for me? Ha, some plan, homeboy. Why'd you let them take Lightning? He was good to the bone. You don't give a shit about us!*

You ain't supposed to cuss and say the Lord's name in the same breath, but who cares.

These people. These officers. They haunt me. I'm terrified to sleep, afraid of what I might see in my dreams—Mom, the hole, Lightning . . . Shorty.

I sob into my pillow. There's only so much nutmeg available to kill this kind of fear.

What would Papa think of me? What about Wilfred, Hilda, and Philbert? What does Reginald think of me—*his* big brother? How could I let Wesley, Yvonne, and Robert down? Does Mom even know I'm here? Before, I never really cared what they thought of me. But now . . . all I know is that this life is not for me. I am not this person. And if I am not this person, then who am I?

Snap out of it. I want to feel something more than crushing guilt, more than the rush of rage that keeps my jaw clenched and my mind awake at night. Where is Papa?

*God, you put me in this shit. How I'm supposed to get out?*

*Just keep busy*, a voice inside me screams.

But that translates into the only word I can really understand: *hustle*.

Whenever they carry out an execution in Charlestown, the lights in the shop flicker and buzz. Cats take off their caps and bow their heads; Big Lee makes a sign of the cross over his chest.

Lightning had no business being killed. Just wasn't right. If an eye for an eye was the reason, we'd have a lot less people with two eyes in this country. Just doesn't seem like anyone has the right to take a man's life. And yet the law allows for execution.

With work done for the day, our unit is allowed outside in the yard for an hour, enough time to stretch our bones, breathe in air not mixed with death, and feel a little bit of the sun on our faces.

The heat is stifling. *Summertime, an' the livin' is easy.* I envision myself at the Cotton Club with Ella Fitzgerald and Louis Armstrong crooning something pretty. Seems we're all singing about the same thing. There's nothing easy about the life we live, in here or out there.

"That Lightning was a decent man," Bembry says as cats gather around him the way you would flock to a preacher. "Strong-willed and kind. Shame, nothing but bad luck had him wind up in this place. Breaking a rule you'd never think existed."

"What he do?" Walter asks.

Bembry replies, "Got arrested for walking."

Someone whistles through their teeth, others shake their heads.

"*Walking?*" I ask. "That's it?"

"Yep. Walking in the wrong neighborhood one night. Lost trying to find his way back to the bus. They pinned some other mess on him. That's all it takes, one wrong turn."

The men mumble to themselves, and a few look over their shoulders at the guards, surrounding us with rifles.

Norm argues, "Well, that's what he gets for thinking he's better than everybody. You gotta pay the price when you do wrong. Everybody knows that. Some Negroes think they special and can walk wherever they want. There are rules in life. He knew he had to follow the rules."

"Hard to follow rules made up as you go along," Bembry

corrects him. "That's like trying to play baseball with no rules. No chance of winning."

"Folks know you can't just walk around neighborhoods you ain't from," Norm snaps back. "That don't make no sense."

Bembry remains calm while cats talk over one another. Norm says the type of stuff that could get a man shot in the wrong places. But Bembry just measures Norm with indifference, like a man would regard a child, unmoved. When everyone settles down, Bembry takes his time to speak.

"Tell you this, Lightning been asking me to help him with his transfer papers. He thought if he could just get from up under their heel, he'd have a fighting chance at life."

"Transfer? We can ask for that?" I ask. I've been here almost six months. Why am I just hearing about this now?

Bembry regards me with a soft nod. "Yeah, they can transfer you to a new unit or to a whole different prison if you ask."

He is always patient when he answers my questions. Thoughtful. Never snaps or loses his temper. Reminds me of . . . someone.

"And if you do ask, you need to ask for this place called Norfolk," Big Lee adds. "That's where my big brother Osbourn is. Says it's like heaven, letting Negroes walk around free. That's where Bembry came from."

There's a longing in Bembry's eyes before he sighs. "But nothing's guaranteed and you can end up at a place worse than here. This cat I knew talked big about getting a transfer, only to end up on a chain gang breaking rocks for the railroad till he died."

Big Lee suddenly stands straighter. "Hey, who's that?"

I follow the stares, peering across the yard. On the opposite end, a man emerges out of a shadowed door, strolling with a cool cat strut as if he was entering the Roseland. But his eyes are dark and don't keep still like regular ones do. They twitch and jiggle in their sockets, the way he looks at everything in his periphery. The same look a brother has when he's about to hustle someone. I recognize the type.

"Oh yeah. That's Chucky," Bembry says. "Just out of intake."

"You met him already?" Walter asks. "What you make of him?"

Bembry takes a long, silent moment. "Hard to say. They put him on my cellblock yesterday, but I ain't seen or heard much of him. Time will tell, always does."

As Bembry and the rest of the brothers continue chatting, I lean on a fence and close my eyes, trying to organize my thoughts. A transfer may be my ticket out of here. But I could risk winding up someplace worse or far from Boston and Ella. What if I transferred to wherever Shorty is? What if he doesn't want anything to do with me? Man, I'd give just about anything to hear his laugh again.

"You the one everyone been calling Satan, right?"

My eyes fly open at the sound of a bellowing voice. Chucky leans against the fence a few feet away from me. He slides a loosie out of his shirt pocket and lights it up. Chucky is tall, stocky, with tight brown curly hair and fair skin like Mom.

My shoulders tense but I keep my voice hard. "What's it to you?"

He sizes me up and chuckles. "Why, you ain't nothing but a baby."

Never show your full hand, Shorty would say. So I keep my expression smooth. Calm. If he wants a challenge, he got it.

"Can I help you with something?" I ask.

Cats are watching us, pretending they're still listening to Bembry, but their ears are tilting in our direction.

Chucky crosses his arms. "You still taking bets?"

The fight. Almost forgot about it.

*Work. Hustle. Always*, the voice inside reminds me.

"Yeah."

He sniffs and spits in the dirt. "What it cost?"

I measure him up, just the way Shorty did when he first laid eyes on me, glancing at Chucky's pockets, knowing he has a few more loosies than the one hanging from his lip.

"It cost what you got."

Chucky leans on the fence a little longer and walks off. He didn't have to say anything, but I knew it wouldn't be our last talk.

Ella keeps her coat, scarf, and gloves on as she sits down at the meeting table, yet her teeth still clatter.

Another visit. Another reminder of my failure.

Ella glances around the visitors' center. Eyes dart to the corner where a guard stands close by, the same one that yelled at us before. Watching. It's only us today but the room still feels tight and tense.

"And you're positive you haven't gotten a letter from Shorty yet?"

"Not that I've seen." She shakes her head. "Malcolm, you don't look well."

My hair has grown out of its conk and I'm stick thin, but I don't think it's my appearance she's referring to. Ella is perceptive, just like Papa was. Whenever Mom was upset about anything, Papa could just sense it like a coming storm. It made him good with people, able to calm their fears of change, of doing what seemed unnatural— wanting better for themselves than what the white man *allowed*.

"Oh, I'm doing just fine," I say with an uneasy smile. Don't want her worrying about me. If I pretend everything is okay, maybe she'll report back to my sisters and brothers, so they won't worry about me either.

Ella peers at me. "You are far from okay. What's going on?"

My mind is heavy with thoughts that I can't put into words. How do I tell her what it's like being in the hole? About the way Norm acts like all Negroes are criminals? The way God has forgotten us? I want her to stop coming here, to stay far away. I don't want anyone to see me like this. But at the same time, I don't want to lose her either. She's the only family close enough to remind me that outside these walls people care about me.

I place my hands on the table, noticing the paint under my nails. If Mom saw me now, she'd lay into me good. She hated dirty fingernails and teeth, always inspecting our hands and mouths before dinner. No matter if we were just walking down the road and back, she made sure we were clean. She made sure we were loved.

I think of her, stuck helpless behind those institution walls. The way I'm stuck behind these walls. Trapped, unable to scream the way we want. Tears fight to come to my eyes and I hold them back.

"Ella, I can't . . . I don't know if I can do this much longer,"

I admit, my throat dry and hoarse. "I know I did wrong, but nothing I did . . . deserves this."

She flinches. Her instinct is to touch, to console, but she knows better. She has seen the way families have been torn apart in this very room.

Ella leans in and whispers, "What do you mean, Malcolm?"

In the corner, the guard moves closer, eyeing us, waiting for one of us to make a wrong move. What if he overhears me talking? What would he do? It's not that I would be lying; everything I'd say would be the truth. But the truth sounds uglier than fiction. These white people in here hate mirrors that show the side of them that the rest of us see.

I shake my head. Can't risk it.

"We have to get you out of here," she says, her voice resolved.

"There's no going home for me, Ella. I'm stuck in this jam."

Ella thinks real hard. "Well, if you can't come home, Malcolm, maybe another place would be better than this."

"Another place?"

She reaches out her hand and grabs mine.

"We'll find a way to get you out of here," she says. "You're not alone. You have family that loves you."

"HEY! YOU!"

Ella steels herself before turning to the guard, stuttering in a make-believe high-pitched voice. "W-we were just saying goodbye, sir."

"Time's up," he spits back, and yanks me by the neck from my seat, throwing me against the wall. Ella looks on, tears streaming down her face.

# CHAPTER 4

*The common goal of 22 million Afro-Americans is respect as human beings, the God-given right to be a human being. Our common goal is to obtain the human rights that America has been denying us. We can never get civil rights in America until our human rights are first restored. We will never be recognized as citizens there until we are first recognized as humans.*

—MALCOLM X

A buzz of excitement envelops Charlestown. All thanks to Jackie Robinson, the first Black man to enter Major League Baseball in America. All anyone can talk about in the shop, the mess hall, common areas, even the chapel is that a Negro is playing baseball.

"They got that boy playing against them white boys now!" someone had laughed when the news broke: April 10, 1947. It was announced over the radio, and the paper even showed his photograph. Had to wait so long for my turn to catch a glimpse of him in black and white that by the time it reached my hands, the newspaper was nearly torn to pieces. I stopped on his picture to catch a good look at him. Wearing a crisp pinstripe uniform, gripping a baseball, Jackie is a tall, dark-skinned man, with determination in his eyes and a bright smile, like Papa.

Crowds pack the colored sections of the stadiums. Folks dress in their church best just to watch him play. Men in their suits and hats. Women in their Sunday dresses and fancy gloves. Can't believe our eyes. And not just Negroes. The white people, too. Kids sitting up in trees outside the fields, concession stands selling out of salted peanuts and soda pop before the fourth inning. White folk never allowed Negroes to play in any major league games.

*Up, up, you mighty race!*

On April 15, Jackie played his first game. Dodgers versus the Braves. All of Charlestown huddled by the old beat-up radio in the mess hall. Felt like the whole world was listening.

Of course, Norm had something to say about it. "Can't believe some Negro wants to play against white folk. He might get himself killed!"

For once, we agreed on something. Couldn't imagine why any white team would let a Negro on their roster to play against other white folk. What would they get out of it? Had to be some type of hustle, which gave me an idea.

After Jackie's first game, I had started making my rounds and taking bets. A few nickels, some loosies, an occasional matchbook of nutmeg. Baseball season has more games, which means more opportunities for bets. So I don't have to rely on the occasional fight.

"Game be on in thirty minutes," someone hollers into the common room.

Back in Lansing, we used to play baseball in our backyard. Philbert would say I couldn't hit a ball if it was tossed a foot from my face, that all the white boys in Lansing were better than me. But he was wrong. I hit a few home runs and even stole a base or two. Or at least I remember doing that. Wonder what Philbert thinks of Jackie. Is he keeping his stats, tuning into every game like the rest of us? I'll have to ask him about it in my next letter.

Today's game should be a good one. Pirates versus Dodgers.

There are three small radios in Charlestown. One in the command center for the guards and one in the larger common area that all the units stack into. But with everyone talking over one another, you can't hear a word the announcer is saying. Plus, all those bodies in one room during the June heat makes it feel like we are inside a funky oven.

So, I convince the kitchen crew to set the last radio by the window and keep it secret, invitation only. Even gave one of the guards a nickel just to let us be for a spell.

"Come on, man," Walter shouts. "What's taking so long?"

Big Lee jiggles the antenna, adjusting a few loose wires in the back of the set.

"Hold on, now! I'm working on it. It took the Lord seven days to create the heavens and earth, and you expect me to fix this thing in just a few minutes."

Walter pushes through the small crowd, pointing in Big Lee's face.

"You keep playing around, we gonna end up missing the game."

As the small party gathers, I play host, selling a few loosies, keeping track of all bets laid over the last few days. Reminds me of working at Smalls' back in Harlem during big fights, and I feel like I'm normal again. Wish we could sneak some whiskey, hooch, or moonshine in here. Make this a real party.

Norm, still on kitchen duty, stops mopping up a spill on the floor.

"Why, they really gonna let him play again? Bunch of fools. What's next? Football?"

"Norm, don't you start with no mess," Walter warns, pointing at him. "Ain't about to have you ruining the game with all that talk!"

Norm shakes his head. "Don't know if he's crazy or just a plain fool."

"Man, if you don't take your ass back to your cell . . ."

Norm grumbles, leaning on his mop. "I'm just saying what

y'all should be thinking. They about to send that Negro to an early grave."

The signal snaps in as the announcer for Ebbets Field swims through the static. A collective sigh of relief calms the room.

Big Lee shuffles his cards. "You know, that boy, Jackie, he used to play for my team back in Kansas City. The Monarchs. Well, in the Negro league, that is."

"And he didn't want to stay there? Where it's safe?" Norm asks.

"Safe?" a big booming voice says behind us and we all turn.

Mack sits in the corner, a newspaper held up to his ears.

"Safe." He repeats the word again with a chuckle. "Boy, ain't nowhere safe. For us."

Everyone grumbles, eyes rolling.

"Man, don't listen to all that mumbo-jumbo talk. He worse than Norm," someone says.

Mack peers at us with his one good eye and goes back to his paper. I barely see him in his cell except for lights-out.

"All right now, y'all, hush. The game's starting," Walter says.

Everyone huddles, shoulder to shoulder, around the radio as the announcer comes on. A few fellas squat on overturned buckets, holding mini pencils and scraps of paper, taking note of stats.

"Man, you know they gonna lose," someone chuckles. Pretty sure it's one of the few guys who bet against Jackie.

"You foolin! That boy Jackie is good! He's saving them Dodgers. That's why they got him, see. He's gonna be rookie of the year, just you wait!"

"That's if they don't run him off the field."

"Making some Negro rookie of the year," Norm spits, standing closer to the door. "You out of your head."

"We'll see. I'm willing to bet on it," someone says.

"You heard what happened at that last game, right?" another says.

"Yup," Walter says. "Couldn't be me. Couldn't have them yelling and throwing rocks and banana peels at me."

Chucky strolls into the kitchen, a smirk on his face. The room calms, cats acknowledging him with a nod. He's made quite a name for himself over the last few weeks—scuffling with a few cats in his unit, acting out in his cell, skipping work duty . . . almost like he's trying to be shipped down to the hole.

He stands beside me, feigning calmness.

"Heard about your little party." He chuckles. "You still taking bets?"

I nod toward the radio. "They still playing, aren't they?"

He mulls it over, then snaps his finger. "All right. Put me down for five."

"That's a pretty big number."

"I'm good for it," he says with a wink, extending his hand.

Papa always said to never buy things on credit. Never owe a man anything, especially one you can't trust. The pinching in my gut tells me I should leave Chucky alone but I ignore it. Instead, we slap skins. Not like he could hide or skip town on me. He got to square up.

Mack watches from the corner and huffs, returning to his paper.

In the brief moment Chucky distracts me, the group gasps, all on their feet, followed by a cheer that could be heard in Canada.

"What! What happened?"

"Did you just hear that?! That boy stole home plate," Big Lee sings. "HOME plate! How about that Jackie! Whoo!"

Cats go wild, hopping and carrying on. All except Norm.

"Oh Lawd, they gonna string him up by his feet," Norm mumbles, eyes wide and staring.

"Relax!" Big Lee says, clapping him on the back. "Ain't nothing gonna happen. He's in God's hands. This is history in the making!"

Norm pales, his mouth gaping wide like he just saw a ghost. He drops the mop, mutters something at the floor, and storms out the kitchen.

"What's with him?" Chucky asks.

"Don't pay him no mind," Walter says. "The man can't stand to see a Negro win at nothing. It's like he wants us to lose!"

"Heh. Sounds like he's playing for the wrong team."

I step back from the crowd, leaning against the counter. It's not that I don't want to celebrate with everyone, I'm just overwhelmed by the moment. Ebbets Field is not that far from Harlem. If I was free, I would've been there, seen Jackie with my own eyes. Maybe Shorty would've driven down Interstate 95 from Boston and gone with me. We could've been a part of history. Instead of trapped in this shithole.

I turn left to find Mack watching me.

"Can I help you with something, old man?" I ask, hard. Always got to make sure no one thinks I'm some soft little kid they can push around in here.

"Your friend there," he says, pointing in the direction Norm headed. "He's got a point."

"Jackie stole that base fair and square. He's worrying over nothing."

Mack sniffs and folds up his paper. Not sure if he was actually reading it, seem like he'd been stuck on the same page for a while. Mack has smooth dark skin like Jackie, with black hair peppered gray. Aside from his eye, he has two fingers missing on his left hand and I can't help but stare at the scars around his temples. The deep, jagged lines like a road map.

"Son, I've seen men killed for less. Some of us are in here for less."

I glance back at the fellas, still on a high from the score.

"What you got to understand is that your friend there," he says, nodding at the door once more. "He's seen some things, shook him up nice and good. Got the look in his eye that he's seen a few live bodies lose their lives. A mob of hate-filled crackers foaming at they mouths for a Negro lynching. That fear . . . it never leaves you. Never. He got every right to be scared."

The next day, after we finish up in the shop, the guards let us out into the yard. Now that it's summer, we're allowed outside a little more often. Except it doesn't keep the nightmares away. It doesn't help me breathe any easier or cry any less. I average less than two hours sleep, if that, most nights. Wish I had something, anything, to take the edge off.

Cats are still talking about the game. Bembry replays it word for word for those who missed it, while some of the other fellas make up a small diamond field in the grass, playing stickball. Everyone's in a good mood so I take my time collecting winnings, tingling from the nutmeg I had this morning.

Mack is out in the yard today. He has a limp I never noticed before. He must have been forced out of the kitchen, the way he inches around the gate, squinting at the sun. His face stoic as if he's itching to be back inside, which doesn't make much sense to me.

I stare out past the fence, out where I wish I could be. Some yards away on a wide-open field is another unit of cats. But they're not laughing and joking like us. They're lugging what looks like large, sharp, heavy rocks that must weigh a ton, while others are pulling up weeds and thick roots. In this hot sun, and their long uniforms, it looks like nothing but hell on top of hell.

"They're getting ready to build another penitentiary," Mack says, standing beside me now. "Making prisoners build their own cage, like digging they own grave."

"Who told you they're building another pen?"

"Heard some of the guards talking about it. They're expanding. Not enough room in here for all of us—they want to bring in more. Hell, they'd gather up all the Negroes in sight if they could pin something on them."

"Well, if nothing else," I quip, "your hearing is sharp."

He chuckles, and it's the first time I see something that resembles a real smile.

"Got to be. Now," Mack sighs, waving at his caved-in eye.

"What happened to you? Some type of accident or something?"

He tips his chin up. "Had me surrounded. Close to fifteen

men. Came down on my head with baseball bats. Must have blacked out 'cause when I woke up, I was in a jail cell. Only reason they took me to the hospital was because I was bleeding all over the courtroom."

"Damn. What'd you do to deserve that beating?"

Mack frowns. "I didn't do a damn thing. Nothing I could ever do would deserve this." He thinks awhile, then closes his one eye. "They say I bed a white woman."

I wait for him to finish the reason and realize he said all there was to say.

"That's it? That's all you did?"

"Boy, you think I'm crazy enough to do something stupid like that?" he barks, gripping the fence to steady himself. "I ain't never slept with no white girl. Ain't even looked at one. But she had to find some reason for that brown baby."

I swallow real hard, thinking of Sophia. How different it all could have been for me. I could've lost more than I already have. Stuck in some kind of prison cell? A rush of rage comes. She betrayed me. Not just in the courtroom, but for all those years we'd been together. I loved her. I loved her white skin. Her silky blond hair. Damn, I loved her blue eyes. Blue, my favorite color.

I pretend she never existed in my world and say, "Man, you lucky to be alive."

"Lucky?" he huffs. "Yeah, that's what they all say. You ask me, they ain't no luck in prison."

"At least we alive though. Could still be picking cotton. Could be dead," I say.

Mack squints and points across the field. "Take a look around you. What do you see?"

I shrug. "See a bunch of Negroes standing about."

"You ain't looking close enough, son. To me, I see a bunch of Negroes, terrified on the cotton field, with an overseer barking orders. One wrong move and they're either whipped or lynched. My granddaddy was a slave. He used to sit us all down and tell us what life was like back then. Wouldn't wish that life on anyone, son."

*Slave.* The word pops through the air, reeking of recent memories.

Mack shakes his head. "They get slaves they don't even need to buy. Just control. They do whatever they want and you can't do nothing about it. Your whole life is in their hands like you ain't got no feelings or dreams of your own. I'm still trying to figure out why they hate us so much. What we ever do to them?"

Something deep in the pit of my stomach turns sideways. "Homeboy, you wild," I say, laughing, trying not to sound frightened, but it comes out forced. "We ain't slaves."

He sees right through me. "Ain't the cotton field but might as well be. We a different kind of slave."

Shaking my head, I say, "No. Slavery ended over fifty years

ago. It's against the law. We're free men, free Negroes." But even as I utter the words, I know he's right.

Mack chuckles. "Brother, when have you ever been free? You ain't been free a day in your life. You don't even know what free is."

"I was free before I walked into this prison!"

He gives me a look that turns my blood cold.

"That wasn't free neither. When have we ever been able to walk where we want? Sit where we want? Drink where we want and take care of our families like we want? Emancipation just off the plantation, but we're still living on someone else's terms, even outside this prison."

I open my mouth to argue, but nothing comes out. Don't have one answer for him.

"Got one eye and to me, it don't look much different." Mack nods his head. "My granddaddy lived out his life on the chain gang, building that damn railroad west. His whole entire life!"

I've heard of the chain gangs. West Indian Archie once told me about them. They line prisoners up like an army, tie shackles around their ankles, then send them out to do hard labor, like building walls or roads. Said it's the type of hard labor that shaves years off your life. It's so hard some people die from it, right on the spot.

What if that's the type of work they have Shorty doing . . . wherever he is.

"No," I mumble, my eyes frantically searching for Shorty in the crowd over there. But even if I find him, there's nothing I could do. I can't even save myself.

And I made Shorty the one thing he never wanted to be: a different kind of slave.

# CHAPTER 5

*Hence I have no mercy or compassion in me for a society that will crush people, and then penalize them for not being able to stand up under the weight.*

—MALCOLM X

The tomato vines in Mom's garden grew tall, some taller than me. I'd stand between them, and they gave a good shade when the sun was high and the breeze low. Mom grew lots of vegetables. So much so, folks in town thought we were rich. Mom knew how to grow food rather than buy it. And she was good with nutrition. She'd give us dandelion root tea with our chicken soup on a cold night. We always ate good. Hilda would make apple and peach cobbler, and we would have homemade ice cream that Mom would make with the fresh cinnamon Papa would find from her native island of Grenada.

The sun was shining rays of light on our home as birds sang from the hickory trees. I plopped down between the rows of crops and lay back in the soft soil to stare up at a crystal-clear, shimmering blue sky. Puffy white clouds—giant horses, elephants, sheep, even bunnies—all floated by. Did people in other cities see the same clouds I did? In other states? I even wondered what it would be like to go to other countries. To travel back to Africa, like Papa always talked about. To fly to—

"Malcolm? Malcolm?"

I sat up quick, shielding my eyes from the glare. "Yes, Mom?"

The sun bounced off the pearls around her neck, her hair twisted up in one of those styles; I think Hilda called it a French twist.

"Young man, what are you doing lying in the dirt like that?" She laughed, adjusting the basket on her hip. "Are you trying to grow, too?"

"I finished all my chores, ma'am," I said eagerly. "See?"

I pointed to the cabbage patch, tilled and weeded.

"Yes, I see. Come, help your mother," she said, shaking a fist like she was about to roll some dice. "Papa will be home soon and we must be ready for dinner."

I sprang to my feet and followed her, passing the back screen door of the house. Inside, Philbert and Wilfred were at the table, their noses in Papa's books. In the living room, Hilda danced with baby Yvonne in her arms. The rosemary chicken roasting in the oven was calling my name.

Mom stopped at a small patch of soil she'd cleared in the herb garden, placing a basket of tools by her feet.

"Look. Come see what I have here."

She kneeled down and opened her hand. In her palm was a pile of small black seeds, gold stripes down the middle.

"What is it?"

She shrugged. "Not sure yet. A kind woman at work gave them to me."

"Mom! You're going to plant seeds and you don't even know what kind of seeds they are?"

She giggled. "Well, we have to find out now, don't we? First, we have to plant the seeds. Then, we must be patient and allow them to grow. Pass me that shovel."

I grabbed the small hand shovel and watched her dig seven deep holes.

"What if they're trees?" I said. "You're just gonna plant them anywhere?"

She shook her head, a whisper of a smile on her lips. "Well, we'll just have to keep nurturing them with water and see what sprouts. Whatever they're going to be will be, my love. But nothing will grow if you don't plant it and allow it a fighting chance at life."


Some days, I imagine it's not me in this place. I'm not really here. I'm outside these walls—in a plush seat, snacking on goobers, sipping pop, watching a picture show. Watching myself play this character I don't recognize: screaming through the night, dreaming of Mom gardening, mopping up filth, walking through this rodent-infested place in a haze. Helps me forget, black out and just float through the motions.

This jumpsuit, these shoes, and this jacket—they are not mine. Yes, they are in my possession. Yes, they have a number inscribed on them. But they are not mine. They were handed to me, branding me a commodity, property. These items once belonged to another Negro. And another before him. And they will be passed on to another after me. They are not my brother's hand-me-downs, and they were never worn with love. They were worn with desperation, fear . . . anger. The recycled rage seeps into my skin, settling like dust I can't wipe clean.

Mack was right: Negroes are trapped, one way or another.

*Up, up, you mighty race!*

Seven more years in this dump, maybe six, depending on parole. I count each day and think how it would feel to melt into the ground. I'm heavy. Not in weight but in mind, like a fog that's surrounding my head, impossible to escape. At night, I write a letter to each of my sisters and brothers. I write so much now that my fountain pen is starting to run out of ink. I try to sound like myself, the Malcolm they know. Upbeat, funny, down for a good laugh, so they won't worry. Ladies used to call me charming. Men used to call me smooth. In here, not sure who I am or what's left of me and if it even matters.

Nothing eases my craving for reefer, powder, drink, or women, despite all the ways I try to distract myself. Time is passing way too slow. Routines and the nutmeg can only take me so far. When will I see outside these walls again?

I think about Mom, stuck in that institution because she refused pork and bad cheese from the government, refused their handouts, wanting better for her children. With Papa gone, there was no one to help her. She was easy prey.

I'm pacing in my cell. A cell? Would I be in a cell if Papa were alive? Would I be here if the KKK didn't kill him? Would I have ever left my family in Lansing? Would I have ever gone to Boston or Harlem?

These are the questions I ask myself over and over, a record on repeat. When you're so used to running from everything that haunts you and then forced to keep still with yourself, the thoughts start eating away at you from the inside out.

"I'm doing everything I can, Malcolm," Ella says from across the table, her hands folded. "Everything. I'm writing letters every day to your parole board, the Department of Corrections, that Norfolk place you were telling me about. I'm trying to get this transfer but they are just slow as molasses."

Reminds me of what Mom said about our father. Papa petitioned President Coolidge to have Mr. Garvey released from prison after he was charged with federal mail fraud. Papa said it was all a ploy to have Mr. Garvey deported out of the country so he could no longer spread his teachings to uplift Negroes.

*Up, up, you mighty race!*

Ella looks over her shoulder. There are more people in the room with us today. Some cats I don't recognize. Maybe from other units. I wonder if Shorty gets visitors where he is. His mother maybe. She came and saw me right before our sentencing. She forgave me, even if I still can't forgive myself.

"I may have another way," Ella whispers. "A friend of mine, Thomas, he owns the drugstore not too far from the house. He's also on the parole board. I'm gonna see . . . what he can do for us if I . . . give him a few dollars for his troubles."

For a moment, I'm too stunned to respond. My straight-laced big sister has a hustle . . . just like everyone else in Roxbury.

"You really think he'll help us?"

"Can't hurt to try." Ella takes a deep breath, then frowns. "Malcolm, did you know a fella named Clay Jenkins? Went by 'Lightning'?"

"How'd you . . . how'd you know Lightning?"

Ella leans forward to whisper. "There's a very young woman out there, in the lobby. Been coming here every week looking for answers about what happened to her husband. Last week, they tossed her out on her knees, she was asking so many questions. I'm afraid she's going to do something silly."

I don't want Ella getting mixed up with these ruthless devils. I press my hands together, shaking my head. "No, don't know him."

"Okay, I need you to stay safe, Malcolm. You hear me? Stay safe and I'll get you transferred out of here."


My spoon is icy to the touch. I have on every layer of clothing I own, trying to warm my muscles, but nothing is working. I sit in the mess hall, surrounded by shivering cats, talking to distract themselves from the cold.

"Man, I don't know," another brother whispers back. "He's been a little out of it. Either he's screaming about the devil or stone-cold quiet. You never know what mood Red's in."

"The boy needs to snap out of it, whatever's eating him. Got no place for it here."

Everything in me wants to snap. I'm ready to knock out anybody who comes my way. But I can barely feel my legs, my head is stuffy, I'm flying in the clouds.

"Fight coming up next week," Walter says from the table next to me. "You taking bets again or what?"

*Hustle.*

Clearing my throat, I put on a smile. "All right. Fight next week. Who's feeling lucky?"

Day of the big fight comes quick.

Sugar Ray Robinson versus Chuck Taylor, in Detroit.

Worried about the fight starting so close to lights-out, cats gather around the radio in the kitchen early, even setting up a quick game of dominoes to pass the time. Meanwhile, I make my rounds, taking bets, selling loosies and nutmeg. It's like I'm running my own bar. Maybe that's something I could look into when I leave this place.

"Ain't you from Detroit?" Walter says to me. "Fight's happening in your hometown."

I start to correct him, but let it slide. Some people never heard of Lansing. Detroit is just easier to say. Been encouraging Philbert to move from Lansing to Detroit in my letters.

"Did you know Sugar? Says he was raised there."

I laugh. "You know, Detroit is a big city. But I may have seen him around once or twice."

Mack is in his same spot in the corner of the kitchen. Not for the fight, of course. Seems like he's just making sure we don't mess up his kitchen. Even Norm is relaxed tonight. I guess because it's boxing, where whites and Negroes have been competing for a while.

Norm's leg shakes. "Hope they hurry it up. Gonna be lights-out soon; no telling what they'll do if they find us in here."

Chucky overhears Norm and throws him a loosie. "Relax, daddy-o. Besides, he got us covered. Right?"

The room stares at me, not seeing Chucky's sly grin as he chews on a toothpick. Somehow, Chucky knows I paid off the guard to let us have this space in peace. Chucky seems to know everything and yet we know nothing about him.

"Ay, Chucky, where you from again?" I ask. "Don't think I caught that."

"Oh, you know, I'm from just about everywhere you'd think," he chuckles.

Chucky always dances around personal questions. Can never pull a straight answer out of him. Shorty used to say, cats like him can't be trusted. Don't ever let them know too much.

"Oh yeah. And what'd you do to get locked up in here with us?"

He says the words real soft and slow. "They say I killed a man."

The room stiffens.

"Well . . . did you?" someone asks.

Chucky gives the group a smirk. "Is any one of us in here 'cause of what they say we did?"

"Quiet, everyone," Big Lee shouts, playing with the antenna. "It's starting."

We huddle closer to the box, silent as the announcer gives us the play-by-play.

*"First round . . . Robinson and Taylor dance around each other, a few soft blows."*

*"Second round . . . Robinson uppercuts Taylor. Taylor, three jabs."*

"Come on now, baby, this is for the championship here!"

*"Third round . . . Side jab, Taylor. Nasty kidney hit."*

"Come on, baby! Come on!"

*"Fourth round . . . Holding."*

*"Fifth round . . . Robinson blocking. Right hook to the jaw!"*

"This is it! This is the one!"

*"Sixth round . . . Sugar hits jaw. Down goes Taylor! TKO, Robinson wins!"*

The room explodes. Cheers and laughter. Everyone except Chucky. He slowly stretches up as if to yawn before glancing at me, his face emotionless.

Chucky placed the biggest bet of all. Against Robinson.

He walks out into the hall. My stomach presses to my back, and I know within an instant that something's not right.

# CHAPTER 6

*I believe in the brotherhood of man, of all men, but I don't believe in*
*wasting brotherhood on anyone who doesn't want to practice it with*
*me. Brotherhood is a two-way street.*

—MALCOLM X

Around three in the morning, I left the Braddock Hotel to head back to my new spot in Harlem. Since I quit working for the railroad (or I should say, I was fired), I was making something of a name for myself as a sort of traveling sales-man, selling reefer to anyone who needed it. But especially by hanging with the hottest musicians in town—Louis Arm-strong, Billie Holiday, Dinah Washington—all of whom I considered friends.

The one hard part about the hustle was keeping a low pro-file. Police liked doing surprise searches, looking for anything to incriminate you. So I moved at least four or five times to different spots since I had started. Even outside Harlem. No one knew where I lived at any given moment, and I liked it that way.

To keep my trail cold, I would jump out of a cab a good three blocks from my home, just to throw folks off my scent in case anyone was watching. But that night, as I turned the corner on my block, I noticed a man sitting on the stoop of my apartment in a thick wool coat, his back to me. From a distance, he seemed anxious, fidgety. Neck arched, peering down the street as if he was waiting for someone, and I knew within an instant, that someone was me. There could be a dozen reasons why a stranger would be at my door, but none of those reasons could be good at three in the morning. I slowed to a snail's pace, my back tensing. Had just a few moments to decide what to do—either face the cat head-on or turn back and jump on the next thing smoking out of Harlem. But something about his build was familiar. I kept my steps light so he wouldn't hear me coming, slipping a hand in my pocket to wrap a finger around the trigger of the gun I carried just for moments like this. Never had to use it or think about using it before. One house away, his ears perked, shoulders tensing. He spun around and I stopped short.

"Reginald?" I gasped.

My baby brother waved his wide hand, smile gleaming in the darkness.

"Malcolm! Boy, am I glad you finally showed up," he said,

grinning. "You know how long I've been waiting out here? Started thinking I had the wrong place or something."

My feet were still frozen to the ground. I was so shocked and happy to see him, I didn't know what to say. "What . . . what are you doing here?"

Reginald hopped down my brownstone steps, swinging a large green duffel bag over his shoulder. His voice was deeper. He had grown at least three feet since I last saw him. Gained some muscle, too. My little brother was no longer skin and bones.

"You're one hard man to find! My ship docked out in New Jersey for some repairs. I tried to write you but you never wrote back, so I figured I'd just come up here, search for you myself, and, well, here I am, brother!"

Reginald, my favorite, my baby brother, was there, right in front of me. My family. The grin on my face spread wider.

"Well, don't just stand there, homeboy, come here!" We hugged, laughing so hard we could've woken the whole block. But I didn't care, I was just that happy to see him. "Man, look at you! How the hell did you find me?"

"Well, I went by Smalls', that spot you told Wilfred you were working, and they said you left awhile back. But this waiter, he pointed me to your friend Sammy and he told me where you stayed."

I chuckled. "Ole Sammy. He's good for something."

"So where are you working now? Why didn't you tell anybody?"

I dodged around the subject, patting him on the back.

"Hey, what's with all the questions, homeboy! Aren't you happy to see your brother? Come on in, let's get something to eat."

Hardly could believe the giant that sat at my kitchen table used to tail after me and mimic every single action of mine back in Lansing. Now we were inside, I could clearly see a mixture of Papa and Mom in his features. He had caramel skin, a square chin, chiseled cheekbones, and broad shoulders. Tall like me, like Pops. Anyone could take one look at us and know instantly we were brothers.

Reginald inspected the freshly fried chicken on his plate with a raised eyebrow.

"Man, you don't cook a thing like Hilda. You sure these birds aren't still clucking?"

I served him another buttered slice of corn bread that crumbled right out the pan. Felt only right that I cook for him, being a special occasion and all.

"My job ain't in the kitchen, but I can throw down a little bit."

"Speaking of that, what are you doing for money?" he said between bites.

I sipped a beer, offering him one.

"Nah, I don't drink."

I thought everybody drank a little booze.

"Just doing my own thing," I said. "Couple of gigs here and there, you know." I wasn't ready to open up and tell him everything just yet. Needed to check his temperature first. We hadn't lived under the same roof in years. He could be a whole new person. I knew I was.

"Man, I just can't believe you're here."

"Me too." Reginald laughed. "Haven't seen you in so long, I started to question if you were real. Like I imagined you jumping on that bus three years ago to Boston or something."

Even though I had the money, I didn't make it back home much to visit. Afraid the memories of my former self would haunt me: Mom in that hospital, where she didn't belong. Papa split in half on the tracks. Teachers saying I'm nothing but a nigger. Instead, I bought suits when I should've bought a bus ticket. Felt kind of guilty now that my baby brother, who had always looked up to me, was sitting right there in my own living room.

"Guess I should've sent a picture or something," I mumbled.

"Yeah. But you look pretty much the same, just taller. That's some kinda hairstyle tho. It looks like white people's hair."

"Oh this," I said, smoothing back my silky conk. "This ain't nothing. I'm due to touch it up soon. We can hook you up with a clean conk. It hurts at first, but you get used to it. Get you some shiny hair like the white folks, too."

Reginald stared at my hair, then shrugged. "Nah, that's too flat for me."

I decided not to push him too quick. It was his first time in the big city, got to take baby steps.

"So how is everyone? Tell me everything!"

Reginald swallowed some corn bread, washing it down with water.

"Wilfred is still teaching trade at the university. Yvonne, Wesley, and Robert—they're still in school. Philbert is talking about getting married, so the family will be expanding soon. And all Hilda wants to do is take care of our family. Always talking about Papa, Mom, and the old days."

"Hmm, everyone is still in Lansing?"

"Yup. Except us. Who would've thought the two of us would be here, in New York City. In Harlem! I love it, man."

He *was* in my world, with me. Aside from Ella, it was the first time I had any family nearby since I left Lansing.

"So what about you, homeboy? What you doing with yourself? Wilfred said something about a ship."

"Yeah, I got a job working for the merchant marine, on cargo ships. Pay's decent, it's a good living."

I raised an eyebrow. "Anyone on that ship know you're sixteen?"

He shot a look right back. "Anyone in Harlem know you're seventeen?"

"I'll be eighteen real soon," I said.

"Not soon enough."

We laughed. Even as a kid, Reginald was sharp as a whistle, served back anything you threw at him. Had his head on straight the moment he was born. You could have a real conversation with him, like talking to an old man.

"How long you in town for?"

"Little under a week."

"Now that's what I'm talking about! Plenty of time to show you around."

Reginald perked up, then checked the time. "Say, man, don't you have to go to work or something?"

"And miss a minute hanging with my brother I haven't seen in years? No way." I laughed. "But, if you gonna stay with me, you gotta get you some new threads."

"What's wrong with what I got?"

"Nothing, nothing. It's just . . . screams that you green as grass."

He frowned. "That I'm what?"

"That you're not from here. Can't show you off to my friends, looking like you all country. See, biggest lesson you learn when you living in the city: In order to get in, you have to look like you belong, you dig?"

Reginald nodded, always listening to understand rather than respond.

By midday we had him in a fresh dark gray suit and a sleek hat. Not the big flashy hats and flashy suits I used to wear in

Boston. Harlem was different. Folks here were sophisticated, elegant, refined.

The whole week, I showed him the town. Took him to my favorite spots, introduced him to friends, even caught a show and met up with Ella Fitzgerald. Everyone loved him. Maybe a little bit more than me, if I'm being honest. Reginald was in awe of everything. The city lights, the people—all different types of colored folk. I remembered feeling the same way when I first walked through Roxbury. Everyone was family.

With us growing so close, I felt comfortable enough to break down my hustle to him, explaining the ins and outs. His eyes widened, not in disgust but more in admiration. He didn't judge me, but I judged myself. I didn't want Reginald caught up in my world. I wanted to be someone he could really look up to.

Next thing I knew, the week was over and he was packing his bag, ready to return to the ship.

"I don't remember much about Papa," he said from the floor of my living room.

A glass nearly fell out my hand. We'd never talked about Papa, he'd never asked. I shifted in my seat, trying to keep cool. Being so far from home, I could avoid talking about Papa. But now that home was here, I couldn't hide from it any longer.

"Oh yeah?"

"You were, what, around six years old when it happened?

But you still probably remember more about him than I ever could. What was he like?"

I didn't want to tell him that remembering made me uncomfortable. That I tried to forget. But I didn't want to lie to him either. Reginald needed memories, even if I didn't. I poured myself a glass of bourbon.

"Well, he was . . . strong. Very strong. Smart. Orderly. Had to be to keep all of us in line. And he had a way with words."

Reginald leaned forward. "What else?"

"Papa . . . he used to host these meetings at folks' houses and minister when he wasn't at the church. You know, the stuff Mom always taught us. But at these meetings, he spoke to these people and . . . I don't know. They really listened. To every word. 'Cause everything he preached was true." I chuckled, the memories flashing back. "The ladies used to be eyeing him, too. He had this long black touring automobile we would ride in. Not too many people had cars back then either, especially not Negroes. And we didn't depend on no white folks for nothing! Papa was the man. You hear me? He was the man!"

"And then . . . they killed him."

I sighed. "Yes."

"Why?"

My mind blanked out. There were so many reasons why they killed him, I guess, but none of those reasons stuck out.

"He . . . he told the truth."

Reginald made a face that looked something like disappointment. He wanted more and I didn't know how to give it to him.

Later, as I walked him out to find a cab, I felt myself wanting to shove him back inside my apartment and bolt lock the door.

"You don't have to stay on that ship," I blurted out. "You can stay here, in Harlem, with me. I'll take care of you. Get you a real easy slave."

"A slave?" he shouted, eyes going big.

I chuckled. "That's what we call a job, homeboy. But what you think? We can go to all the best parties, hang out with the prettiest dames, live together, take over this city. You and me!"

I tried to make the offer real enticing. I wanted him to stay. Wanted someone I loved and trusted near me for a change. Who can you trust more than family? It wasn't until that moment that I realized the restlessness, the constant moving from show to show . . . was nothing more than homesickness.

But the idea of Reginald pushing reefer, carrying a gun, ducking cops every other block? I didn't know if he had the heart for it. He'd always been so . . . honest. Not that it's a bad thing, but you need a certain ruthlessness for that type of work.

Reginald looked off into the distance as if he saw someone he recognized, and cracked a small smile.

"Maybe," he said with a shrug. "I'll think about it."

He hugged me tight, as if it would be the last time I'd ever see him. I held him, not ready to let go but knowing I'd have to. He gave me one last nod and headed down the block. My eyes locked on the bag hitched over his shoulder, tempting me to yank him back, keep him safe with me forever. Goose bumps scattered across my skin as I tried to move my feet, to chase after him, but they wouldn't budge.

Out of all my siblings, I worry about Reginald the most. It's what I'm supposed to do, being his big brother and all. Haven't heard from him for a few weeks now. I should be out there, protecting him from the world. But it seems like the world is trying to protect him from me by shoving me into this box. I really have no business worrying about anyone. Nothing I can do from inside a cell.

Nightmares during the winter bring a different type of pain. The sharp kind that leaves your teeth chattering and body aching from the cold. Winter reminds you that you're in prison and there's nothing you can do about it. No amount of letters, lawyers, or begging can spring you. Nothing. All I'm doing is nothing.

I am Nothing.

What if that's it? What if I haven't heard from Reginald because I lost his respect? Supposed to be setting the example for him, but it seems like all I am now is a cautionary tale.

What will happen to us when I leave this place? Will he visit me like before? Will we live together like I've always wanted?

Will we ever be a family again?

"Hey, where's your head, young brother?"

Bembry's voice snatches me back to the shop.

"Huh?"

"You got paint all over your hands," he says, shaking his head.

My palms are covered in green, the streaks on the plates uneven.

*6KD-101. 6KD-102. 6KD-103. 6KD-104.*

"Uh, yeah," I say, clearing my throat. "Still a little under the weather, that's all."

It wasn't much of a lie. Bad flu going around, everyone catching and passing it like a baseball. Fevers, chills, vomiting, and diarrhea, our whole unit had it. Four of the older men were sent to the nurse's office but only two came back. A guard said there ain't no use wasting medicine on us.

During Ella's last visit, she said I looked grayer than an elephant. She's been writing letters nonstop, begging for my transfer. But what's the use. If we couldn't free Mom out of that hospital when I was still free, what makes anybody think they could free me?

Mid-shift, we're allowed a five-minute break. Most of the other cats hang around, stretch their legs, or grab a quick smoke in the hallway. Others sit by their stations, minds heavy.

Myself included. The fight was a little over a week ago, and Chucky's been hemming and hawing about his debt. Knew I shouldn't have trusted him.

Bembry sits on his stool by his station, holding a wrinkled piece of beige paper, the folds sharp as a soldier's pants crease.

"Takes me a while, sometimes, to read my brother's letters," he says without looking at me. "Not that I can't read. Just my eyes ain't what they used to be."

From afar, his brother's cursive doesn't look so bad. Mine could use some work.

"It's good to keep in touch with your family," he says. "Keeps you balanced. Reminds you that you're you. A man can lose himself in here without even knowing it. Family's important. Probably the most important."

"I write letters, too," I blurt out. Don't know why, just felt the need to share. Something about Bembry makes me nervous, almost afraid to say something wrong around him.

"Oh yeah. Family ever write back?"

"Uh, most of them," I say, thinking of Reginald. If I come up with enough excuses, I can start to believe that he's just been too busy to write me. But still, I write.

# CHAPTER 7

*Fools try to ignore facts, but wise men must face facts to remain wise. Fools refuse to change from their old silly ways and beliefs, but the mental flexibility of the wise man permits him to keep an open mind and enables him to readjust himself whenever it becomes necessary for change.*

—MALCOLM X

At the first sign of spring in Lansing, a cavalry of beautiful invaders always surrounded our home. Butterflies—blue ones, white ones, yellow ones—climbed out of their cocoons, spread their wings, and took flight.

The monarch butterflies were my favorite. They looked like freshly erupted volcanos, hot lava streaming down black mountainsides. Their wings were massive yet they made no sound as they fluttered and landed in the patch of black-eyed Susans that grew on the side of our house. One flew right past my nose. Inching toward the patch like a lion, I held my breath and pounced, cupping the butterfly in my small hands.

"Got it," I yelped, its wings tickling my palms. Perfect catch for my new collection.

Mr. Wallace told me all about collecting butterflies. He owned the fabric store in town and had his own collection framed in his store window, about a dozen at least. His own miniature rainbow of delicate insects. I had to have one for myself.

"See, you have to catch them with a net," he had explained. "So you won't ruin their wings."

The only net we had was for fishing, not fine enough to stop them from slipping through. "Just use what you have," Mom had said, wiggling her fingers at me.

Gently, I peeked inside my cupped hands and the monarch grew frantic at the sight of light, bouncing against my fingers, frightened and panicked. In an instant, my skin grew cold, overcome by a wave of sadness. It thinks it's back in its cocoon, I thought. After all the work it did to move freely in the world, it's trapped again.

And as much as it pained me to lose a good catch, I opened my hands. The butterfly fluttered, danced above my head, then flew away and up toward the sky.

"Higher!" I screamed to it. "Fly higher!"

Fly all the way up to God.

A whistle shrieks in the early morning light. Guards run past, shouting at one another.

"Cell 118. Open up!"

"You got him?"

"Shit! No. He's gone."

I press my face into the bars of my cell, trying to peer down the row. Dark hands reach out through the bars of neighboring cells, waving.

"What's going on?" Norm shouts.

"Don't know, can't see," someone says, his voice distant.

Hysteria fills the air. I hold my breath, afraid to catch it.

"Hey! What's going on down there?"

"I think it's Jimmy . . . I think he hanged himself!"

"What! Oh no, Jimmy!"

"Jimmy!"

Metal plates and cups bang against the bars, a chorus of cries. I sit on my bed, listening to everybody's voices echoing at once.

*That you again, God? Some God you are.*


*A man hanged himself today*, I write in a letter to Wilfred. It's the only thing I can do.

During the night, death came for Jimmy. He lynched himself using his bedsheets, leaving a letter to his lady by his uniform. You can sense it from the protocol, the way the guards react, the way they make us walk past his swinging body toward the mess hall . . . They were used to this. Just another day.

"Why you leaving him like that?" someone in the line cries. "He a man!"

"Shut up!" a guard shouts back. "One more word and I'll throw every last one of yous in the hole!"

I haven't seen a lynched body since I was on that bus leaving Lansing headed to Boston. I was fourteen. Saw so many of them just hanging limp and blowing in the wind. I didn't understand what they did or why they had to die that way. Most days, I didn't want to think about it. So I pushed those questions deep inside. Feels like a million years ago and I've lived a million lives since.

"Slow! Walk slow!" they shout, poking our backs with batons, making sure each and every one of us sees him.

I try to shut my eyes, pretend I am home, back in Mom's garden, chasing butterflies. But hearing the sheets creak, my lids refuse to merely listen and they stretch open. His body dangles, swinging soft as a willow tree in the breeze, tied to the sheets that once crumpled across his thin cot. His eyes are closed, jaw slack, lips purple like a bruise.

My stomach contracts, fighting to keep the few pieces of bread sitting at the bottom of my stomach from shooting out my mouth. Just ahead, Norm keeps his head and shoulders slumped, dragging his feet.

"My God," someone whispers, and we keep walking, the

air of a funeral, a silent service as we file into the mess hall for the repast.

Death slows down time in this place, makes the seconds tick like hours. Ghosts work along with us. They never leave, never go home. They are stuck within these walls of hell.

A thought that tastes like the sweetest whiskey sprints through my mind . . .

He found a way to escape. He found a way to be free.

What if I follow that man's lead? What if I could be just as free as he might very well be?

That night, I write to all my brothers, telling them of the man who found a way out and how a part of me envied him.


With Jimmy gone, I slip the kitchen crew two nickels for two matchbooks of nutmeg. I need more than a measly seasoning that barely takes the edge off, but this is the best I have.

I sit at a table with a couple of other cats from the shop, eating silently, then their faces harden. Across the mess hall, Chucky sits alone, pretending not to see me eyeing him. He has yet to square up for that fight. Where does this fool think he's gonna hide in here?

Norm drops his spoon on his tray. "I just don't see what killing yourself is gonna do."

The other men at the table glance up at him, then return to their soups.

"Leave it alone, Norm," someone says.

"It's just foolish," he carries on, looking for an audience.

"What was he in here for?" I ask.

"Dodging the draft," Bembry says with a huff. "They don't take kindly to that."

Walter shakes his head. "Bembry, you think he really killed himself?"

"Who else could it be?" Big Lee asks, scratching his bald head. "Another Negro? The guards?"

Bembry sips water, taking his time with the words. "Wouldn't be the first time a man was hung and they say he did it to himself."

Something cracks like an egg and shatters inside me. I swallow back thoughts of Papa. How the police swore he threw his own self on the tracks when everyone knew otherwise.

It was no suicide. They killed Papa 'cause Papa was sharp. He wasn't scared of anybody. He was a God-fearing man. They killed Papa for being bold, smart, and speaking truth. For doing the work that would wake us all up. Negroes respected Papa. White folks, too. I remember that all the town, Negroes and whites, were at his funeral.

*Up, up, you mighty race!*

The truth killed him. Could it have killed Jimmy, too? I think of how he tried to save me in the chapel and shiver.

"Ha! Man, you foolin'," Norm chuckles. "Only person who carried out that sin was Jimmy."

"Norm's right, you know," Big Lee says. "Don't know what be possessing folks. Killing yourself ain't the answer. You know if you kill yourself, you don't get into heaven."

Walter snorts. "Who told you that?"

Big Lee is so outraged, he could spit. "Well it's right in the good book!"

"The good book? You mean that book written by the white man," Walter says.

"Careful now! You sounding like Satan!"

*Satan is not my name*, I want to shout back at every single one of them.

"Last I read," Bembry says without looking up, "God didn't talk about killing yourself won't get you into heaven. He talked about finding salvation. Whether in this life or the next. That depends on you."

The table quiets, and I'm in awe of how Bembry silences a room in just one breath.

"So, you really think he killed himself, don't you?" Mack stands at the head of the table, his face damp with sweat, voice raspy. We all freeze, not used to seeing him anywhere but the kitchen during the day.

He leans forward, face inches away, slurring and spitting as he talks. "Let me ask y'all something. Have any of you seen an empty cell around here?"

Everyone looks at one another, shrugs abound.

"No," he demands. "There are no empty cells. Beds don't

stay cold more than a day before they're occupied again. And there's a reason." He leans in closer. "The more of us they have, the faster we make them money."

Folks squirm, mumbling among themselves as my mouth goes dry. Norm cocks his head to the side, indignant.

"What you talking 'bout? We don't make them money!"

"Oh, you think them license plates y'all making are free? Them rocks you chopping down to nothing and them roads they building out there cost nothing? You getting paid for that?"

The room feels colder and my body goes numb. I glance down at my fingernails, at the green paint dried underneath, and think of Papa.

Norm waves him off. "They just putting us to work 'cause there's no sense in us just sitting around like it's a picnic. Might as well be useful. We strong and able. Gotta do something with these lowlifes."

I can't help but blurt out something I know everyone is thinking.

"Wouldn't that make you one, too?"

Norm scowls.

"I done told you for the last time," he barks, pointing a finger at me. "It ain't nothing but a misunderstanding."

"A pretty big misunderstanding if you ask me. You've been in here longer than I have."

Norm presses his lips together, as if holding in steam boiling up.

Mack stares at him for a long moment, then cackles. "You one stupid little nigger." He taps the table, letting out a sinister laugh as he hobbles back into the kitchen.

When death comes to Charlestown, it drops on our heads, bringing back memories and images of other men who've been lynched, inside and outside this place.

Wild thoughts flood my mind. I think about that first bus ride from Lansing to Boston. The smell of the man named Earl (same name as my father), who was squeezed next to me; the bumps on the road; the roar of the engine; the silhouette of a man swinging from a tree in the distance, leaves falling around him.

Jimmy lynched himself. Living here can force anyone's hand to do the same. Or maybe this place is lynching all of us, slowly. Maybe Mack is right about it all.

Wonder if it hurt or if he had second thoughts or was it instant. And if there's no God, would the other side be any different from in here? But anywhere seems better than here.

What would everyone say about me? Probably something like: *He went home, went back to where he's from. Thank the Lord he's gone.* It'd be a relief to most, given all the trouble, pain, and embarrassment I've caused. Shorty probably wants me dead.

No one would miss me.

I start counting things I've counted a dozen times before: The bars in my cell . . . twelve across, five rows down. Over and over again, I count them. Do they need so many bars to contain me? To contain any of us?

My hand shakes as I try to write a letter to Ella, what may be my last. Struggling to scratch out every word in the low light.

What if the guards are reading my letters, tearing them up so no one knows about the dead bodies? Or the old men they say are dying from the plague? The mold in our food or the way we're thrown into a dark hole with no hope of seeing light? We were sent here to rot like fruit in the summer sun. How does that teach us right from wrong? What lesson are we to learn?

What if death comes for me next?

My heart beats like a hammer in my ear; I hug my knees to my chest, rocking on my bed, jumping at every small sound. The sheets feel so warm under my hand. Soft. If I were to take them off the bed and—No.

NO!

Pacing, I hit my head with my hand a few times, feeling the tip of my hair, the end of the conk, the end of my old life. Need to stay awake. Need to keep the nightmares away.

This isn't real. This place is a dream. I'm dreaming.

But if I'm not dreaming, I never want to wake up again.

I can't be here, I can't be here, I can't . . .

"Little! Mail!"

I hear my name called, bursting through the zipping thoughts.

"Huh?"

"Mail," the guard says again, frustrated.

As soon as the letter touches my fingertips, I recognize his handwriting. Reginald. I palm the letter like a lifeline.

At lights-out, I sit on my bed, thinking of all the reasons why it's taken so long for Reginald to write. What if he's angry with me? Would it be in this letter? Will it be the straw that breaks my back, sending me over the edge?

Quickly, I open the envelope. The letter is nothing more than a few short sentences, but it fills my heart with the type of hope I haven't felt in years.

Malcolm,

When you're ready, I can free you from prison. First, don't smoke any cigarettes. Don't take any drugs. And don't eat any pork.

I miss you. I'll show you the way free.

Your Little Brother,

Reginald

# PART 2

# CHAPTER 8

*By any means necessary.*

—MALCOLM X

"Lansing! Lansing! Everybody off."

The bus to Lansing was smaller than I remembered. Or maybe I had grown several inches. I had just about outgrown all the clothes I bought the year before. Still had the same baby face. Pretty boy, the gals called me. Never thought being called pretty would be such a compliment for a man.

I slept for most of my journey. But somewhere along the route, the heat went out and the cold smacked me sober. I watched the sun come up, light bouncing off the miles and miles of snow-covered fields as we turned down the familiar roads into the old blue bus depot. With two steps, I was back on Michigan soil, the icy wind flicking my ears, welcoming me home. I grabbed my bag from the undercarriage, flipping up the collar of my coat to block the brutal Midwestern wind.

Across the road, Philbert stood by the door of his black

Ford Pilot, made in a factory in this very state. He had his hands in his pockets, and his hat sat low as he scanned the small crowd.

"Excuse me, there!" I called out to him, grinning. "What's happening, daddy-o? You looking for Detroit Red? 'Cause if you are, then here I am!"

Philbert eyed my conk and both eyebrows arched to the top of his forehead. "What on earth did you do to your hair?"

An uneasy silence hung between us. So I put my fist up, quick jab, jab, uppercut through the air, just like Joe Louis. Philbert didn't move.

"What? No love for your brother?" I asked with a laugh, trying to cut the tension.

Philbert stilled, his face unreadable, before he swung and punched my arm, sending me flying.

"Ow! What the—? What you do that for?"

He chuckled. "Still can't take a hit, I see," he said, and clapped my back. "Come on, Hilda's at the house making breakfast. Let's get you home."

Home. The word sounded like the sweetest tune. This really is home, I thought. The place my soles first took root. The place where my memories take form.

Though my soul belonged in Harlem.

The heat in Philbert's car was on high, but it felt like I was back on that bus. Almost forgot what winters were like at home. Outside, the hills and plains were covered in a good six feet of snow. Some could confuse Lansing for Antarctica if they didn't look too hard. I rubbed my hands together as he drove through town, the streets untouched by time. Even the little grocery store I took that chicken from still stood at the end of the road. Have to walk up in there, I thought. Wear my best suit, then buy five chickens just because. Make sure they remember my face, my name. The one they tried to lock up, throwing away the key, and leave for dead at just twelve years old.

"So, Detroit Red," Philbert started. "That's what they're calling you now?"

"Yep. It fits, don't it?"

"Doesn't," he corrected. "Folks do know you're not from Detroit, right?"

"'Lansing Red' doesn't have the same ring to it."

"Malcolm's not a good enough name for you? Just how many nicknames are you willing to take?"

Philbert hadn't lost his touch. He could still make me feel like a small, insignificant kid who didn't know nothing from nothing, despite him being the one living in the hick town. I've seen more than he can ever imagine.

"Hey, you know when you come to visit, we'll hook you up with a cool name, too."

Philbert's upper lip jerked as he turned down a newly paved road. His mustache had grown in thick, made him look real proper and refined. Reminded me of Papa. Tall and stocky but not taller than my six-four frame. The ladies in Harlem would love him, though.

"So how long you in town for?" Philbert asked, ignoring my suggestion.

I squirmed in my seat. "A week or two, maybe."

His head snapped in my direction. "Oh really? And to what do we owe the honor of such a long visit?"

I shrugged, staring out the window. "Just felt like being around family, that's all."

It wasn't a total lie. It had been a few weeks since I had seen Reginald and I longed for the comforts of home. But something else had held a match under my feet that put me on the first bus smoking, and fast. Just wasn't ready to talk about it yet.

"Dang, Philbert, it's cold in here," I said, hugging my arms.

"You must not remember what Februarys are like here," he said, breath puffing in front of his face. "Didn't think anyone could forget."

Philbert had a hard time keeping his eyes on the road, glancing at my conked head every few minutes. I raked my fingers through my hair, feeling the thick, kinky new growth under my silky bronze strands. Needed to touch up my conk a few weeks back but didn't have the chance . . . with everything going on.

"How's Reginald?" I asked. "You see him lately?"

"He wrote home about his visit with you. Said you're real popular around town. All the big celebrities love you."

The hint of judgment was unmistakable.

"Yeah, we had a fine time. Took him to all the best spots. He and I are gonna live together soon."

"Is that so," he said with a knowing smirk. "You are going to let your baby brother leave his good job to come hang around you?"

"I'm not just hanging around," I snapped. Not back thirty minutes and he was already diving under my skin, criticizing.

Philbert pursed his lips, shaking his head. His disapproval could always be counted on.

"Ran into Stacy George the other day," he said.

"Stacy George?" I perked up.

Stacy was the prettiest girl at school, a few years older than me but I remembered her. She always wore her hair in two long pigtails with bangs.

"How's Stacy doing?"

"Good. She asked about you. Said she's having a party next week and that we should drop by."

"A party? Well. Don't mind if I do," I chuckled, already thinking of how to convince Hilda to press my suit. "Can't imagine the types of parties y'all have in these woods. Definitely don't have the newest sounds."

I told Philbert all about my famous friends in the big bands and the music back in Harlem, some the likes of which he'd never seen but had undoubtedly heard of. Sarah Vaughan, Duke Ellington, Billie Holiday. He nodded and grunted, unimpressed. Good Ole Philbert.

"Well, I'm sure you can tell everyone about it."

But I couldn't go into a party at Stacy's house without handling my hair first.

I cracked two eggs into a jar, mixing them into the other ingredients I'd picked up from the store. After I did just like Shorty taught me, the jar turned hot right away, the smell fierce, searing my nostrils. I layered my ears, neck, and hairline with Vaseline, stretched my fingers into my gloves, and took a deep breath.

Ready.

*So you know it's going to burn when I comb it in—it burns bad. But the longer you can stand it, the straighter the hair.*

Shorty's words stayed with me as I cupped a handful of the jellylike concoction, slapped it down, and combed it through my hair. The burning was instant, my scalp sizzled. I bit down on a towel, tears in my eyes, until I could take no more. I rushed to the washbasin and turned on the water. It creaked, letting out a loud screech but not a drip of water.

"Come on, come on!" I screamed, my head on fire. I slammed my palm on the side of the faucet.

Nothing.

"Shit. Shit!"

*Knock knock knock.*

"Malcolm?" Philbert said from the other side of the door as I banged on the faucet. It only sputtered out a reply. "You all right?"

Nothing.

"Malcolm? What's going on in there?"

The blaze on my head felt like the deepest parts of hell. An inferno.

*Knock knock knock.*

"Malcolm, open the door!"

I spun around the bathroom, knocking over bottles, towels, yelping.

Water. I needed water. Needed something to put out the flames.

*Knock knock knock.*

"Malcolm!"

I tripped over a towel, my knee almost knocking over a vase beside the sink.

Oh God, the flowers!

The water inside the vase was old and grimy. The flowers

had wilted. But in desperation, I poured it all over my head, soaking my hair clean until my scalp cooled.

*Knock knock knock.*

"Malcolm, don't make me break down this door!"

I swung the door open, toweling my head.

"Dang, Philbert! What the hell's wrong with the water! I almost died in here."

"What?" Philbert tested the faucet and huffed. "Hm. Pipes must be frozen."

"Frozen? Dang!"

"What's with all the ruckus? And what did you do to your head that got you—"

He stopped short, staring at the water dripping down the side of my face then at the empty vase.

"No," he said, laughing. "No, you didn't." He laughed harder.

"I had to! The pipes were frozen, like you said!"

His face twisted up, enraged. "Man! Look at yourself! What got you putting your whole head under that dirty water? Your kinks aren't good enough? You wanna destroy this crown? You hate yourself that much?"

He plucked at the wrong nerve. "Well, you're the one with frozen pipes, living in this old hick town."

I spun away from him, drying off my hair while facing the mirror, my fingers gliding right through. Straight and smoother than silk. Perfect.

Philbert stared, hard. Shaking his head.

"What? What you looking at me like that for?"

He crossed his arms. "You remember Samson and Delilah?"

"Oh, now you wanna break out the Bible? Don't you—"

"Samson had Godly strength. Could kill a lion with his bare hands. His power was stored in his long, kinky locks. It was a gift from God. So his lover Delilah betrayed him, cut his locks while he was sleeping, rendering him helpless enough to be captured by the Philistines. They gouged out his eyes and enslaved him. He had to call on God to save him."

"What you getting at?"

The lights flickered as he narrowed his eyes.

"What would happen if I pinned you down, Mr. Tough Guy, and cut all that stuff off your head? Would this big and bad attitude of yours die? Would my real brother come back? Would he remember Mom and Papa and what this family stands for?"

I yelled back at him as loud as I could. "What this family stands for? Mom and Pop are gone! All the people they fought for? Where were they when Papa got killed? Huh? Where were they when Mom was taken and locked up in that institution? Where were they?"

The lights flickered and I could barely see Philbert now. His voice soft, like a whisper that stung my ears.

"Man, you're not my real brother. You're nothing but a drunken buffoon with dirty water in your hair and rotten flowers stuck to your shirt. My real brother wouldn't do this!"

That swift kick in the stomach knocked the wind right out of me. "What you talking about 'real brother'? This is me!"

"Is this *you*, Malcolm?"

"People don't call me Malcolm!"

"But that's who you are."

The lights blinked again, the bathroom grew darker, the tiles under my feet mixed with lye and ice water.

"Oh I see, you gonna leave me, Philbert? Huh? Is that it? You gonna—"

The jar rolled off the washbasin and slammed on the floor, glass shattering. I jumped back.

"Dang! Philbert, I—"

But he was gone. Vanished.

"Philbert?"

I stepped forward, right onto a piece of glass, and screamed, falling to the floor—water, glass, and lye everywhere.

Lights choked to darkness. Blood on the tiles, my heart raced . . .

. . . until dawn hit the bars of my cell.


*When you're ready, I can free you from prison. First, don't smoke any cigarettes. Don't take any drugs. And don't eat any pork.*

I read Reginald's note over and over again. Keep it in my pants pocket, taking it with me to fold and unfold whenever I have a spare moment. Strangely, having his words close to me brings me some comfort. Some peace. If that's such a thing in Charlestown.

The mess hall is humid, the musty smell of body odors erasing all traces of food. Loud voices, pots clashing echo from the kitchen. But today, nothing bothers me. Even the dream I had last night doesn't linger in my head for long.

My brother's found a play.

I knew all that time in Harlem would do him some good. No wonder I hadn't heard from him. He'd been working things out, plotting a way to break me out of here. That's gotta be it. I'll be free, soon enough.

My brother's found a way out of here.

I stand in line, thinking about all the things I want to do the moment I'm outside these walls. First, shower. A real hot shower, with all the soap I can find. A shower might not be enough. Probably could sit in a tub for a week and still not soak all this dirt off of me. Next, a fresh conk. May even start growing out my hair now so it'll be long enough to take. Then, some food. Good seasoned food. Fried chicken, candied yams, black-eyed peas, and a whole pot filled with greens. Well, maybe not the greens Ella makes, since she doesn't eat pork . . .

Pork!

Reginald's letter comes back to me in an instant. *Don't eat any pork.* It wasn't impossible. Mom never gave us pork. But . . . what kind of play is Reginald coming up with? Why pork? And how would anyone even know if I ever did eat some pork?

*Wake up, Malcolm!*

I spin around, the sound of my mother's voice calling me. But she's not here. Just brothers and guards.

"Here," a voice says.

In a blink I'm at the counter. A cat who took Jimmy's old spot hands me a plate for my tray. On most days, I can't tell one meat from another. But today, a skinny frank and a sad slice of bread stares up at me.

Pork.

I swallow, Reginald's voice fresh in my mind. How badly do I want out of here, enough to keep up with his plan?

"You got anything else?"

The cat leans forward, cupping his ear. "What? I can't hear you."

"I can't have pork," I say louder. "You got anything else?"

He frowns. "You . . . Muslim now or something?"

"No. I just . . . just . . . don't eat pork."

The servers exchange a few confused looks. At the sink, Mack raises an eyebrow, watching on.

Behind me, the line of men curses under their breath.

"Hey! What's the holdup?" someone barks.

A guard starts heading over, antsy hand on his baton, and I swallow hard. Reginald told me not to eat pork, so that's what I'm gonna do. If I'm going to trust anyone, it will be him.

"You got anything else?" I ask again, stronger than before.

The cat grabs the plate with a shrug. "Uh, yeah." He reaches behind him and spoons some red beans onto the plate next to the slice of bread.

"Here you go," he says.

Mack shakes his head but if I didn't know any better, I would've sworn there was a grin forming at the corner of his mouth. The guard reaches us just as I walk away. And for the first time in a long while, I feel a familiar sense of hope and pride ballooning in my chest. Growing up, we weren't allowed to eat pork. Out of all my family members, I was the only one who'd ever tried it, an act of defiance. Even when we didn't have enough and the government tried to ram food down our throats, Mom wouldn't allow it. She would say the United States was in the Great Depression. She'd rather us starve with nutrition, even if that meant eating only morsels. Said God created pig to eat the dirt of the land. That it wasn't meant for human consumption. That the human body can't digest it.

They called her crazy. Locked her up, took our land and our home.

One thing I know, with every ounce in me, Mom wasn't crazy. And if she was willing to stand in her truth, there must be something to it. Something I don't yet see or remember.

Reginald's letter was the bucket of cold water I needed. For over a year, I felt like I was just floating, wading, waiting to drown. Now I feel the need to stretch, to kick, to swim and try to save myself, imagining what freedom really tastes like.

Today, it tastes like burnt beans and stale bread.

Across the mess hall, I see Chucky. He's been dipping and dodging me for weeks now. Still ain't square up his bet. If one Negro thinks he can disrespect me, they all will. I don't want to fight him but I can't *not* fight him at the same time. I have a reputation to keep . . . in and out of Charlestown.

*When you're ready, I can free you from prison. First, don't smoke any cigarettes. Don't take any drugs. And don't eat any pork.*

How did he know what I was up to in here? Or maybe he knows me better than I could ever imagine.

Pork wasn't much to give up, but . . . nutmeg. It's one of the few things that balances me in this hellhole. I try to tell myself that maybe he just means reefer and powder, not nutmeg. Shame wants me to imagine it's anything but.

I toss the last of my nutmeg into the half-filled bucket of piss just so I'm not tempted to dig it back out.

Maybe whatever play Reginald is cooking up can work for Shorty, too? That's the first thing I plan to do when I'm out of here—find Shorty, set him free, spend the rest of my days making all this up to him. I owe him that much. More than that. I owe him my life.

I hope Shorty is doing better than I am. Wherever he is.

*8KD-723. 8KD-724. 8KD-725. 8KD-726.*

Shop moves slow today, but it doesn't stop cats' mouths from moving quick.

"You aight over there, Little?" Walter chuckles. "You sweating good and it ain't a bit hot, kid."

I wipe the sweat dripping down my forehead and ignore him.

"You know he's coming off that junk," Big Lee mumbles.

It's been only a few days, but I'd just about tear off my arm for a high. Cold turkey quitting. Feels almost as bad as them first days they threw me in the hole.

Well. Almost. Nothing could ever feel like that.

"Or maybe he's sweating 'cause Chucky got him looking the fool!"

The shop cackles, a flurry of voices talking over the machines I try to ignore.

"Y'all let the young brother be," Bembry grumbles. "We all have to start somewhere."

The fellas laugh, taunting, as my hands stiffen over the paintbrush. I try not to let them get to me, try to focus on

Reginald coming to save me. But the pent-up pressure of the last few months pushes on my skin from the inside.

"Chucky better watch out," Big Lee cackles. "Satan is steamed now."

Just as I'm ready to explode, I hear Bembry's voice. "If he's Satan, who are you, Jesus? You God?"

The room stirs. Big Lee hooks his hands on his hips. "What kind of craziness you talking? No, sir. Can't go around calling your own self the Lord."

"Then how you going around calling someone Satan?"

The men exchange a few confused glances.

"Lay off the kid, he's coming into his own. He'll be all right," Bembry says.

"Sure, the boy special, right? He goin' somewhere, right?" Walter snorts. "Man, Bembry, you be saying some wild stuff. He locked up just like us. He ain't better than nobody. He ain't goin' nowhere. He a nigger like the rest of us."

Bembry pauses, his fist clenching slow in a way that makes me nervous for Walter. But we all know Bembry doesn't have an ounce of violence in him.

"Why you have a beef with everybody? Fighting over turf when you don't even own the land. You only see life through the eyes of the white man."

His gruff reply leaves Walter speechless.

I, too, am mesmerized. He has a tone right below a shout, never cursing, always direct, like Papa.

*My Dearest Brother,*

*I pray you are safe, in both good health and spirits. I received your letter the other day and I could barely read it. Your penmanship has declined. When you were little, Mom would make you practice your cursive every single day. What happened?*

*I've read that some of the prisons have English Studies. Perhaps it will be good for you to take a class while you are there. When you come home, your penmanship will be sharp and you will be able to get a good job.*

*Things are fine here in Detroit. It's busier than Lansing, so much to do and see. But, I worry about you. Please write soon, and make sure it is legible so your big sister can read it.*

*I love you so much,*

*Hilda*

The warden is a tall man. Wrinkled, pale face with big open pores. Thin glasses that sit right on the bridge of his long pointy nose, hair slicked back, eyes black as coal.

My first year here, I didn't see him but once. Usually he

stayed in his office, his voice only heard over the loudspeaker. But lately, he storms around like a hurricane, inspecting the place. Sometimes he brings outsiders, showing us off like we're a bunch of circus freaks. Other times, he's surrounded by guards, barking commands.

"Take that nigger to Cellblock C . . . Put that nigger in the hole . . . Why is that coon out of line? . . . Need more hogs on the field . . ."

*Nigger* this, *nigger* that, as if they know no other word to call us. As if our only purpose is to be squashed.

The warden stands off to the side of the mess hall and cats become real quiet. One wrong move and he'll throw all of us in the hole without a single care. Mack's voice creeps in my head, and I try not to compare him to a plantation owner. We're not slaves, but it's hard to imagine this place as anything less than that type of hell. How does one live his life desiring to terrorize another?

Today's lunch is kidney beans and brown water. The stench in the air is to the point that I rarely crave food anymore.

Mack sits down at our table, still in his apron, eyeing the warden. If looks could kill, that warden would be a dead man walking. Never seen Mack so filled with rage, but the silent kind.

"Must be auction time," Mack mumbles under his breath.

"What's that?" I ask.

"He comes around here every so often, inspects his property, and POOF! One of us disappears or gets transferred to God knows where."

A lump rolls up in my throat. I ain't mention to anyone how Ella has been campaigning for my transfer out of Charlestown. Not even to Bembry. Too risky. Sometimes you have to keep your business close to the chest. But the warden must know by now. Maybe he knows about Ella working with her friend, arranging things . . .

But thanks to Reginald, I won't need a transfer anymore. I'm about to be a free man.

A cough rips up from the bottom of Mack's stomach. He hacks into a handkerchief, seeming weak and out of breath.

"Say, daddy-o, maybe you should go to the nurse's station or something," I say. He's been like this for the last few weeks, in bed long before lights-out. Not to mention, him coughing around our food doesn't seem too sanitary. Not that it would make much of a difference to the quality, but it will spread germs.

He waves me off. "What good will that do?"

"Better than you being like this, that's for sure," Norm butts in. "What you need is some good ole fashion soup and some cough medicine."

Mack laughs him off. "Is that so? You think they gonna make some homemade soup and hand out cough medicine to someone my age?" He stirs his cup of coffee with his finger.

"Well, brothers, looks like my time has come. Not sure if I'll make it through the night so I'll say my goodbyes now."

Some of the other cats laugh, but I don't see nothing funny about death. Not in here, where it seems so . . . possible.

"And if I don't make it to morning, you can go on and help yourselves to my notepads and pencils. Make sure you scoop them up before they throw them out."

Bembry stretches to look Mack square in the eye.

"Stop talking like that, old man. You ain't dying today or no time soon."

"You never know in here."

A hush follows that statement. Some nod and continue eating.

Mack's words roll around my head again. How we're all so disposable. How we're nothing but machines making *them* money. There are no empty cells. I don't want them taking anymore from me than they already have. I don't want to be a number or a slave, and I sure don't want to die in here. Damn! They'll suck you dry if you let them.

Reginald is my only chance.

And yet, I can't help but think how we all should be free. How no one, not even stray animals, can survive in a place like this.

# CHAPTER 9

*If you aren't careful, the newspapers will have you hating the people who are being oppressed, and loving the people who are doing the oppressing.*

—MALCOLM X

Mom's kitchen hadn't changed much since she was taken away from us.

Hilda stirred a pot on the stove as a record played on the phonograph in the living room. Stewed chicken, rice and peas, a medley of greens, and Mom's secret ingredients for homemade buttery sweet bread with the fruit preserves she stored in the cupboard. My mouth watered so much I almost drooled on the floor.

"Can you tell that stomach of yours to stop hollering at me?" Hilda teased. "Dinner is not quite ready yet."

I patted my belly. "It has a mind of its own."

Hilda giggled, wiping her hands on Mom's apron. I wondered if she knew how much she behaved like Mom. How she had her high cheeks and bright eyes. I felt like a child again just being in her presence, ready to follow behind her knees, snacking on the sweet pea pods or pieces of bread Mom would sneak to me before supper.

Hilda peeked at herself in the mirror, patting her short bob, making sure every curl was in place. She smoothed down her navy dress, checking for runs in her stockings. Just like Mom, her appearance was tall and stately.

I rubbed my arms, then blew into my hands. You'd think after two weeks at home, my skin would be used to the cold again. Instead, it ached for the warmth of Harlem. Not that Harlem was much warmer in temperature, but there was that spark in so many people that felt like an ongoing family reunion, that fire, that rush of adrenaline coursing through my veins always kept me toasty. I missed that *what's-up-homeboy, how-you-living, slap-me-some-skin* type of life.

"So what time is this fella coming over?" I asked.

Hilda smirked. "Be nice. He might be family soon."

"Not if I have anything to say about it," I chided.

She slapped my shoulder with her hand. "Watch your manners."

Hilda never talked about this beau in any of her letters. I wasn't one to pry but I couldn't imagine her dating anyone. Or having a good time. Ever since they took Mom from us, she had fallen into the mother role, always just a little too serious for her age. Don't get me wrong, I was happy she was making a life for herself. But I was also nervous about what her new life would look like and if she would forget me.

"What's for dinner?" I joked. "Pork chops?"

Hilda pursed her lips and returned to her pot. "Malcolm, the pig is not for human consumption. God created it to clean the garbage. You need to keep your body clean. Mom taught you better than that."

There wasn't a knife in the entire house sharper than her words.

"I stand corrected, Big Sis."

Even though I couldn't see her face, I could tell something was on her mind, just by the way she stirred the pot, ladle scraping the bottom.

"You've been here for quite some time, you know."

My shoulders tensed. I sipped some water, nodding, not knowing where the conversation was going but desperate to run away from it. I decided to play it cool, defuse whatever was coming.

"Sick of me already? First you complain I don't come home enough, now you worried about when I'm leaving."

"No, not worried one bit," she said without looking at me. "I know you won't stay. Just wondering if there's any particular reason why you came home?"

"Like I told Philbert and everybody else that keeps askin', just felt like being around family."

Hilda gave me a look, and I knew right away she wasn't buying what I was selling.

"Malcolm, what's wrong, my love? Why are you really here?"

And there it was. Mom's tone, the way she could walk right through your lies. Hilda had it down to a science. I straightened and blew out some air. Guess no getting around the truth.

"Well, about three days before I left Harlem, this tall, red Negro, wearing a woman's stocking over his face, walked into a bar, held up a bartender and managers doing the night's close. Wiped them clean. Bartender was so mad, he hired some hit men to go hunting for whoever did it. Who would've known they'd show up on my doorstep."

Hilda stopped stirring to stare at me. I had her full attention.

"They came to my apartment," I continued. "They tried to intimidate me to get some information. I played it cool and I let them know it wasn't me. Really, Hilda. I don't roll like that. I was working until real late that day. Cats saw me. And I had a solid alibi."

My alibi was a petite blonde who I was in bed with for most of the night, but I thought it was better to leave that part out of the story.

"So you ran off?" Hilda asked, puzzled.

"Just for a little while. Just until the heat dies down. They're big-time and they'd just about settle for anyone to pin it on. Told my boy Sammy to send word when the coast is clear."

"Why didn't you just tell them it wasn't you; why didn't you head up to Boston to see Ella?"

Hilda was naïve. She hadn't seen what I'd seen.

"Would've found me too easy," I said. "That's the first place they'd go look."

Hilda grumbled. "But out of all people, why would they think it would be you?"

I chuckled. "You'd be surprised how many tall, red Negroes are up in Harlem. Black folks of all kinds live up there. Someday, I hope you'll come visit. Sometime soon."

First Reginald, then Hilda. Maybe the whole family could visit. We could all be together again, like we were before.

Hilda stared at me, her eyes narrowing. She placed two hands on the table and leaned real close.

"You must take me for a plum fool."

"What?"

"They'd only suspect you of doing wrong if you've done wrong before. What else are you not saying, Malcolm?"

There were only a few times in my life that I could remember Hilda being cross with me or anyone. She was always composed, formulaic. The last thing I wanted to do was upset her. I leaned back in my chair, my eyes sweeping the floor.

"Nothing. Nothing!"

"Malcolm, you're my brother. And no matter what, I'm

going to take care of you because we're family. But you need to be honest with me, now. If you are in some kind of trouble, you should stay here. Where it's safe. Where you can be with your family, who loves you unconditionally, and who will protect you the best we can."

I loosened my tie, the back of my neck dripped with sweat. It was bad enough being nagged to death by Ella, now I had to add Hilda to that list. She wouldn't understand, not in a million years, what it's like outside this little hick town.

"You've changed, Malcolm. And not for the better."

My Dear Brother,

I'm sure you're surprised to receive this letter so soon after my last, but what I have to tell you simply cannot wait any longer. You see, the men in our family—Philbert, Reginald, Wesley, Robert, and I—have been following the teachings of a great leader. He is a prophet who speaks as a messenger of God. A God like no other and a God that is for the well-being of our people. His Arabic name is Allah.

We are following the teachings of Islam, working alongside brothers and sisters who are just like us. They are also working to protect and uplift our people through holy scriptures that teach us about our identity and heritage. Our real history, Malcolm. We are the original people. The characters in the Bible, the Torah, and the Holy Quran. And we must be obedient to our Creator, God, Jehovah, Allah—one God with a different name depending upon the language you speak or the religion to which you subscribe.

I pray Allah will continue to comfort and guide you over the coming days. More soon.

Your Big Brother,
Wilfred

Philbert and Reginald have been writing similar stuff in all their letters. How they found a God who looks out for Black folk.

A God named Allah.

"Heard you got a big problem," Walter mumbles, not looking in my direction, but I know he is talking to me. "Heard that Chucky is going around saying he ain't paying you back shit."

Bembry glances at me from across the line, and I pretend not to notice.

"Oh yeah," I say, real smooth like. "Who'd he say that to?"

"I don't know. Just word around town."

Of course I've noticed Chucky dodging me every chance

he gets, but I didn't think there was much to worry about. Where could he go? He can't hide. Yet, judging from the looks on cats' faces, I haven't been paying close enough attention and got this whole place looking at me like I'm some chump.

Walter purses his lips with a smack. "So, what you gonna do about it?"

Everyone in the shop stares, waiting for my next move.

"What'd you mean what I'm gonna do about it? He needs to pay what he owes!"

"Yeah, but if he don't, then what? What you gonna do then, Red? Gonna let him disrespect you like that?"

I know what he's getting at. If word spreads that Chucky stiffed me on a bet and didn't suffer consequences, then anyone will think they have the space to do the same.

"Back in my day, cats would lose a few fingers if they stiffed me," Walter says.

"Chucky ain't stiffing nobody," Big Lee says. "He just pressed on his luck."

"Seem like he got plenty of luck to me," Walter shoots back with a laugh.

"Man, now he got Satan after him," someone says behind him. "Sheesh. Good luck, Chuck!"

The men roar with laughter. Chucky's making a joke out of me. Hasn't laid a finger on me but I'm already TKO'ed.

"Hey! Leave him alone, man," Bembry warns the others.

"He doesn't have to do anything if he wants to leave this place the way he came in. Alive."

Don't think anyone can leave here the way they came, that's for sure.

Someone sets a hammer in front of me, whispering in a deep voice, "What you need to do is take *care* of him, you dig?"

The hammer glistens under the overhead lights, the steel cold and smooth, as the room grows quiet. He means "handle him" the way West Indian Archie would handle someone who owed him money. The way he almost handled me, but Shorty saved my life.

Bembry taps his brush on the counter like a judge's gavel, lips in a sharp straight line.

"Young brother, let it go. There's no turning back from violence. You'll be on a road that will lead you nowhere fast."

His words aren't aggressive or hostile, but authoritative.

"What y'all don't seem to understand is, in here, we all in the same boat. We're taking our fear and frustrations out on each other when we should be smarter than that."

The room stirs. My skin is hot, hands sweaty.

"Now what we need to do," he says, holding his palm up. "We need to form together, like a tight fist. That's the only way we all gonna survive and get ahead."

The other men in the shop stop to listen to him, his voice

carrying over the machines like a speaker. "We are not each other's enemy. We're just pawns. Acting like animals trying to take each other out. For what? More time. We gotta be smarter than that. We need to control our own damn feelings so we make it to the outside. Get that hammer outta here."

It reminds me of Papa. The way he used to talk about creating for ourselves. About working in unity to improve our conditions. Building a nation to be independent and manage our own affairs. To be free.

*Up, up, you mighty race!*

But then I think about what Mack said in the yard, talking about how we're slaves, and it fries my blood all over again. Papa lied about us being free. Papa left us for the wolves to rip our family apart. And if I'm going to be stuck in here, ain't no way I'm going to let some Negro disrespect me.

The hammer, it's a small tool, easy to hide in my pocket and walk right out of here.

By the end of the shift, as the other brothers leave the shop for dinner, I hang back, wanting to be the last to walk into the mess hall, a blur in the crowd so Chucky don't see what's coming. I know I should just cool my head, wait for Reginald to save me, but there's some things you can't let go.

At the door, Bembry stands like a wall in my way. He points to my pocket. "Say, what you got there?"

"Don't know what you getting at."

He sighs. "Young brother, you don't want to do this. It ain't worth having blood on your hands and spending the rest of your life in this dump."

I get straight to the point. "Chucky's late squaring up. He's walking around disrespecting me. Can't have that, no way. He needs to pay what he owes."

"You really wanna ruin what's left of your life over this? You won't even know this fool ten years from now. You have to learn patience, man."

He doesn't know me! All everybody sees is some kid they think they can get over on. A fire blazes under my skin. My hands ball into fists.

"Move out my way, old man. This ain't none of your business."

He hesitates before saying, "All right then, fight me."

"Why? You wanna take the beating in his place?"

He sighs, tilting his chin up. "If that's what it takes."

I raise my fists, knowing nothing I'm doing makes a bit of sense, but I'm in a blur of rage.

"Aight then, come on!"

He looks at my hands but doesn't move his. "I ain't gonna try to stop you. You do what you have to do."

"What do you mean, old man? Come on!"

From the corner, the guards are watching us, mumbling to each other. Any other time, they would've jumped in, taken control of the situation. But they're waiting. Waiting for us to attack each other, to fight like animals, for any excuse to beat us bloody and throw us in the hole. Or worse, kill us. Even knowing this, it doesn't stop the waves of anger rolling over me.

Bembry shakes his head, voice firm and steady. "Do what you have to do, son."

Chucky crossed the line. If just one Negro crosses me, they will all think I'm here for the picking. And yet, there's Bembry. He's never raised his voice, never thrown a punch or even lost his temper. Yet the respect he receives . . . with just his words. It's powerful.

Just like Papa.

In an instant, the realization sucker punches me in the throat. It's what I couldn't put my finger on all this time. This man IS Papa. And I'm about to fight him. My chest heaves, heart racing.

"I'm not your son!" I roar, the words searing my tongue. "I'm not your son! I'm not your son!"

Bembry only nods. "All right."

"I'm not your son!"

I'm not my father's son. I'm not acting like it. The fact that I'm here, in this place . . . makes it all the more true. I don't know who I am anymore. This hammer in my pocket, the nutmeg, the reefer, the weed . . . What am I doing? What have I done?

I hold back the sob building in my chest as my feet carry me away fast, out the door, straight back into my cell, before I release it. I'm swinging at the air like Sugar Ray, cursing, screaming until I can barely breathe. A tornado touches down in cell sixty-one. Mattress flipped, sheets ripped, everything tossed about. Papers fly like snow, letters from my family, dozens of them. When the dust settles, I fall to the ground, tears streaming down my face. Breathe.

*You don't belong here*, a voice inside me says. But where do I belong?

"Little?! What's going on in here?" the guard barks.

The real enemy walks in, his voice tight and loud. For a change, I don't feel the cold. I feel no pain. The guard looms over me, same one that threw my boy Lightning in the hole. When I don't respond, he lifts his foot, aiming at my eye.

"Nigger, you hear me talking to you?" he hisses.

My Harlem instincts come back quick. I reach in my pocket, fishing for a gun I no longer have. Only the hammer, piercing my thigh.

"Oh, so you deaf now?" He points the tip of his shoe, aiming it square at my forehead.

The thoughts rip through me: If I kill this man, I'll be killed. I'll never see my family again. But I can't let him treat me like this.

I shift onto my knees, meeting his glare, and press my cheek against his heel, knowing it's a shoe that has stepped through every square inch of this filthy place. Don't care. He needs to know I'm not scared of him or no one, and I look him in his eye.

The guard frowns, eyes softening to something close to fear. His Adam's apple dances under his tie, uniform tightening around his neck. He sets his foot down, then kicks my pail, piss spilling out on the floor.

"Clean this mess up, nigger," he shouts, shutting the cell door, and I'm a caged animal once again.


I'm not Satan. I'm not Detroit Red.

I'm not sure who I am anymore. And it scares me. I became many Malcolms to survive. Survive living without Papa, survive living without Mom and my family. Survive the streets of Roxbury and Harlem, survive prison. If I don't find myself and quick, I could wind up staying lost forever.


Today, Bembry is talking about life out west in California. He's been all over this country while half of these cats haven't made it out of Roxbury. He doesn't mention the other day with the hammer and so neither do I. It'll remain that way.

When Bembry speaks even the guards listen to his stories. You've got to be smoother than smooth to have these white boys' attention without breaking a sweat.

On the way to lunch, I walk behind him, questions buzzing

around my head. Not knowing how long I have before Reginald frees me, I jump right to it. Whatever Bembry's gimmick is, I want to know.

"Hey, Bembry, how you know all that stuff?"

"What stuff?"

"That stuff you always talking 'bout."

Bembry laughs. "Books. Lots of books."

"Books?" Seems too simple an answer. I read books. Well, sometimes. "How do you know which ones to read? Where do you get them?"

Bembry turns to face me, his eyebrow arched. "You know, I know you ain't a dummy. In fact, you got some good brains up there, if you'd just learn how to use them right."

Bembry also knows how to cut you without so much as a curse.

"So where are these books you're talking about?"

"Young brother, you been to the library yet?"


The library has a recognizable scent. Rich with a hint of dust and wet wood. Mom and Papa had a lot of books. We all used to read together at the kitchen table. Mom with a baby in her arm. Papa teaching us about identity, empowerment, and self-reliance. About the right to want more out of life than the scraps and limitations thrown at us. He said the captor will never tell you your worth, especially when they've taken your identity for their own. Their voices ring in my ears.

*Wake up, Malcolm . . .*

Bembry slams a pile of books on the table in front of me. The books are old as dirt, torn and worn down. The library has nothing but a few shelves of them, and they all seem to be in the same condition.

"You want to gain some knowledge, you need to start here." He taps on the top book, grinning. "You smart, Red, I can see that. But you got to read more than just a little here and there. You got to read every single day, whenever you can. Absorb all this knowledge like a dried-up sponge in water."

"I read a lot," I say. "I used to be class president, man. Just got a shitty hand, you know."

"That's all right. You still growing, kid. But to grow a tree, you gotta start with the seeds."

I think of Mom's garden and the butterflies and start sweating. The smell of those books . . . the smell of home.

"Seeds?"

"Seeds, meaning the foundation. The root. Words!"

He slides a few books into my hands—*Moby-Dick*, Shakespeare's *Macbeth* and *Romeo and Juliet*. He then slips a large book from the bottom of the pile, flipping it open to the first page. *Oxford English Dictionary*.

"This will be your guide for when you get to a word you

don't know in these books. Words have power, Red. The more words you know, the more power you gain."

Power. Exactly what I'm looking for. Exactly what he has.

"Well, where do I start?"

"Where everyone starts. From the beginning." He flips to the first page of the dictionary.

"All right, all right, I got it. You want me to remember all these words?"

"Yep. Write them down. Each word and its definition. Whenever you write something, it takes to memory."

There's probably hundreds of thousands of words in this book. I scan the first one, struggling through the pronunciation.

**"'Aardvark . . . noun. A large burrowing nocturnal mammal of sub-Saharan Africa that has a long snout, extensible tongue, powerful claws, large ears, and heavy tail.'"**

Bembry smirks. "It's a start."

I have two more weeks to kill until Reginald arrives. Outside of Ella, he'll be the only family member I've seen since coming to Charlestown. I never wanted anyone to see me dressed this way, living in this dump, in this state of mind. But maybe that was a mistake. Maybe it's family that I need most. To remind me who I am at my core.

In my last letter to Ella, I asked her to send some new pens. I'm using mine up quickly writing all those words from the dictionary. I'm already at *B*.

**Buoyant. Adjective. Capable of floating; cheerful.**

Studying the dictionary helps pass the time. It feels familiar, like I'm back home at the kitchen table. My brothers and sisters surrounding me. Mom telling another story about her voyage to Canada, where the Marcus Garvey convention took place in the early 1900s. That's where she met Papa. I've got my books in hand, we all do, and we're absorbing her every word like a gospel hymn.

The bell rings for lunch. "Line up!" the guard calls.

In the mess hall, I spot a brother who looks just like Shorty. Enough for me to almost ask if he is related to a Malcolm Jarvis. Pretty wild that Shorty and I are both from Lansing and both named Malcolm. Two needles in a haystack found each other like a couple of long-lost twins, years apart in age, destined to meet that day Fat Frankie hustled me out of forty dollars. Back then, I was so green, they couldn't call me Red. Shorty knew I was young, probably because I was tall and lanky and always had a book in my back pocket. But after he showed me the ropes, he never treated me like some kid again. He respected me.

I wouldn't be who I am if it weren't for Shorty teaching me everything he knew and then some.

"Heard you ain't eating pork no more."

Chucky stands in front of me, blocking my path to the tables, and I reel back from the stench of his hot breath and rotting teeth. Most of us don't have toothbrushes, but I keep my teeth clean with a piece of washrag. He has some nerve coming up in my face about anything but what he owes. Then I remember, Reginald will be here soon. I'll be free. And this fool will still be in this filthy cage. Just have to play it cool, like Shorty taught me. Like Bembry showed me.

"Yeah, who you hear that from?"

Chucky is startled by my response, probably expecting me to beg him to pay up. He digs deeper.

"Oh, you know everybody talking about it," he says, a laugh in his voice. "'Little don't eat no pork no more.' Folks trying to figure out what you getting at."

"Nothing. Except wondering why everybody is all in my business. Most of all, you."

"Strange, that's all. You ain't have a problem with it before."

"Just staying away from it. Never ate it as a kid. Not eating it now."

"So you and your family too good for what's being served here? Thinking you better than everyone else?"

I grip the tray tight, swallowing back the urge to shove it in his face. I have a fire pit deep in my belly. Especially when it comes to my family. Chucky is trying to coax that fire out of me, trying to push any button to set me off.

And it's working.

Right as I'm about to shove my tin plate down his throat . . . I hear my number called.

"22843. Little! Visitation, line up."

My blood is racing as I head into the visitors' center. Ella is early. But that's not what's on my mind. I'm wondering how I'm going to deal with Chucky. He keeps pushing me to the edge, and now he's bringing my family into it. I'm so lost in my own thoughts that I don't see her right away. If I was paying attention, I would've noticed the way she stood out in her blue dress. And Mom's blue coat.

Hilda.

My feet stop dead in their tracks and the guard pushes me forward. Hilda smiles at me, her lips painted a dark red.

This is a dream, I tell myself, looking for all the ways I could make myself wake up. I pinch my arm, bite my tongue, hold my breath.

"Hello, Malcolm," she says.

Her voice. It's exactly how I remembered. Stern, crisp, yet soft around the edges. I blink once. Then again.

We sit at the table and I watch her examine the room, carefully. Taking in every detail.

"You're . . . here," I blurt out.

She smiles slightly.

"I told you I would come, and I've always been a woman of my word."

She takes a handkerchief out her purse, holding it to her mouth and nose for a brief moment, and she dabs each corner of her eyes.

"I . . . I didn't know nothing about you coming."

"Anything. You didn't know *anything* about me coming. Ella didn't tell you? You didn't get my last letter? I said I was buying a ticket. Would've come sooner but I had to find a proper place to stay. Whatever happened to your *Green Book* we sent you east with?"

"It's at Ella's," I say.

"Well, I can see why you changed. This city is just so . . . busy. It's even busier than Detroit."

"Wait. A place to stay? You moved to Boston?"

"Didn't want Ella taking on all the trouble of seeing you. Must be wearing on her. But, more than anything, I didn't want you feeling abandoned by your family. Everybody needs their family, Malcolm. We're always with you. Don't you ever forget that."

At that moment, it didn't matter where I was or what Chucky knew. My eldest sister was with me now. Not just in letters. In the flesh.

"Thank you," I whisper, unaware of how badly I needed to hear those words. I want to hug her but I'm too afraid.

Hilda doesn't look as stressed as Ella does when she visits. She's composed, regal, radiant. A light this place has never seen. Hilda and I were always close. The sister I knew since the day I was born, my sister who took care of me longer than Ella, Papa, Mom, or anyone else.

"Well," she huffs. "You're nothing but skin and bones. We need to fatten you up once you're home."

"Home? You're working with Reginald, too?"

Her face falls.

"Reginald? No, my love, I'm working with Ella. We've been writing letters, petitioning for your transfer. You don't belong here. This is no place for any human being to live. I don't care what they say you or any of these young men did. Who died and made them God?"

I swallow, my heart racing. "Oh. Yeah, yeah. Right."

She doesn't know. But if Reginald has a hustle that will get me out of here, I don't want her caught up in it. I nod my head, smiling. I'm just so happy she's here. That I have more family nearby than I've had in years.

"Although, I know Reginald wants to talk to you. Some things . . . well, it's better that he shares his plan with you himself."

"By order of the president, the Executive Order abolishes discrimination on the basis of race, color, religion or national origin in the United States Armed Forces."

Norm grips the edges of the newspaper, sitting on top of the table in the common area, a big smile on his face as he reads aloud. I'm still stuck on the headline splashed across the front.

## PRESIDENT TRUMAN WIPES OUT SEGREGATION IN ARMED FORCES

Norm sounds like he's chewing glass as he reads, wincing through every word. It's painful to the ear. Maybe he should study the dictionary, too.

One table over, Big Lee and Bembry are playing dominoes. On the opposite end of the table, Chucky's head pops up as Norm reads, almost in disbelief at what he's hearing.

"So that means we colored folk can join the army and fight with the white boys?" Big Lee asks from behind me.

"Yup." Norm folds the paper. "No more *all-Negro* units. Equal pay, equal rights, equal everything."

"Man, I can't wait. I'm going to enlist first opportunity I get," Norm says, grinning.

"You want to join the army?" Walter asks. "Why in the world would you wanna do that?" We all turn and look at Norm, waiting for his answer.

"Man, why not?" Norm scoffs. "That's good honest work right there. They dress you up in a fine uniform. You get to travel the world. Fight for our country. Fight for freedom. You get to be a *real* man alongside them white folk!"

"Freedom?" I snap. "Whose freedom?"

The question catches us both off guard. I wasn't sure where it came from. Someplace I had long hidden from myself.

Norm trips over his words, fixing his mouth to defend himself.

"Well, ours. From the . . . well, you know." He clicks his tongue, real nervous like, avoiding my eyes. "Hey! Come on y'all, the game's about to start!"

It's 1948. A new season of baseball. Means I've been here for two years. Guards stop letting us use the kitchen. They've been tightening their grip around our necks the past few weeks. Random cell inspections, lineups, head counts, clean-ups—more heavy-handed than usual. They've even started confiscating things they once let slide. Reefer, nutmeg, loosies. We always had an understanding of sorts. But all those unwritten rules vanish. Something has spooked them.

Everyone gathers around the small radio propped up on the table. It'll be impossible to hear the game in here today. Not that I'm not taking bets anymore, it just doesn't have the same meaning.

"Not interested in the game?" Bembry asks as he cleans up a set of dominoes.

"I am," I lie. Don't want anyone to know about the storm brewing inside me. "You hear Norm talking all that junk about joining the army?"

Bembry silently puts the pieces away as I join him.

"Wild, right?" I continue, trying to distract myself. "I just don't understand why Norm would want to fight for a country that doesn't even consider him equal. I don't get that. A slave . . . I mean a job he's willing to risk his life for? Not like they're gonna make him a general, or give him back a piece of the land his ancestors toiled in return, so he can have the freedom to mind his own business and care for his family. He thinks he's gonna see the world from a free man's perspective? He'll probably just end up mopping the barracks or washing some white soldier's dirty briefs. Why wouldn't he want better for himself?"

I can feel my father's teachings like a beating drum through my bloodstream, coming alive, threatening to come out my pores, but I fight it. Who am I to tell anyone who they should or shouldn't be?

*Up, up, you mighty race!*

Bembry pins me with his eyes. A look I'm not used to. He folds his hands on the table with a sigh.

"You hear that boy Jackie Robinson there?" Bembry says, nodding over his shoulder.

I glance at the other cats, gathering around the broke radio, faces tense, leaning in to hear as best they could.

"Jackie's showing them white boys what we made of."

Bembry stands up, dusting his hands before tucking the domino set under his armpit.

"Sometimes, you got to play to beat folks at their own game. Not focus on showing them up, but showing them another way of winning. We win more when we are together. That message is worth more than all the words you can ever muster. But you can't win nothing from outside the field, and you can't win alone."

Always prided myself on being a good student, taking detailed notes, and asking the right questions. When I was a kid, I began writing a book, but I kept starting over every time I made a mistake because I needed it to be perfect. I'd sit with my mom when she was working on Mr. Garvey's *Negro World* newspaper or I'd go out in our backyard when I really wanted to gather my thoughts.

But it's hard to concentrate knowing Reginald is only a few days away. I've done everything he's told me. Stopped smoking, stayed away from reefer and nutmeg, and haven't even touched an ounce of pork. I sent him a simple letter: *I'm ready, I'm clean, come get me.*

I'm ready for whatever Reginald is cooking up.

**Finite. Adjective. Having definite or definable limits; having a limited nature or existence.**

I write at least ten words a day. Already gone through two notebooks and I'm trying to write smaller, fitting more than one word on each line if I can. My penmanship is improving in just a matter of weeks. I feel lighter, knowing that at any moment, I'll be free from this place.

Hilda comes to see me twice a week. Every other visit, she tries to tell me more about the Nation of Islam, but I'm really not interested in any type of religious talk.

"Well, Yvonne and I haven't joined the NOI, but all of your brothers have because it's much like the work that Papa was doing and it's the closest religion out here that offers salvation to Black people. Everybody in Detroit says this man is the messenger of God in the flesh and that he is a savior.

"The Honorable Elijah Muhammad is helping us discover our history and how to thrive in the world together. That's important to every human being, Malcolm. He's helping our people. Maybe he really is a Black savior."

I listen, but really all I'm interested in hearing is how Hilda is enjoying Boston. Maybe when Reginald gets me out of here, I can convince her to stay. We can find a spot together or maybe we can all move in with Ella. She has three floors plus an attic. Her house is big enough. We can all live under the same roof, and be a real family again.

"The smartest people in the world have the best vocabulary," Bembry says as we gather in the common area, waiting for suppertime. "You don't win fights with your fist, you win fights with your words. Doctors, lawyers, politicians, theologians . . . they all use words to prove their point."

Growing up, I wanted to be a lawyer. Had the grades and the résumé for it. Best in class. They even voted me class president. But then my teacher asked what I wanted to be; his answer haunts me to this day:

"Don't be ridiculous. Niggers can't be lawyers."

**Felicitous. Adjective. Very well suited or expressed; apt.**

His answer made me question all that Papa and Mom taught me. How could his words contradict theirs? How could I be anything, do anything if to the world, I'm just a nigger? If being "just a nigger" while believing I can be my best self could get me killed—like Papa—then why bother trying?

From that day on, the thought of being in school made me sick to my stomach. But here I am, learning again.

Except, I'm still in Charlestown. I'm in a prison.

Soon enough, though, Reginald is going to bust me out of here.

I'm itching for freedom and I can't sit still. I can almost taste home. Hilda's homemade lemon pound cake. A glass of bourbon with my name on it, calling me.

**Felicity. Adjective. The quality or state of being happy;** *especially*: **great happiness.**

The warden walks into the unit with a crew of guards surrounding him. He's been walking around with more white businessmen in black suits, white shirts, and hard pudgy faces, talking in fast, hushed whispers. I can spot a scheme cooking from a mile away. Something is about to go down, just wish I knew what.

Today, they seem to be measuring the height and width of the cells, taking notes and muttering plans.

"Hey," I whisper to Bembry, nodding over my shoulder. "What's happening there?"

Bembry sighs over his domino pieces. "They're about to add more of us in here. Soon enough, you won't have your own cell anymore. There'll be two or three more bodies in there with you."

My cell is six by seven feet. I can barely fit in it alone. The walls have inched in over the year, and just the thought of three of us sharing that one bucket makes my chest tighten and my blood boil. They can't add more of us! We're filled to the brim. Overflowing. Drowning.

Reginald can't come soon enough.

# CHAPTER 10

*Children have a lesson adults should learn, to not be ashamed of failing, but to get up and try again. Most of us [adults] are . . . so cautious . . . and therefore so . . . rigid and afraid that it is why so many humans fail.*

—MALCOLM X

When I was fired from my slave with the railroad, I became my own boss. Everyone knew me at the best clubs and shows around Harlem.

My daily routine: wake up sometime in the afternoon, grab some breakfast, check in with friends, head to the movies to kill time, and then check in at the supper club to watch the big bands or catch cats for dinner and a drink before making my final rounds for the evening.

Movies were my obsession. Ask me about a movie, and I'd probably seen it! Maybe even twice. When you hustled, it was best to keep a low profile. The dark cover of the movie theater was the best way to keep money in your pocket, stay out of sight from the cops, and get in touch with the rest of the world. I never traveled in a large circle. Being loud and greedy would put you on the quickest road to prison.

And ain't no way I ever wanted to end up in there. Not ever.

In the picture shows, there were a lot of white women. Beautiful ones. They all made me think of Sophia. Especially that Lana Turner. She had Sophia's big eyes, her silky strawberry blond hair, her porcelain white skin, even her raspy voice. Harlem had plenty of fine Negro ladies. But Sophia . . . was one of a kind. She loved me like no other. I missed her up in Boston. The way she purred my name and made me feel . . . invincible. Man!

One afternoon, I walked out of *Casablanca*, headed home to give her a call.

"Hey there, stranger," Sophia said, and I could almost picture her wrapping the phone cord around her little pinkie. "I thought you forgot about me."

"Oh, little lady, I could never forget about you. In fact, why don't you pack a bag and come on down and visit me? Getting kinda lonely in Harlem. Could sure use a pretty thang like you to brighten up the place."

She giggled. "Say, that wouldn't be such a bad idea. I can take the train down this weekend. Will you meet me at the station?"

"I got you!"

"Then . . . I guess it's settled," she said, but something caught in her throat.

"What's the matter? You sound a little . . . reluctant."

"Oh no, darling, never that, I just . . . well I just wonder are you ever coming back home, back to Boston?"

I didn't expect her to sound so pained without me. It had been a few years and she'd always seemed sharp as a knife when it came to us. That's what I liked most about her—her cunning confidence—but maybe the distance had changed things.

"My home is Harlem," I said, urging myself not to fall for her games.

"But, I miss you."

The way she said it, I almost believed her. But then, how badly could she miss me when she acted as if there wasn't a chance we could really be together?

Not that we could. Not that the world would allow it.

The doorbell rang downstairs. I looked out the window but saw no one on the stoop.

"Hey, doll, someone's at the door. I'll call you right back."

"But I—"

I hung up fast, slipping the pistol out of my jacket pocket.

I held my breath, inching toward the front door.

"Who's there?" I barked.

"Malcolm?"

Stunned, I lowered my pistol.

"Reginald?" I gasped.

I slipped my gun into my waistband and swung the door open.

"Well, homeboy, you like a stray cat. I can't seem to get rid of you!"

Reginald brightened at the sight of me, duffel bag slung over his shoulder.

"Whew, man, I'm glad you're home. Wasn't sure how long I was gonna have to camp out here."

He'd gained a few more pounds of muscle and had the faint shadow of a rusty beard growing in.

"What are you doing here?"

"Thought you said you missed me," he chuckled.

That's Reginald. Always ducking and dodging any direct questions you threw at him.

"I haven't missed you that bad," I said, slugging him in the arm. "I go from not seeing you in years to seeing you, what, every few months?"

"Well, uh, there's been a little mix-up," he said, scratching the back of his head. "I, uh, missed my ship."

"You lying."

"If I'm lying, I'm buying." He laughed.

"Well, guess I'm treating you to dinner!"

We dropped off his duffel and headed to the Braddock Hotel. I was so excited to see my little brother again, I could barely stop grinning. We talked about everything, from news back at home, his travels around, to my wild stories about Harlem.

The next ship wouldn't be back for another two weeks.

That meant Reginald and I had plenty of time to hit night-clubs and speakeasies all over the city. Creole Bill's, the Roxy, the Apollo, and the Paramount. Reginald loved music and, with my connections, I was able to bring him backstage to some of the best shows in town. The guys from Lionel Hampton's band told him stories of their exploits. Billie Holiday hugged him with the biggest smile, singing "baby brother." Everyone took to him. We were the tallest with the broadest shoulders wherever we went. Just like Papa. No one would've guessed he was just sixteen and I was seventeen. My brother was just that cool.

"Heh. Well, I'll be," Reginald laughed, scooping up copies of my two books, *The Green Book* and *My Bondage and My Freedom* by Frederick Douglass. Both had fallen from my pocket right outside Dickie Wells's spot. "Still carrying around books, I see? What is your obsession with these things?"

I snatched them out his hands and tucked them back in my jacket pocket.

"Old habits," I mumbled.

He raised an eyebrow. "*The Green Book?*"

"Yeah. Sometimes I need to hit the road and go down south at a drop of a dime. Need to see it on the map before I agree to follow the bands. You gotta know your living options. I don't want any problems."

Reginald shook his head. "That book is mighty thin. Not many places Negroes are safe."

I pressed my jacket, hugging the book to my side as a man stumbled out the door, laying eyes on me with a grin.

"Red! I've been looking for you," he slurred, turning to Reginald. "This man right here trying to take Bumpy Johnson's place in Harlem." He cackled loud enough for the whole block to hear. "Say, man, you got a little something for me?"

Reginald nodded and stepped aside, always turning a blind eye as I sold reefer to customers. He never asked questions, just went with the flow. Something the rest of my family wouldn't do.

When I finished up business, I rejoined Reginald at the corner, leaning on a streetlamp, watching the taxicabs pick up customers. White men stumbling out the bar, Negro women on their arms, hailing taxis to the nearest hotel. They loved coming up to Harlem, loved the warmth and excitement of being with Negroes. But only late at night, under the cover of darkness.

"You and Wilfred should've gone to college," he said after a few minutes. "All those books you two read. Would've gone real far. Maybe even become a professor or a lawyer."

I shrugged. "Wilfred was always the smart one."

"I was talking about you, too," he said, a smirk on his lips.

The hairs on my arms stood up. Quickly, I changed the subject.

"So, uh, what's the plan, daddy-o?" I said with a laugh. "You trying to get back on that slave ship or you trying to stay. 'Cause it's been a week and you're fitting in pretty good around here. Taking to Harlem like a natural."

He shrugged with a grin. "I wouldn't mind staying for a spell."

It had been a long time since I felt the type of happiness that bloomed in my chest. The type of happiness that made me fear losing it.

"Well, all right. That's good. But first, we need to find you a hustle."

Reginald winced. "You know, I'm not into all that stuff."

"I see what you getting at, homeboy. We'll keep it cool and find you something even better! Just will take a little creativity. All you gotta know is how folks move and think out here. Then find whatever they need more than you do. You can sell water to a well if you meet the right well."

He smiled, sipping some whiskey. He had started drinking during this visit. Nice to see him cut loose with me. "How else you think I'm able to keep up with you and all that running your mouth do?"

Reginald was smart, he'd learn his own way. But I didn't want him following in my footsteps. I wanted to find him a nice safe hustle, 'cause the white man made it difficult for Negroes to have dignified jobs where you could make a good living. You had to create your own hustle, if you were smart. Then maybe eventually, I'd start looking for a steady, legit slave. Find us a better place, someplace stable for my family.

"Malcolm, do you ever feel alone out here, all by yourself?"

*Sometimes*, I wanted to say but didn't.

"Last visit, you, uh, said you wanted to know about Papa," I said as we head to the next bar.

"Still do. Sometimes, when I'm out at sea, I feel like I'm out there all alone, sinking."

"Anyone tell you that Marcus Garvey would stay at our house . . . when Papa was president of the Milwaukee chapter?"

Reginald brightened. "What! Really?"

"Yes, really. Come on, time to celebrate this new life we about to live in Harlem!"


Around 4:00 a.m. on Friday, coming home from celebrating Reginald's decision to stay, was when it hit me: Sophia.

"Uh, hey, homeboy, we gotta find you a room to rent for next weekend," I said as we entered my place. "Company's coming."

Reginald laughed. "Company that long I have to stay away? Must be a fine piece of company."

"Well, Boston ain't exactly around the corner, you know. It's Sophia."

The spark left his eyes. "Oh."

Reginald knew about Sophia. Overheard me talking about her to some fellas from the big band backstage at the Apollo.

He sobered up cold at the mention of any white woman since.

"But, hey, we'll still break bread this weekend. I want you to meet her! Looks just like that movie star Lana Turner. You'll like her."

"Um, nah. I think I'll just catch a picture show or something."

The apartment steamed up as he turned his back to me. I moved to the kitchen, throwing a couple of ice cubes in a glass with some whiskey, trying to find the right words without sounding bruised.

"You . . . don't want to meet her?"

Reginald didn't mince words. "No. And you shouldn't want to meet her either."

My back tensed, the base in his voice jolting. He shoved shirts into his duffel bag, ready to leave.

"So what is it, because she's white? You know how many Negroes would kill to be in my shoes? To have a fine white woman like her, wanting ME!"

Reginald shrugged. "It's about a lot of things. But I'll tell you this, though; you stay with that woman for too long and she'll ruin you. You can kiss this life goodbye."

I swallowed.

"And maybe that's a good thing," he continued. "Maybe you'll come back to your senses. Maybe you'll finally . . . wake up and find that woman isn't good for you."

The visitors' center is glowing blue with the sun beaming streams of light inside as I sit waiting anxiously for Reginald to arrive.

The thoughts turn over and over again in my head. Thinking of all that time Reginald stayed with me in Harlem, the hustles he picked up, the moves he made. Just as I suspected, he learned quick. He could talk himself out of a jam, easy. Everything he learned led us to this moment. Maybe it's fate. Maybe God hasn't forgotten about me after all.

The moment Reginald walks in, I have to pick my mouth up off the floor. I have never seen him look so good! He always dressed sharp but, boy, my brother looks CLEAN, slicker than okra juice in his fresh tailored charcoal-gray suit.

"Ooooh-weeee . . . looking good, daddy-o!"

I reach back to slap him some skin but quickly straighten, glancing at a guard in the corner, forgetting for a split second where we are.

"It's good to see you, Malcolm," Reginald says, real proper like, a steel rod in his back.

"Uh, yeah. Good to see you, too, brother," I say, playing along.

We sit at the table and I rub my hands together, nerves like firecrackers. Reginald remains poised and placid (words I picked up in the dictionary). We talk about family, about his new move to Detroit with Philbert, Hilda and her move to Boston. I'm so anxious after weeks of waiting, I nearly explode out my seat.

"Aight, homeboy, spill it," I whisper, speaking fast. "What you got cooking? What's with the no pork, no cigarettes riddle?"

Reginald stares off into the distance for a moment. Then, as if a surprise thought occurs to him, he looks at me and smiles.

"Malcolm, if a man knew everything imaginable that there is to know, who would he be?"

My stomach drops to the ground with that quick, sinking feeling I'm about to hear some bad news or worse, no news at all.

"Well, um . . . he would have to be some kind of God—"

"There is a *man* who knows everything, and he says he is the messenger of God."

The calm and patience in his voice makes me sweat. "Who is that?"

"God's name in Arabic is Allah."

Allah. I recognize the name from Philbert's letters. From Hilda's talks. From the guys in the shop. I'm confused so I don't say nothing, because I don't want to seem stupid in front of my little brother. Reginald takes pity on me.

"The Honorable Elijah Muhammad is a Black man, just like us! Lives in Detroit, that's where we met him. A small, kind, gentle man who knows the true knowledge of the

Black man. That we are descendants of the first man, the original man, in Africa. He is powerful, Malcolm, and he genuinely cares about the welfare of our people. Much like Papa did."

There's a brightness in his eyes I didn't notice before. The same peacefulness that shines from Hilda. As if they both ate stardust for dinner.

Reginald goes on to tell me about this Elijah Muhammad, who proclaims himself the Messenger of Allah. About his practices and his vision.

"The Honorable Elijah Muhammad says Negroes must be taught the knowledge of self, our real self. He said during slavery we were systemically taught that God did not create us as equals to the white man. That He created us to be their slaves. They are corrupt, brother, not you!" He looks me square in the eye. "They forced their ungodly ways on us and created this desperation in us to survive and thrive, a desperation as men when all we really want is to take care of our women and our families. The Negro was taught to take THEIR names, their fake religion, and their identity . . . We don't know where we came from, or who we are, or our true family name."

"Little," I counter, baffled.

"No. That was a name given to our father, which was given to his father and his father. We had a clear identity before the white man went to Africa and disrupted our sovereignty;

kidnapped millions of men, women, and children; and imposed HIS savagery and corruption on us, Malcolm. Mom used to tell us similar stories. Remember? This is the same work of Mr. Garvey and Papa. Strong men, Malcolm, who are powerful, organized intellectuals. Elijah Muhammad is the messenger of God and HE is going to help you get out of this place."

My head is swirling. My entire body is on fire, the disappointment and anger raging through me. All this time . . . I thought he had a plan—a real plan.

I stand up quick and Reginald leans back to look up at me. My fist balls up, tears pinching behind my eyes.

"You have no idea what I've been through," I say through clenched teeth and walk away.

I should have known; if they couldn't get Mom out of that hospital, how in the hell are they going to break me out of this shithole?


The nutmeg in my system makes it hard to focus on the monotony in the shop. Bembry frets over the paint I'm spilling, but I'm too numb to hear or care.

I receive letters almost daily from Philbert and Wilfred, urging me to become a Muslim and join the Nation of Islam. All my brothers accepted this new religion. They were together. I was once again on the outside, alone.

Reginald was smart; he leaned into my hustle spirit and knew the only way he'd get me to listen to anything he had to say. He snatched the rug out from under me. Of all my siblings, I trusted him most to understand. I may never forgive him.

Reginald visits again. Explaining more about Allah and Elijah Muhammad, how the acts of white people were systemically designed against us and against the coloreds in the world. That they are the acts of the devil and that their time is up. Black people are waking up from hundreds of years of self-loathing and brainwashing.

"It's what Papa would've wanted," he says.

I feel myself tip into a fit of rage. "How do you know what Papa would've wanted? How do any of us know? He was lynched by those crackers!"

"Yes, Papa was killed by a mob of white people who were enraged by his independence and success," Reginald corrects. "The mob beat our father like an animal. They tied him up and placed him on the tracks and stood there to watch an oncoming streetcar sever his body. Cut one of his legs off entirely. There's a pattern here, you must see it. That's evil and criminal, brother. We're expected to remain helpless and love the people who were our kidnappers, our torturers, our lawmakers. The same people who disrupted our livelihoods are also our educators, too." My brother remains composed as he speaks. "Just think about every white person with whom you've ever come in contact. What good have they done for you or for these people in here?"

When I think of all the white people in my life—the Klan who killed my dad; the government officials who threw my mother into an asylum; the social workers who systematically tore apart our family and took our family land; the kids that I genuinely liked but who called me *nigger*; my favorite teacher, Mr. Ostrowski, who called me foolish for thinking I could be a lawyer to help people; the guards; the police who harassed me; the judge who sentenced me; Sophia . . .

My mind races down a rabbit hole in my tiny cell with no way out, stomach twisting until I vomit into a half-filled bucket. Yeah, I took that watch, but there was not one white person in my life who treated me with decency, who respected me wholeheartedly . . . as an equal, as a human. A human being with feelings.

I had believed everything they'd said as if they'd earned Black people's trust. But I see now they could never imagine us being anything more than niggers. I conked my hair to make it as flat and smooth as theirs. I even put all my hopes of freedom into Sophia.

Papa taught me better.

I look up, noticing Bembry standing outside my cell.

"Boy, you were going down a good path," he says, disappointment in his voice. "Making improvement. Whatever's haunting you, young brother, don't let it take you under again. Don't let them win. What sense does it make leaving this place the same way you came in?"

He softly lays a booklet on my bed. *David Walker's Appeal to the Coloured Citizens of the World.*

Fearing new nightmares, I stay awake, pacing in my cell. Despite the pain of my disappointment, Reginald's words are hard to ignore, ringing in my ear like the loudest bell.

But I have at least six more years here. His truths don't bring the same comfort as the taste of freedom.

The booklet stares up at me, untouched. I have to save myself. I have to start at the root. If I stay this way, feeding into the darkness, I'll either end up in the hole for life or hanging from the ceiling. Either way, they win.

They win again.

I pick up the booklet Bembry left, sit by the bars, straining to see in the low light as I open to page one.

The rainstorm picks up speed. Hail rocks slap the windows and bars with buckets of water. With our shop flooding, they assign us to cleanup duty, to mop up water and patch leaks throughout Charlestown. The funk of wet bodies mixed with mold and humidity is suffocating.

"Maybe this place will flood and turn into Noah's ark," Big Lee says, staring out the window, mop in hand.

"God has no business saving us sinners," Norm says matter-of-factly.

Walter clicks his tongue. "Oh, so God don't have to show no compassion for us that He insists we must have for others to enter His heavenly kingdom. That's some bull!"

In an instant, a debate erupts. More religious talk. But this time, I don't want to run away. This time, I pay attention.

"Maybe a flood would wipe out all the white devils and return the land to its rightful inhabitants," Walter says smugly. "The Honorable Elijah Muhammad is a messenger of Allah in the flesh. He says the time of the white man is running out. That he committed the greatest sin against humanity."

"Elijah Muhammad is no messenger from God." Big Lee laughs. "Jesus is white and He is the flesh-and-blood Son of God."

"The *Honorable* Elijah Muhammad," Walter corrects him, "says Jesus was a prophet. Allah is the Arabic name for God."

There are only three followers of Elijah Muhammad here at Charlestown.

Thunder cracks, lightning flashes through the sky. Now knowing that my brothers are all Muslim, I listen with both ears to the conversation, but I can't make heads or tails of it. Still have to question, though. Mom used to say I was a born leader, always searching for the answers before I make a final decision.

After I finish David Walker's *Appeal*, I begin reading W. E. B. Du Bois's *The Souls of Black Folk*.

*The equality in political, industrial and social life which modern men must have in order to live, is not to be confounded with sameness. On the contrary, in our case, it is rather insistence upon the right of diversity;—upon the right of a human being to be a man even if he does not wear the same cut of vest, the same curl of hair or the same color of skin.*

Reading in my cell brings a familiar comfort I thought I had forgotten. I remembered hearing Papa mention this man, W. E. B. Du Bois, before. Unlike Garvey, who wanted us to be a self-sustaining people, Du Bois believed that Black people should have the same rights and were entitled to the same benefits as any other American citizen. He sounded just as frustrated with the economic conditions that Black folks have been forced to tolerate. While Garvey ultimately wanted us to return to Africa and control the wealth of our own resources, Du Bois wanted to stay here, to integrate, and be acknowledged for having an American identity.

But like Reginald said . . . How can we be expected to work, trust, and break bread with the very people that criminally and psychologically enslaved us?

The bell rings. Dinnertime. I shuffle through the mess hall, get in line waiting for the unidentifiable mush they call food. Haven't slept nor eaten much of anything in days. But I keep moving and keep reading. Can't let them win. I won't let them win.

Guards stand close, batons in hands. New fresh-faced guards to replace the elders. The type that waits for anyone to take one step out of line. Hit blindly, ask questions later. I steer clear of them.

From my table, I watch Chucky enter the mess hall with an innocent skip in his step. A guard's bright blue eyes follow him. He steps in Chucky's direction.

"Hey. I said, hey, you! Come here. What are you doing?"

Chucky doesn't seem too concerned. Not like the rest of us. He has a fool's confidence.

"Who me?" Chucky says with a smile. "I'm just walking. Sir."

"Shut your mouth," the guard screams, spit flying out his mouth.

Chucky's grin straightens to a thin line. A hush comes over the mess hall. A few of the other guards surround him.

"Hands on the wall. Now!"

Chucky looks around the room. "I was . . . I was just going to get something to eat."

"I said quiet!" The guard slams him against the concrete wall.

Mack steps out from behind the counter. The rest of us keep our heads down over our cold broth. Hearts pounding fast. Instinctively wanting to protect Chucky from this bully. Though Chucky's not what you'd call a friend, a bully's a bully in uniform or not.

But all we can do is just sit, seething.

"What seems to be the problem, Jefferson?" a guard says.

"Inmate here is having trouble following orders."

They throw him against the wall again, shoving his face hard as they search him.

I glance up in time to see one of them pull a pile of loosies out of his uniform pocket. My heart stops as thunder roars over our heads.

"Well, what do we have here?" Jefferson says with a smirk.

Chucky looks over his shoulder, his eyes flaring, face oozing blood.

"What?!"

"Is that why you skipped work duty? Peddling around this stuff."

Chucky's eyes go wilder as he tries to shake free.

"I didn't! I didn't skip work duty. Those are just mine. To smoke, you know? I'm not selling nothing."

"Don't lie, nigger!"

They let him up off the wall and he whimpers. The five guards surrounding Chucky don't look much older than me.

Jefferson smiles. "Time-out. Let's go."

He turns to one of the young guards with him, smiling. "What you think? A couple of nights in the hole would help him remember who's in charge here?"

In an instant, Chucky's bloody face turns gray.

"Nnnn-ooo, I can't do that," he mutters, "I c-c-c-can't do that."

"Are you challenging me, boy?"

Chucky starts breathing funny, hyperventilating. The rest of the brothers at the table sit stunned. He looks over to us, screaming at the top of his lungs. "Help me!"

But there's nothing we can do.

"Please, you . . . you don't understand. I can't do that. I can't . . . I can't be in the dark. I don't like the dark. I can't be in the dark."

The guards look at one another, laughing as they reach for him.

Chucky's fists ball up, swatting them away with a grunt, air whistling between his teeth. "You son of a bitch, I said NO!"

The entire mess hall turns, all the air leaving the room at once.

Jefferson frowns.

"What did you say?"

I don't like Chucky much, but I can't take knowing he's about to die right in front of my eyes.

Batons are drawn, and Chucky backs into the wall, a trapped animal. Walter attempts to stand but Bembry holds him back, shaking his head. Mack steps forward, his bottom lip quivering.

"No! Please, NO! I'm not going. I'm not!" Chucky wails like a baby as they inch closer to him.

I close my eyes and try to hum, but all I can hear are batons hitting skin and bones, blood splattering, until he stops screaming.

Until he's silent.

"You think he's dead?" Norm asks, picking at his bread.

No one at the table answers or has to ask who he's talking about. Last we heard, Chucky was sent down to the hole directly from the nurse's station. That was almost two weeks ago. But with a beating like that, it's hard to say how he'll come out. If he'll come out.

That could've been me, I think, still shivering at the thought. I sent a letter to Hilda, telling her about the new guards. How they've become even more vicious and savage. How we all walk around on eggshells. She sent a short letter back:

*If you take one step toward God, He will take two steps toward you.*

I don't know what type of step I have to take, but I'd give anything to be saved.

Bembry sighs. "Isolation down in that hole is torture. They put brothers as young as fifteen down there."

My mouth goes dry as I picture myself in Chucky's shoes. Lying on that freezing concrete, in pitch blackness, the filth, the rodents, the tears, the agony. Time no longer existing.

"I just don't understand why he was fighting back," Norm flusters. "If he just did what they said, they wouldn't have taken to beating him like they did."

Mack hobbles out the kitchen and leans on the table. "He's still alive."

There's a collective sigh of relief from the table.

"Is he all right?" Big Lee mumbles.

"Hard to tell; they didn't do much to patch him up. Even when they dragged him out of here, they were still pouncing on him and I think he was already knocked out. Could have lost his mind before he went to the hole, with that kind of warfare."

Norm scratches his head. "Mack, what you know about him?"

Mack sits at the table, folding his hands.

"He served in the war. Fought for that freedom you think we have."

I nearly drop my cup. The entire table leans back as if Mack placed a bomb in the middle of it. Even cool-as-a-cucumber Bembry is stunned.

"Yup. Wasn't even drafted. Went willingly."

"Then . . . what happened?" Norm encourages him, hand covering his mouth.

Mack shrugs. "He came home."

"He came home" had a sting to it. A sting of knowing that overseas, where you're killing people, you're treated better than in your own country. That you can fight for your country, risk your life for your country, but you have no rights *in* your country.

"He should've never come home," I say softly. "That could've been any one of us in that hole right now. He don't deserve that. None of us do."

"Inmate 22843!"

The entire table jumps at the guard's bark. Mack rushes back to the kitchen.

"Yes, sir," I say, standing, trying to remain calm.

"Warden wants to see you. Now."

196

Two of the new guards lead me to the warden's office. My hands are clammy, pinched in front of me, the cuffs tight. Mouth full of cotton, I rack my brain, trying to figure out what I've been called to the warden's office for. In all my time here, I've only heard of a few people being called, then never seen again. From what I heard, the hole is nearly full. And they're not just throwing cats in there for a few days but weeks and months at a time. We may never see Chucky again. What if that's it? What if they read my letter to Hilda, talking about Chucky? What if they do the same to me?

*If you take one step toward God, He will take two steps toward you.*

In a flash of panic, I hold my palm upward as best I can, like I've seen Walter do, and bow my head.

Allah, I don't know what you want from me. I'm trying to take a step, but it's hard to take a step in that hole. I can't go there again, Allah. Please, I am begging you.

I don't know if I'm praying right or how you're supposed to pray to Allah. I've heard the other brothers pray in different languages. But as I'm praying and pleading, the words actually calm me.

The warden doesn't look up as we enter his office. He continues scratching some notes in a file on his giant desk while we stand there in silence for fifteen minutes.

Heart pounding through my ears, my knees begin to shake, thoughts of the hole come rushing back. Except this time, I'm ready to fight, just like Chucky. Not out of insanity, but injustice. Chucky, who fought in a war that had nothing to do with him, is lying in a dark cell, broken and scared, all for some loosies? I shouldn't be punished for telling others the truth about this place. People need to know.

"Malcolm Little," the warden says finally.

I clear my throat, not allowing an ounce of fear to taint my voice, even with a stomach full of dread.

"Yes, sir."

He looks up, then adjusts his tie.

"You are being transferred."

I release the breath I didn't know I'd been holding. "Transferred, sir?"

"Your so-called petition has been approved. You've had two infractions but mostly good behavior. You'll be moved in three days. Pack your things."

"You'll have to read up about Concord yourself. But boy, that place is something."

I swear, you'd think Bembry was paid by Concord's local government to give such a glowing endorsement of a place he's never been. But Concord, Massachusetts, is the town of my new home: Norfolk Prison Colony.

"You've been given a real chance. Not a lot of people leave Charlestown before they supposed to. You ready?"

I glance around my cell. Nothing to take except my letters, notebooks, and a few pens.

"Just about."

Bembry nods. He looks like he's going to say something but then changes his mind.

"There's a good library at Norfolk, thousands of books, the kind they don't have here. The kind they don't have at many libraries either. You better use it. Classes, too."

"Okay, thanks for this."

I hand over *The Souls of Black Folk.*

"Right, yeah," Bembry says with a laugh, palming the book. "What'd you think of it?"

"Well, it helped me to read about history from the perspective of such an accomplished Negro. But it's hard to understand how any man, especially a Black man as educated and committed to the struggle as Mr. Du Bois, would want so desperately to be respected by his oppressor. I don't get that. Don't think I ever will, not anymore. A new set of standards should be established by people who have integrity, who see the universal brotherhood of people. I mean, on what ground did God give white people the authority over man, the authority to dehumanize us with the law on their side—but no law to protect our rights as human beings? On what ground? I don't get it."

My heart is beating hard and fast, my fist shaking.

He smirks. "A Garveyite! Well, it all makes sense now, brother."

For the first time, I don't disagree. I am my father's child.

"To your point," he says, holding his chin. "Hard to imagine a world that considers us equals when the core of our very existence is human and they don't even consider us that. What have I been telling you, son?"

"Everything starts from the root."

"Yup. And if they don't consider us human, first they'll never consider us equal, no matter how we paint the picture. But that's their problem, their shortcomings—not ours."

"So . . . how do we get them to recognize our humanity?"

He smiles. "Keep reading. You'll see."

# PART 3

# CHAPTER 11

*So early in life, I had learned that if you want something, you had better make some noise.*

—MALCOLM X

*Wake up, Malcolm!*

The bus stops short and I'm wrenched out of a hazy sleep. Outside the windows, layered with thick metal mesh, the sun is peeking over the horizon.

Two guards board the bus and unhook the chains from around our seats, then order us off. As my feet touch the gravel, I smell . . . trees. Blooming greenery, morning dew on the grass. The smells of my childhood. The smells of Lansing.

It's a sprawling property. No large gates, no hideous bars, just a wide, open quarter, surrounded by tall buildings. Like a college campus.

My mouth dries. Am I dreaming?

"Everyone, line up!"

I steel myself, breath quickening, remembering my first

day at Charlestown. The fear that entrapped me from the moment I stepped through its gates. Won't let them see that same fear in me here. This time, I'm ready.

We enter through a pair of double doors and are led down a long, brightly lit tunnel, with various-sized vents scattered above. The guards leading us are all empty-handed, their weapons still tucked safely in their belts. Eyes forward, head straight, I suck in a breath, the last bit of clean air, before we come to what appears to be the main hall.

A group of prisoners—white, some Black—walk past, wearing denim and white T-shirts, carrying books, talking among themselves as if it were perfectly normal to do so. I'm gaping, then I recognize a familiar scent—coffee. Brewing somewhere nearby.

A guard stands waiting in front of a massive gated window. He's tall with bright red hair and a crooked smile. We line up in front of him.

"Hello! Welcome to Norfolk Colony! This here, where you're standing, is the heart of our facility. It leads to all dorms, classes, the recreation center, gardens, and the canteens."

The terms he uses are bewildering. Dorms? Classes? Recreation center?

"If you ever get confused about where you're supposed to be, you can come find me right here. Just follow your heart," he says with a laugh. "We will be giving you your bedding, uniforms, and ID numbers. Go on ahead and line up to your right."

Beside us, a delivery window opens in the door of a supply room. Inside, inmates are working alongside guards to prepare our items. Last in line, I let the others collect their gear as I survey the spot.

Outside in the courtyard, inmates roam, taking what looks like leisurely walks. They pass a set of guards and tip their hats. None of the guards are alarmed or threatened by our presence. They almost seem at ease, courteous, respectful . . . friendly.

This must be some type of trick, I think, clocking every person I see. What's their play? Then I hear a voice that sends chills straight down my spine.

"Here you go, homeboy!"

No. No way in the world . . .

Inside the storage room, his back is turned as he digs through a bag of laundry for another set of uniforms. Haven't seen him in so long, I almost don't recognize him. He's lost a good thirty pounds, has grays in his new beard as if he aged twenty years. But if I could spot him in a crowded ballroom at Roseland, I could sure spot him here.

I clear my throat. "What's happening, daddy-o?"

He jolts, spinning upright. Face matching my shock.

Shorty.

The air here isn't soaked with the same heaviness it had in Charlestown.

Nor the revolting stench.

My uniform feels soft and new, like no one else wore it before me. My shoulders ease out of their tense hold. The guards and prisoners speak . . . peacefully. Giving eye contact, saying "good morning" and "good afternoon." There's no segregation here. The white prisoners talk to Negroes. Almost like . . . equals.

Two guards show up at my cell later that week. "Come on, Little, this way."

"Where are we going?"

"Processing."

Straightening up, shoulders back, I walk erect and confident, despite my mind racing. What's processing and why am I the only one going?

On the way, I scan the hallways, hoping to see Shorty again.

Shorty and I . . . we're family, we're brothers. Not by blood but by bond. Feels like I've known him my entire life. When I think of home, I envision Shorty there. And yet he hasn't said one word to me since our trial. Been here at Norfolk, alive and well. All that time I spent worried about where they sent him, sick with guilt that he was thrown on the chain gang, and turns out he's just fine. Better than me. Prisoners can't write to other prisoners, but surely he could've found a way to let me know where he was and that he was okay.

I want to be angry, but mostly I feel relieved . . . and a little scared that he might hate me.

"Hello. Malcolm Little, right?"

The superintendent stands as I enter the room. Immediately, I'm on guard.

"Um, yes, sir."

"Good to meet you. My name is Winslow. Please, have a seat."

Did he just say . . . *please*?

Winslow sits behind his desk, resetting his thin silver eyeglasses. Dressed in a brown wool suit, he's tall, pale, with soft features and shiny brown hair.

"Did I . . . did I do something wrong, sir?" I ask, even though I couldn't see how that was possible. Only got here a few days ago. Haven't even been outside my cell.

He laughs. "No need to be nervous. Nothing's wrong."

I'm not nervous. I'm distrusting and with good reason, Reginald's warnings sinking deeper into my skin.

"I just like to meet with every individual who comes to our facility," he says, motioning to the chair across from his desk.

Hesitant, I peer around the room before slowly taking a

seat. Winslow's office is full of landscape paintings, books, plants, and polished mahogany furniture. It feels like a home, like he lives here.

He smiles again, opening a file.

"Says here you're twenty-two and originally from Lansing, Michigan," he reads, looking up at me. "What's it like out there?"

Unnerved, I'm almost too stunned by the kind question to respond. "It's . . . a nice place."

"I bet you have a big family. Am I right?"

"Yeah, I do. There's eight of us."

He nods. "I'm the youngest of nine. A lot of mouths to feed."

"We did all right," I say quick, lifting my chin up. Even in the hardest times of the Depression, we were far from destitute, if that's what he's trying to get at.

Winslow notices my change of tone and smiles warmly.

"Well, I bet you have a lot of questions, so I'll jump right into it. As you've already seen, especially coming from a place like Charlestown, Norfolk Colony isn't your typical facility. Here we have a different goal in mind for men who join us.

"The goal here is rehabilitation. Do you know what that word means?"

Of course I do, but before I can answer, he says, "It means to restore back to a healthy state so if and when you reintegrate into society, chances are you'll be more of a productive citizen."

I shift in my chair. "How?"

"By providing opportunities that may not have been available to you before. Educational courses and other services of your choosing. I'm sure we can both agree, if a man is trying to survive by any means necessary because opportunities are scarce, taking a course in literature would be last on his priority list."

I nod. "So what's the catch?"

He laughs. "There's no catch! You are the captain of your own ship here, young man. How you spend and use your time will be in direct correlation to your success."

Makes sense. Almost too much sense.

"Sounds like you're asking me to trust you," I challenge, hoping to see him drop the act. It's risky, but I'm curious.

Winslow smiles. "More like, trust each other. Only thing I ask is that you follow the rules. Report to work duty, stay out of trouble, and take your courses. Let me show you one more thing."

He opens another file, full of large photos. He flips through the portraits, mostly white men and just a few Blacks. All dressed in well-fitted suits.

"These are our success stories. We take a photo of every man who is released from here. Send them on their way cleaned up, in a suit, and with skills in hand. I've been here since the very beginning. Helped build this place! I've seen the fruits of our labor and I believe in our mission. Severely punishing a man when he's already down doesn't rectify the larger problem or prevent repeating offenses. But giving them back their dignity? That elicits real change."

Through the window behind him, I see inmates tending to a garden in the courtyard and think of Mom.

"So what do you think, Malcolm? Think you can work with us?"

I have a name again. No longer just a prison number. This stroke of luck must be a sign from Allah. I barely escaped with my sanity from Charlestown, but here, at Norfolk, it feels like a bright new beginning.

"Okay."

"Great! And now that you've been in intake for about a week, I think it's time we get you started. Transfer you into your official dormitory assignment. Place you on work duty and enroll you in classes."

Intake at Charlestown was thirty days of solitude. I wonder how long I'll be comparing this place to that hellhole.

"So," he says, scribbling some notes. "Any questions?"

I have a billion questions, but only one is at the top of the list.

"Yes. Is there any way to be assigned to the same unit as Malcolm Jarvis?"

He frowns. "Jarvis?"

"Yes, he's an old buddy of mine."

"Hm. Well, I'm sure it'll be nice to have a familiar face. Maybe he can also give you a tour."

There are no units but dormitories, in which each prisoner has his own cell that is three times the size of the ones at Charlestown. Instead of dark, tiny concrete boxes, we have rooms with a window, cushioned bed, sheets, and blankets. My cell gets good light in the morning. Above all of this, there are toilets. Real toilets that flush, showers with proper water pressure. In comparison to where I've been, this place is the heaven I was promised.

There is no mess hall. Instead, each dorm has its own canteen where we eat. It's like one great big dining hall. That's where I finally see Shorty again.

He approaches my table, standing on the opposite side. My tongue feels burnt, at a loss for what to say to him. Really, I'm afraid to say the wrong thing. Can't blame no one but myself for the crack in our bond. He has every right to blame me, but how many times or ways can I say I'm sorry? Sorry that I got us caught up. Sorry I ruined your life. Ruined *our* lives. But maybe the damage is not beyond repair; it just needs time.

"Hey, homeboy." I raise my hand, thinking maybe if we

slap some skins, the spark would help us reconnect. But Shorty remains still. Sullen. Thick nerves build in my throat.

He takes a deep breath, then sits. "So what slave they got you working?"

His voice. Haven't heard it in so long, I never realized how much I missed it.

"Um, k-kitchen," I stutter out.

He chuckles. "Boy, you lucky. Can get yourself an extra cup of joe whenever you want."

First, he comes over all cold, now he's talking about coffee?

"Is that all you got to say?" I snap. "Man, what the hell happened to you! You could've gotten word to me that you were all right."

He palms his cup of water, his face stoic. "I ain't gonna lie to you, homeboy, when I got shipped off, I took it rough. My mind played all kinds of tricks on me. And I was mad as hell. At you."

The words I was most afraid of hit like bricks.

"Yeah," I sigh. "Figured as much."

Shorty's eyes narrow on me. "You got us hung out to dry. I should've never listened to you! Should've never trusted them broads!"

I wince, wondering if it's too late to switch dorms again.

"But then," he continues, his voice softening. "Thought real hard about everything that happened, and we didn't deserve the break we got."

I nod, letting the moment pass between us.

"This is just . . . wild, man," I say, looking around the room. "That we end up at the same place and at the same time?"

"Yeah, and this place ain't all that bad either, Red. You'll be all right."

"So what you been up to ALL this time?"

He smirks. "Keeping out of trouble. I'm actually heading to orchestra rehearsal now."

"What! Orchestra?"

"Yeah, homeboy. They got an orchestra and a theater, too. Sometimes I help out in there."

"Wow. Well, what else they got?"

He gulps back his water and sets it on the tray, standing.

"Come on. I'll give you a tour."


Work duty doesn't feel much like work. More like chores I would've done if I were back home in Lansing. Here, I'm given more responsibility and somehow, it makes me feel alive again. Even a crumb of dignity can change the way you look at the world and the way you see yourself in it.

I'm assigned to the kitchen. I used to scrub plates back when I was fourteen at Mason Junior High. Went from being the only Black student, working kitchen cleanup, to becoming class president and playing on the football team. They didn't just give those opportunites to me, I worked hard for it. Studied every chance I could get and always gave 100 percent. Hoping that's some kind of move I can pull off here, too. I would feel good about that.

Most of the other inmates I've met ask about the outside, eager to know what they're missing. They quickly lose interest once they discover I'm a transfer and have nothing to report.

"Easy, fellas," this cat named Alfred says from the sink next to me. "He's tall for his age but young. Fresh meat. Don't scare the poor boy!"

Here they go. They think I'm some green-as-okra cat they can take advantage of. The way Shorty did, all those years ago when I first found my way to Roxbury. I always seemed to stand out in a crowd, he told me, like I didn't belong on his side of the tracks.

"Not that new to the way things go around here," I correct him. "From one prison to another, it's all the same."

I say it like this was just another walk in the park.

Alfred raises an eyebrow at some of the other fellas in the kitchen, smirking. "Well, don't we have a *live* one here. Introduce yourself, fellas."

"How you doing? Frankie," an older white man says with a toothless grin. He has sandy blond hair and a scar across his left cheek.

"Frankie, he helps with the cooking. Ozzy handles the deliveries."

A tall Black man with a bald head, who is carrying crates to the back, stops by the sink.

"The name's Osbourn. Folks call me Ozzy."

I can barely hear him. Too busy staring at the eggs in his crate. Eggs! It's been so long since I've seen them.

"Say, you come from Charlestown? You know my brother, Big Lee?" Ozzy asks.

"Yeah, sure do."

Ozzy smiles. "You'll have to give me the news then."

I nod.

Alfred goes on to show me around the kitchen. It's big, high ceilings, white walls. New everything and sparkling clean, just how I like it. They have milk, cereal, coffee . . . and even fresh vegetables. Real food . . . not processed slop. Alfred's been here since the place opened more than two decades ago. You'd think they paid him to be a part of the welcoming committee.

He reminds me of Bembry in some ways. Almost the same height, same weight, same freckled skin. If he were as smooth as Bembry in the way he talked, I would've mistaken them for cousins.

"So you see, when you been around like me, you know a little something."

I shrug. "Perspective doesn't guarantee wisdom." Something Bembry would say.

An "oooh" comes from behind us. For a split second, a dark

look comes over Alfred's face that he quickly pushes away with a laugh.

"All right now, we got an educated Negro here!"

The way he says it, it doesn't feel like a compliment. I have to keep my wits about me with this one.

"I'm just surprised how wide open and spacious it is here," I say, pretending not to be put off by his tone. "I can see the road from my window. Haven't had a window in almost two years."

"Yeah. This is one of a kind. Not like any other prison I know," Frankie says. "But you still got folks hell-bent on breaking free. There were two of them a few weeks ago."

"They escaped?"

"Didn't get far." Frankie laughs. "Remember that tunnel you came through before intake? It got vents, with tear gas. They'll set them off the moment you try to fly the coop. That's one thing about Norfolk: You step out of line, they'll make you regret it."

My first letter at Norfolk is from Bembry. He must have sent it to his nephew, who sent it to me the day I left, or even a couple of days earlier, because it comes during my first week:

*Young Brother,*

*Not sure when you'll receive this letter, but as promised, here is a list of books you should read. They'll help you grow into your true self. Help you do better. When the mind is engaged, the heart heals.*

*Keep reading. You'll find what you're looking for.*

*Bembry*

I open the heavy wooden door and stare in awe.

The library has high cream ceilings and oak wood shelves. The room is bright and is a perfectly shaped square, like a cottage chapel. There are more books here than I've seen in my entire life. The shelves are overflowing. Bembry had the whole world at his fingertips in here. There's gotta be well over ten thousand books.

"Hey, there," a voice says behind me. "Can I help you with something?"

A white man with a heavy beard stands with a stack of books in his hands behind a desk. Doesn't seem like an inmate. He must work here.

"Uh, yeah. I'm looking for a few books." I take out Bembry's letter and read. "Um . . . The Story of Civilization by Will and Ariel Durant. Volume one: Our Oriental Heritage and volume three: Caesar and Christ. *The Outline of History* by H. G. Wells. *Twelve Years a Slave* by Solomon Northup. *Sex and Race* by J. A. Rogers."

"Oh, we have those, for sure," he says. "But first, let's set you up with a library card."

I nod. "Okay."

"You must be one of the new intakes. My name's George. I run the library."

George goes over the rules of the library while writing out my name and prison ID number on a small card.

"There you go," he says, blowing on the ink to dry. "Your ticket to the world!"

We tour around the aisles while picking up the titles I need. I'm in heaven.

At the checkout, George asks, "Studying for something specific?"

"No," I mumble, collecting the pile from him. "Thanks."

"Anytime." He pulls on his beard a little. "You seem like an avid reader. We have a book discussion club that meets here on Thursdays, before supper, if you want to join." He gestures over his shoulder. "Akil, over there, never misses a meeting."

At a table on the far end is a brother with an olive-toned complexion, black curly hair, and thick-framed glasses, wearing one of those knit kufi crowns I've seen another Muslim brother wear. My stomach tenses, thinking of my family, their letters, and endless requests to join them.

"Uh, thanks," I say as something on George's desk catches my eye. It's some sort of newspaper, but unlike the ones I've seen from the outside. It's titled *The Colony*. George notices me staring and smiles.

"It's our own paper," he says, handing it over to me. "Comes out biweekly. You can have it if you'd like."

"Prison paper?"

"Yeah. Inmates submit articles, short stories, poems, anything we'd like to publish."

I take the paper, turning it over slowly, reading in disbelief. I'm back at my kitchen table, reading over Mom's shoulder as she typed articles for *Negro World*.

"Thanks."

I glance around until I find what I'm searching for. It's the exact copy Bembry had at Charlestown, which makes it easy to find my place.

**Pertinacious. Adjective. Adhering resolutely to an opinion, purpose, or design; perversely persistent.**

As I sit there facing the door, soaking in each new word, more and more inmates pour in. Some reading books, some studying, and others copying and taking notes. Men with whom I had no ties a moment ago, immediately become brothers in the love of reading. Is this a dream, too? Or the lifeline I need to keep from sinking? For the first time, I let go of what feels like a real sigh.

**Pliant. Adjective.**

**Pliable, 1) Easily bent; flexible. "quality leather is pliable and will not crack"**

**2) Easily influenced. "pliable teenage minds"**

Somewhere around midnight, as I huddle near the bars of my cell, struggling to make out words in the darkness, a siren blares, and the cell doors open simultaneously.

A troop of guards come running in, batons in hand, yelling over one another.

"On the ground! NOW!"

Every prisoner wakes up in a fright, shuffling quick outside their cells.

"What's going on?" I ask Shorty as he steps out of the cell across from mine.

Before he can answer, a guard approaches, his boots stomping.

"I said on the ground," he screams, shoving Shorty's face with his hand. "Ground! Now!"

I drop to my knees, lying flat on my stomach with my palms on my head. Shorty and I exchange a worried glance. They ran these types of drills at Charlestown. But I've only been at Norfolk a few weeks and this intensity is unfamiliar. Disorienting. For a moment, I wonder if this has all been a dream.

"You find it yet?" a guard yells.

"Nope. Search them."

They pat us down, hands grabbing every inch of our bodies, then begin shifting through our meager belongings. Uprooting bedsheets, ripping down photos, throwing everything into a pile in the middle of our cells. I glance to the left and right at the men on their stomachs, confusion and fear in their eyes.

"What are they looking for?" I whisper.

"Shhh," Shorty warns.

The guard in my room shuffles through my letters, throwing them on top of my mattress, now bare on the floor.

He picks up the composition book, tucked inside the dictionary I had shoved under my bed. I take a deep breath as he flips through it.

"What's this?" he asks.

I keep my eyes down. "My workbook, sir."

"What the hell you doing copying the dictionary?"

"For reading purposes. Sir."

"Who reads a dictionary," he mumbles, shaking his head before tossing it on the mattress.

I take another breath to fight the rising anger, realizing it doesn't matter how nice a place is, they still think we're less than nothing and not worthy of mere dignity.

The classes at Norfolk are constructed to mimic schools on the outside. We take courses like history, literature, civics, and mathematics. It's thrilling to be back in the classroom, back to learning. I do the majority of my studying in the library. But I'm not just focused on classwork; I read everything and anything that sparks my interest.

Shorty is taking classes, too, between his work detail and orchestra practice. We often find each other in here, nose deep in the pages.

"They keep us busy in here, don't they?" he says from across the table, setting his open book down. We're not hanging out in Roxbury smoking reefer or sharing a bottle, but this feels just as cool if not better.

"Well, that don't look like English homework. What you got there, homeboy?"

"It's a book on Egyptian hieroglyphics."

"What?" I chuckle, reaching over to flip a page. "Man, this thing looks like sheet music. You understanding it?"

"I'm getting there, homeboy. Don't rush me," he says with a laugh. "You ain't the only one putting these books to work. I've been studying, too. I figure, you know, with all this time, it's best to accomplish something good for yourself. No sense walking out this place the way we came in."

Sounds like something Bembry said once.

"You . . . you came in just fine," I correct him. "It was me that got you caught up in this. It was me messing with people that never . . . never were for us."

Shorty shook his head. "I'm a man. I made my choices. I had two infant sons and a wife to feed. This wasn't my first, Malcolm, but it was my last. I'm sorry I got you entangled in this, man."

I nod, knowing that we both made mistakes, knowing that's what he truly feels in his heart.

"So, what you reading?" he asks.

I hold up a book. "Trying my hand at Latin."

"Another language? Whewww . . . that's tough stuff."

"It's not that hard, man. It helps you figure out how words are built, like the root of a word. And when you know the etymology of a word, the roots, you can figure out what anything means. Look, I can teach you what I learn, and you can teach me what you learn, especially this hieroglyphics stuff. We can test each other. What do you say?"

"Sounds like a fair shake." His smile fades. "Hey, you think this is all gonna matter?"

"What you mean?"

"Do you think we can be saved? They have us in here like

college students, learning things. I'm just wondering if it's really gonna make a difference when we get back on the outside."

"Shorty, if we had known, really known everything like we do now, you think we would've wound up here?"

The walls of the Norfolk visitation hall are a soft yellow with white molding. The windows are spotless, letting in bright sunlight and fresh air from lots of beautiful trees. A few guards stand about, hands folded behind their backs, not itching to grab their weapons at your slightest move. But now I know that behind their facade of kindness sometimes lies the devil itself.

Philbert sits across from me, nodding. "I like the new digs."

I shoot him a glare. "Real funny."

He cracks a smile. "Easy there, slugger. I'm not here to fight you."

"Then what are you here for?"

"We're here to set you free," Reginald says, next to him.

Free? I think, letting the unfamiliar word roam around my head. I'm no freer than when I was first locked up. But now . . . the concept almost seems possible. That when I leave this place, I'll be in a suit, armed with knowledge, ready to take on the world.

Still, I shake my head at him. "Can't believe I let you trick me into thinking that you had some power to get me out of here."

Reginald's eyes grow big. He slowly opens his hands on the table, like in prayer.

"I never meant to trick you, Malcolm. I love you. You're my brother."

Philbert cuts the tension. "Well, this place is a far cry from where you've been. How are you feeling?"

Despite the recent hope that has blossomed from a stark change in scenery and reconnecting with Shorty, nothing seems to help me forget that my every move is still controlled by someone else. I'm still trapped. And worse, I'm tormented by the conditions my brothers in Charlestown are living in. I can't stop thinking about them and there's nothing I can do to help them.

I'm reading day and night until my eyes hurt, hoping to tame the anger, but it's still there. And I don't know what to do with all the anger, empathy, and compassion living deep in my gut, eating me from the inside.

This is what I want to tell my brothers, but I don't because they'll never understand. Philbert measures my silence then clears his throat.

"You've been lost for some time, Malcolm. We've all seen you . . . lose yourself. I'm grateful to Allah that you are alive." He gives me a hopeful smile. "You are looking more like my brother again, man. And we need you to come on home."

"We love you, Malcolm," Reginald adds.

"Your family needs you to be whole again, brother. You're already on your way. Look," Philbert says, waving around the room. "Allah has brought favor to your life. You take one step toward Allah, and He'll take two toward you."

"So what am I supposed to do?"

"Write to the Honorable Elijah Muhammad," Reginald says. "He will guide you."

# CHAPTER 12

*My alma mater was books, a good library . . . I could spend the rest of my life reading, just satisfying my curiosity.*

—MALCOLM X

The streets of Lansing were empty, as they should've been for the late hour, but the backdrop of snowcapped mountains was glistening under a star-filled sky. The ground was wet with mud. A streetcar bell rang in the distance. I turned quickly to the sound of someone standing next to me . . .

"Papa?" I gasped.

There he was. In his dark double-breasted coat, hat, round spectacles. His coal-dark flawless skin shined in the moonlight. It had been so long, I wasn't sure if I would remember his face, but it was him. I knew it in my bones.

Papa didn't say a word, his eyes steady on me, full of wonder. Like he didn't recognize me.

"Papa? It's me. Malcolm," I whispered.

He looked me over, as if he were inspecting a property he never meant to purchase. I had disappointed him.

"I'm sorry, Papa."

We stood under the stars of which our people were made.

Without a word, he turned and then the mob swarmed around him, barking slurs. They began slowly walking ahead . . . toward the streetcar tracks.

"Papa? Papa, what's going on? What are they doing?"

One hit him on his head with a metal pipe. His hat tumbled in the wind. The streetcar bells jingled. Closer than before. They were forcing him onto the tracks. I yelled, but no sound came out. I shut my eyes.

"Don't make me watch this! Please don't make me watch," I begged.

They wrestled him onto the tracks and tied him down.

I tried to scream again. But nothing came out.

I heard Mom's voice. Hilda's voice. Reginald's voice.

"Remember who you are. Remember who you are."

"It's what Papa would've wanted."

*Up, up, you mighty race!*

"It's time to wake up, Malcolm."

I fell to my knees, covered my ears, and waited for the streetcar to pass, crushing his giant body, as they watched in delight.

The silence came fast.

And I find myself once again on a cell floor, sobs tearing from my chest.

Tears and sweat roll down my face, splashing on the floor like a rainstorm.

I climb to my feet and jog in place, kicking up my knees, higher and higher as the darkness of my cell creeps in closer. I have no idea how long it is until sunrise, but I can't sleep again.

I can't face Papa again.

He's seen all I've done. He's watched me plummet, away from everything he taught me. He saw me steal. Lie. Fornicate. Drink. Smoke. Snort. Eat swine. He saw me pretend I couldn't read, and, worse, deny Marcus Garvey's call . . .

*Up, up, you mighty race!*

And yet he loved me. My brothers—Wilfred, Philbert, Reginald, Wesley, Robert—they love me. How can anyone love someone like me?

I swing at the air like Joe Louis.

Sophia's piercing laugh floods my ears—then there are the big bands onstage with forced smiles; Billie Holiday's wailing melodies; empty souls clinking glasses; young Black prostitutes looking for someone to love them; the pained cheers of Jackie Robinson stealing base; cell doors closing one after the other; panic-stricken young men in the hole weeping for mercy; Mom—alone with no one to protect her. Railroad tracks, clang, *clang*, CLANG . . . *Up, up, you mighty race!*

"STOP!" I yell into the silent world.

Slowly, through the silence, Papa's speeches begin to play in my head, full of static like the old radio in the living room. And I remember. Every word. Every. Single. Word. I remember being a little boy watching my papa at the pulpit. I remember it all.

My chest heaves. The blackness in my cell easing.

But the anger is still heavy inside me. I need something to expend it upon.

Hours pass, until sunlight hits my window.

In desperation, I write to the only person that may understand. It's a shot in the dark but it's the only shot I have left to take.

The return letter comes in a cream-colored envelope. Typed in black ink, addressed to me: *Mr. Malcolm Little*, neat and perfect, like I'm worthy of something good.

I hold the letter in my hand like it's a message from God, sent from the place where my father is, where all the great ancestors from the beginning of time are. Ausar, Noah, Moses . . .

I stare at his signature, *Messenger of Allah.*

His words are echoes of my childhood. Echoes of what I've seen and where I've been. What I've always known deep inside of me to be true.

As-Salaam-Alaikum

In the Holy Name of Almighty Allah, the Beneficent, the Most Merciful Saviour, Our Deliverer, Master of the Day of Judgment. To Allah alone do I submit and seek refuge.

Dear Brother Malcolm,

The Black prisoner symbolizes white society's self-righteous crime of destroying the Black family. White society has kept the Black man ignorant to the knowledge of self and, as a result, it has been able to keep him oppressed. When the Black man lacks knowledge of self, he may be unable to get a decent job and properly care for his family. Out of an urgency to cope and survive, he may turn to drugs, alcohol, or criminal behavior. White society uses its authority to police his community, causing him to become incarcerated and made into a slave of the State.

Young man, you must remember that Allah is the only Judge—not the white man! Do not focus on what he thinks of you but on what Allah thinks of you. Focus on your whole self, your heart, thoughts, and deeds. Read the Holy Quran. It does not matter who you have been up until now.

Accept your own and be yourself, which is a righteous Muslim. Turn to the East and pray, to Allah only. He will guide you. We are forever here to support you.

Your Brother,
Elijah Muhammad
Messenger of Allah

And just like that, I am free. Cast from a long spell of self-loathing, the Messenger of Allah has reached deep inside me, grabbed my spine, and shaken me awake from a long, dormant sleep. Time is on my side again.

His words, although new, feel like the encouragement of my father. He genuinely cares for my well-being. Even sent me five dollars to put on the books. With his letter, he welcomes me into the true knowledge. He understands me, and he welcomes me home.

He is just as my brothers and sisters said he would be. His philosophy reminds me of Papa's and he's a Garveyite, too. Why didn't I listen and write to him sooner?

Maybe I was afraid. Maybe Elijah Muhammad will help me be the man Papa wanted me to be. A man who can help our people.

As-Salaam-Alaikum

In the Holy Name of Almighty Allah, the Beneficent, the Most Merciful Saviour, Our Deliverer, Master of the Day of Judgment. To Allah alone do I submit and seek refuge.

Dear Brother Malcolm,

One thing you must understand is that the history of the Black man has been rewritten and falsely documented. When the white man came to these shores to conquer, he eliminated the Black man from history. There is a reason. For if the Black man thinks all that is white is better than his own, the white man's desire to control the world's masses and environmental resources will be a success.

Allah has sent me to open his bewildered

children's eyes to see the truth of their heritage and therefore restore their identity. They will see the white man's corruption and his fear of being the true minority in the world.

The white man has stolen our history and replaced it for his own. We need true believers, like you, son, who have experienced firsthand the injustice against the true chosen children of Allah.

Ground yourself in the glorious history of the Black man who is the father and mother of civilization. Seek true knowledge by learning the Holy Quran's scriptures.

Awaken your mind. Trust in Allah. I am here for you upon your return.

Your Brother,

Elijah Muhammad

Messenger of Allah

The Honorable Elijah Muhammad's letters make me want to learn everything there is to learn. Bembry set the course for my studies, and Mr. Muhammad added the gasoline. It's hard to explain what it feels like to have someone of his caliber willing to speak to someone like me—a prisoner—and show me my heritage as a Black man. I take none of his words for granted.

I start with the first volume of *The Destruction of Black Civilization*. It details the journey and horror of the slave trade. How millions of Black people had thriving societies and democracies and were strategically conquered, tortured, raped, and even murdered during the Middle Passage. How the West undermined the rulers of Africa, and then greedily portioned control to the British, French, Spanish, Portuguese, Belgians, Germans, and Italians for its natural resources. They required unity of the smaller European nations. I learned that of all the land on this earth, God blessed Africa, the second-largest continent in the world, to be the birthplace of humanity and the foundation of the wealthiest natural minerals and resources.

Every day, I take out as many books as I can get my hands on and read with a fiery urgency. The sense of purpose is invigorating. Every atom in my body is coming alive. The more I read, the more I learn. The more I learn, the more I see how this white man has made just about every person of color in the world suffer under his reign. After taking the indigenous peoples' identity and history, they inserted themselves as the founders and scholars of civilization instead.

How do people not know of these truths? Why aren't we talking about it? Mr. Muhammad thinks that people will listen to me. I will not let him or my people down. This is my mission now. My purpose is clear, and days at Norfolk become almost bearable. Any task to which I'm assigned, I do with expedient accuracy, so I can return to the library and resume my studies. I was always a reader but now I'm a purposeful reader.

"Bet Fresh Meat don't even realize how far we are from our very first ancestors." Alfred's voice competes with the running sink water during kitchen duty.

"What's that?"

"I said, did you know we aren't that far from Plymouth Rock? That's where the first ship came. Crazy, right? We so close to where it all started, yet so far."

Alfred is giving another lesson on Norfolk and the surrounding areas. Most of the time I ignore him. But today, my soul thrums with the blood of my father and begins to boil.

"Landed right over yonder on what they call Plymouth Rock."

"Yup!" Frankie says. "We are where the Pilgrims first discovered America, where this country first started. If it wasn't for my ancestors, y'all wouldn't be here."

"You got that right," I snap.

A pot drops out of Alfred's hand before he can catch it. The room turns to me, the air changing with it.

"Sounds like you disagree," Frankie hisses.

Ozzy sets down a crate, as if preparing himself to intervene. I wipe my hands dry.

"You got that right, too. But your people didn't discover

America. America already belonged to the indigenous people. Your people stole it with fake treaties. And you also brought disease, trickery, and crime with you."

Alfred's mouth drops. Frankie flusters, his face growing red.

"But . . . your people landed there, too. Ain't you proud of that?"

"How can I be proud when my ancestors came to this country in chains, tormented in the bottom of a ship?" I say. "We were hunted, kidnapped, and stolen from the Empire of Benin, which today has been divided into Ghana, Nigeria, Sierra Leone, Senegal, Mali. We weren't pilgrims who willingly migrated for a better life. We were already living it. We were among our kings and queens living on a land of mineral wealth. We were enslaved and traumatized at the hands of your ancestors—real criminals. So, yes, if it weren't for you, we wouldn't be locked up in here! We'd be cohabiting peacefully."

The room holds a breath. My chest heaves, heart pounding.

Frankie takes a quick survey of the room, realizing no one is going to stand up for him, and storms out, madder than mad.

"Well, well, Fresh Meat," Alfred says, and laughs. "You got some real intellect held up in them bones. With all that mouth, you should just go on ahead and join the debate team."

I feel the frown take up my face. "What's that?"

Norfolk Prison Colony Debating Society meets twice a week in the classroom adjacent to the library. It's not a large group. About six or so men plus two coaches, Coach O'Connell and Coach Nash, who teach the day classes. One of the men is Akil, from the library. Shorty and I wait outside the classroom for the meeting to adjourn before entering.

"Little . . . Jarvis," Mr. O'Connell says with a smile. "What are you two doing here?"

"We're here about the debate team," I say.

The men gather around. Akil sits on the desk.

"You ever been in one before?"

"Yeah. I argue with people all the time." I smirk.

They laugh.

"It's not just about arguing," Mr. Nash says. "It's more of a . . . discussion. It's about articulating your point or position rationally, making a case for it."

"And if you're able to prove your point, you win?" Shorty asks.

"Yup."

"How do you do that?"

"Building a case with research, facts, and statistics," Mr. Nash explains.

"Books, Malcolm," Akil adds. "You know, I've seen the books you've taken out the library. This is right up your alley, brother."

Suddenly, I see how my brothers are right. Everything is put in order, by Allah.

"Who do we debate?"

Akil smirks. "Rich college kids. Usually once per semester. We got one coming up in three months that we're starting to prepare for. You in?"

I laugh. Oh, I'm going to love the debate team.

Dear Brother,

Receiving your letter has brought me much joy. I am elated that you are asking for advice on how to pray to Allah. You can pray anywhere, even standing where you are. All you have to do is open your palm and bow your head.

Seek council and guidance.

We pray daily for you, brother, and can't wait until you are back at home with us.

Best,
Wilfred

"So how do you know this cat, again?"

After lunch, Shorty and I head to the visitation hall

together. At Norfolk, Shorty and I can have a visitor at the same time. We can even hug someone if we want, real human contact.

"He's an old music buddy of mine," Shorty says, excited. "We've been writing to each other ever since I got here."

"But why does he want to see both of us?"

"I told him how we've been studying Islam and want to become Muslims, and he said he wanted to visit. Came all this way so be cool, okay?"

We enter the hall, already crowded with visitors. I think of Lightning's last days before he was executed, how they stole him from his wife and son without hesitation.

"There he is," Shorty says, pointing across the room. A brown-skinned Asian man with shiny black hair smiles and gives us a slight wave.

Shorty rushes over, and while they laugh and shake hands, I hang back, taking in this stranger. He has on a sharp black suit and tall black kufi hat with a long string tassel hanging from the top that swings whenever he moves.

"Red," Shorty calls me over. "Meet my old pal, Abdul Hameed."

Abdul nods with a beaming smile. "As-Salaam-Alaikum."

I freeze, turning to Shorty.

Abdul laughs. "It's a greeting we say. It means, 'peace be unto you.' Please, let's sit. It's good to finally meet you! Shorty has told me many things."

"Hope only the good stuff," I chuckle as we gather around a table. "So how do you two know each other?"

"We jammed at a few clubs in Roxbury," Shorty says, beaming. "Abdul here is mean on them piano keys!"

"I miss Shorty's sound and pray for his freedom, always."

"Where are you from?" I ask, noting his thick accent.

"India," he says. "I came to this country some years ago."

"The man was classically trained in London!"

"I have loved music all my life," Abdul agrees.

He talks more about his musical journey that brought him to Boston. There's a calming presence about him. He seems at ease, even inside a prison, everyone staring at that wild hat of his.

He folds his hands on the table. "So, Shorty says you two are studying Islam?"

"That's right," I boast proudly. "Do you know the Honorable Elijah Muhammad? Have you met him before?"

Abdul shakes his head. "No, afraid I don't know much of him nor much about this Nation of Islam. I'm a member of the Ahmadiyya Movement in Islam. We are orthodox."

First I've heard of other Muslim organizations. Wonder why Reginald never mentioned them. Or maybe he didn't know.

"I thought if you have any questions, I can be of assistance. It is the will of Allah to carry out His teachings to anyone eager to learn. But first, I must ask, do you know how to pray?"

Shorty and I share a quick, uneasy look.

"Well, sort of. From what I've been gathering from my brothers and some of the books I'm reading."

Abdul nods. "It's good that you are praying. I will assist you so you are praying the right way to honor Allah. That is one of the most important steps in our faith."

Shorty leans in. "All right, so what do we have to do?"

"You must pray five times each and every day without fail," Abdul says, taking a brown leather-bound book out of his satchel. "First, make sure the area you plan to pray in is clean. You, too, must also be as clean as possible. Wash your face, ears, nose, hands, and feet. Then lay a mat or blanket on the floor, facing the east, toward Mecca, the Al-Ka'bah. If you are ever unclear, remember, the sun rises in the east and sets in the west.

"Before you utter a word, have a prayer in your heart and drop down to your knees and bow unto the Creator, the Lord of the Universe, the God of our ancestors, God of the righteous."

He slides the book across the table. "This is the Quran, filled with the sacred words of Allah."

"Is . . . is this for me?" I ask.

He nods. "Every Muslim man should have one of his own."

"But I don't even know you," I say in disbelief.

"It is one of the pillars of our faith, to help our fellow

human beings and give to those in need. When you leave this place, it will be your duty to help your fellow brothers, even strangers. Allah will reward you twofold for your generous and selfless acts."

I grip the book tight, tracing a finger against the engraving, overwhelmed by its power.

"Thank you," I whisper.

He smiles wide. "Shall I go over some prayers for you to master?"

"Yes!" I blurt out. "Yes, please."

Brother Abdul lists the steps carefully, saying more Arabic words I don't know how to pronounce yet.

But I will learn, and very soon.


Reading is my sanctuary. In some ways, it always has been. I'm back at the kitchen table in Lansing. Studying books. Remembering facts. Preparing for deliberations with my brothers and sisters. I think of the essay assignments Mom would make us do. But she didn't position them as debates, more like a game of fact-finding, asking us questions and letting us flip through encyclopedias to find the answers and create summary narratives. Felt like I was preparing my whole life to be part of something larger than myself.

Every book helps to mend Papa's teachings in my

heart—the ones I ripped up and discarded, hoping to forget. At lights-out, I sit by the door of my cell, using the faint light of the hall to continue reading. I read everything I can lay my hands on. It's like I am under a spell.

Reading also helps me better articulate my thoughts in new letters to the Honorable Elijah Muhammad. Every time I receive a reply, I am hit with more clarity.

Nothing can stop me.


"Here's how it works," Mr. O'Connell begins. "There are two teams . . ."

He scribbles on a blackboard in front of the class during our last practice before the big debate. They set up two podiums on opposite sides of the room to help us become familiar with arrangement and protocol.

"Each side speaks for and against the proposed argument. As you know, our topic is Should Capital Punishment Be Abolished?, which Norfolk Colony is arguing in favor of."

"What a question to throw at us," Akil says, shaking his head. "As if we're not already fighting for our lives every day."

I breathe in and think of Lightning. The look on his face, his desperate plea for another chance at life.

As the affirmative team, we've spent the last two weeks researching historical facts, quotes, and studying the law, finding every possible reason to do away with the death penalty. I'm so well versed that once free, I might even be able to represent myself if I ever have to go back to court. Not that I plan to.

"Once you're at that podium, you will have five minutes to present your argument. Boston University will present their case. Then you will have a small break to prepare for your rebuttals. This will be your chance to attack every single point mentioned by Boston University."

"How do we score?" I ask, even though the better question would be *How do you win?* because that's all I really care about.

"The judges count the number of points raised in your argument, and subtract it by the number of points refuted by your opponents. The team with the most points at the end of the debate wins. Now Mr. Nash is going to give you a few pointers."

Mr. Nash stuffs his hands in his pockets and takes center stage. As always, he looks real serious.

"Right. So there are a few things on which you need to focus. First things first, all these college kids are going to see is a bunch of criminals. That'll be their first mistake and you should use it to your advantage. Assumptions are their weakness. Second, you can support anything with the right amount of evidence. It's why we've had you study on your own. These kids are being spoon-fed their facts. You have an intimate knowledge of every point. You'll find yourselves making points which you weren't even prepared for.

"Third, and most important, time is of the essence. Five minutes doesn't sound like much. However, be accurate and concise, with the right inflection, and you can make anyone believe wine is water. It's all about the delivery. Okay? Let's go through a few practice rounds."

Akil goes first, then I follow. Each of us taking turns with our practiced talking points. Nash paces around the room, hand on his chin as he listens. Our fellow teammates take notes while O'Connell clocks our time.

When done, Nash turns to me. "Malcolm, intensify your tone, speak as if you don't have a mic. Pronounce every word with authority. You've been to church, I'm sure. You want to speak like a minister addressing his congregation with conviction and passion."

I think of Papa and swallow hard.

*Up, up, you mighty race!*

Papa didn't just speak. He roared. I clear my throat, tilt my chin up, and try again.

"The irreversible act of taking a life does not set this democracy apart from its barbaric predecessor. No, it only confirms their propensity for ruthlessness and lack of respect for life . . ."

Everyone in the room shifts back in their seats with stunned expressions.

"Whoa," Akil mumbles.

Nash nods. "Better. Much better."

After we wrap up our session for the day, Shorty and I head back to our dorm to prep for supper.

"Ain't gonna lie to you, homeboy," he says. "I'm a little nervous."

"You? You were born for the stage!"

"But this here . . . is different. Bigger. You realize what we get to do? We get to tell off those white boys and not lose our tongues. We get to show out and let them know they ain't as smart as they think."

He laughs, an almost delirious laugh from deep in his gut.

When lights are out for the night, I stay up, studying. Shorty's right. We get to educate the miseducated. Show them that despite our circumstances, above all things, we are made of the same material.

Mr. Muhammad would be proud.


The debate takes place in the Norfolk Prison assembly hall. With three hundred seats filled, the place is packed not just with inmates, but college kids, locals, church groups, and even press. All smiles and joyful interactions. The Norfolk Colony's orchestra provides music for the affair, with instruments played by inmates, including Shorty on the sax. It's remarkable, a real sight.

The debate will air live on the radio. I imagine what Sugar Ray thinks before entering the ring, knowing that the whole world is listening, waiting for the big fight. This is a different type of fight. Instead of our hands, we're using our minds.

I spot Alfred, Ozzy, and Frankie sitting in the middle row, along with other brothers from the kitchen crew. George sits in the same row as Nash and O'Connell. In front of the audience is a panel of three judges, three white men in suits and wearing black-rimmed glasses. Winslow is busy greeting some of these academics and businessmen in sharp navy suits, the kind I wouldn't mind scoring on credit back in Harlem, when I was Detroit Red.

Standing on the auditorium stage under the hot-white lights, I reshuffle my notes. Across the stage are our opponents from Boston University, three tall, lanky white boys, all dressed in dark gray suits, crisp white shirts, and burgundy bow ties. Sharp contrast to our prison uniforms.

My collar feels tight. I fidget with my pencil, instinctively go to smooth my hair down . . . then remember my conk is long gone.

"Relax," Akil whispers next to me. "Don't let them scare you. We're just as worthy."

The room grows humid and sticky. Feels like we're standing on the surface of the sun. I reshuffle my notes again, notes I don't really need since I've just about memorized everything on the pages.

"What if I . . . say it all wrong?"

He shakes his head. "You got this, brother. You know this stuff better than all of us."

I glance at the opposing team again as they stare around the hall, eyes wide and leery. Bet they never dreamed of being inside a prison before. Can't imagine why they would agree to challenge us. Then I see it, the way they look across the stage at us, the smirks of preemptive satisfaction. They think this will be an easy win. They are sadly mistaken.

Educate the miseducated. I am no longer afraid.

I pray to Allah before taking the podium.

"The whole history of penology is a refutation of deterrence theory, yet this theory, that murder by the state can repress murder by individuals, is the eternal war cry for the retention of Capital Punishment . . ."

Behind me, the Boston boys are taking copious notes, preparing for their rebuttals. Once I'm done, the first Boston boy steps up to the podium. He turns, giving us a once-over before a slick smile spreads across his face.

"The death penalty is about one thing only: justice. Justice for victims and their families. It's a debt that is owed for the crime committed. Numbers show that setting examples deter criminals from repeating the same offense. These lessons, while hard, are the only way the criminal will learn . . ."

The pencil in my hand snaps in two. I scan the audience for a reaction. None of them ever knew a man who was sentenced to death, knew someone whose life was minimized to nothing more than a "lesson." In the front row, Nash gives me a small nod and I wait for my turn back at center stage, notes long forgotten.

"Killing people to show killing is wrong is the very definition of hypocrisy! If we intend that violence will deter more violence, then we haven't paid attention to the history of the world . . ."

The judges stare up at me, their faces remain unmoved. But the audience gazes in awe.

At the end of round three, we wait for the judges to tally their scores. In the band section, Shorty is biting his nails. But I am not worried.

The moderator takes center stage, rereading his note. "Ladies and gentlemen, the winners are . . . Norfolk Colony!"

Victory. The crowd cheers. Everyone is clapping. All I can do is smile at the unbiased support.

We're given a celebratory dinner, which isn't much more than regular dinner and a slice of pound cake. Smiles upon the faces of my fellow inmates fill the room. Proud smiles. Congratulations come from every direction.

"Well done, Malcolm," Winslow says, greeting me in the main hall of the Colony, the heart.

"Thank you, sir."

"It's amazing how in such a short time, you've learned so much and have become so articulate. I knew you were going to be one of our brightest stars!"

"Well, actually, sir, I studied much of this before. Just didn't know what to do with it."

Winslow frowns. "But, you don't even have your high school degree. I'm sure you can see how this place has *really* shaped you."

I hold a steady face. "Sir, with all due respect, I was shaped long before I arrived here. Have a good night, sir."


Debating is my superpower. With every debate, I become stronger and stronger. You can dismantle a man's rhetoric solely and simplistically with facts. That's what Bembry meant by the power of using your words. That was my parents' secret and their greatest gift to me. It's all making sense. Every book I read helps add to the arsenal of words and facts I can use against my opponent to disprove his unfounded arguments.

It is the first time I can confront a white man and knock him out without lifting a finger. But I don't just want to beat him. I want him to know that I'm just as good, if not smarter, than he is. The proof is in my victories.

The proof satisfies my soul.

# CHAPTER 13

*To me, the thing that is worse than death is betrayal. You see, I could conceive death, but I could not conceive betrayal.*

—MALCOLM X

Sophia's soft fingers danced up my neck, her red nails like delicate drops of candy. She hummed a song I couldn't place and snuggled against my chest, squeezing me tight.

"I've missed you," she cooed.

The bedsprings creaked under us as I stared at the ceiling, the fan spinning round and round. Her hair smelled like lilac, and I wondered if Mom's garden grew such a flower or if all women's hair smelled like hers. Maybe even Laura's.

Laura. I hadn't thought of her in years. The pretty girl who walked into that soda shop where I worked up on the Hill. All she wanted was for us to go to a good Negro college together. But I couldn't see that dream, not when Roxbury was thrumming with energy. What would my life have looked like if I had gone home with her that night instead of with Sophia?

I must have stayed quiet too long. Sophia looked up at me, hurt in her eyes.

"What's wrong?"

"Nothing, baby."

"Well, something must be wrong." She pouted.

I didn't want to talk about what had really been on my mind—Mom, home, family. I also wondered if Sophia liked to garden and if she would be happy in a small house out in the country. Crazy thoughts. Dangerous thoughts.

I slipped from under her arms and scooped up my T-shirt and slacks. She lay on her side, watching me.

"Did you mean what you said the other day?" I asked. "About me moving back to Boston?"

She sat up and smiled. "Yes."

"So you want me to leave Harlem?"

Sophia hopped out of bed and leaped up on top of me, throwing her arms around my neck and her legs around my body. I had no choice but to hold her.

"I want you to come home with me," she said, beaming.

"And what about you? Will you leave your husband and live with me?"

Sophia blinked, as if waking up from a dream. She stared at the floor, slowly untangling herself from my lanky body.

"We . . . we have a good thing here, don't we?"

In so many ways, her no was crystal clear.

"I guess," I muttered.

Sophia stepped away before throwing her hands up. Collecting her clothes tossed on the floor.

"I didn't come all the way down here just to sit in some Harlem apartment and fight with you."

She leaned back in a chair, dressed in a lace slip, and lit a cigarette. Her puffs of smoke engulfed the room in a haze. I grabbed the bottle of whiskey off the side table, drank it straight. It ran down my throat like liquid fire, the same way I remembered my first drink with Shorty, back in Roxbury. I looked at Sophia, the memories of our times together flooding back, out of order and shaken.

"Don't you want . . . more?" I asked her.

She stared at the carpet, a scowl on her pretty little face.

"I don't know what you want from me?" she said matter-of-factly. "It's not like I can change what . . . is."

"But . . . you can try. We can try, together? Right?"

She picked up her pointy brassiere, almost the same color as her skin, ivory cream. I used to love kissing her beautiful white porcelain skin.

"I have to do what's best for me."

"And what about me?" I asked, then coughed, the smoke thickening in my throat.

"You're a good time," she continued. "But you're asking for the impossible."

She had years on me, but I didn't know this Sophia. I didn't know that monsters could hide in pretty white skin.

The kitchen is a beehive, preparing for supper. Shorty is here now. We got him switched off laundry duty. He helps Frankie with the meal prep, watching the ovens so that nothing burns. Ozzy loads in crates of fresh carrots, tomatoes, and romaine lettuce to have with our turkey slices. Even Alfred is busy taking pans out of the broiler.

What am I doing? Pretending the pot in the sink is Sophia, trying to scrub her power of six years off me.

Alfred walks by and laughs, touching my arm.

"Hey, man, don't break my pot now. It didn't do nothing to you!"

My arms ease out of their tight flex. Been in the kitchen almost all afternoon. The thought of sitting still in the library today made me want to rip my hair out in chunks. I'm angry with Sophia, but most of all I'm angry with myself, for never really knowing her in the first place. Never knowing who I was becoming with her.

"Something on your mind, young man?"

I spit out my first thought without thinking.

"You married, Alfred?"

Alfred cackles. "Well, I'll be, I knew it had to be lady troubles! Yes, sir, I got me a woman. And just like with you, she makes me want to hit a few tin pans myself sometimes. You married?"

I let out a relieved laugh.

"Married? Man, I'm too young. I doubt I'll ever get married. I don't have the best record when it comes to the ladies. But . . . how'd you know that your lady was the one for you? How do you know somebody that well to trust them?"

Alfred dumps more dirty trays in the sink.

"Ain't how much you know about them, but how much you know about you. When you know yourself, you can sense what type of character anybody is made of just like that!" He snaps his fingers. "My momma always used to say, if you don't have a good sense of who you is, you can't love anyone the way you supposed to. You see, you got to love yourself first, Red."

"My mom used to say something like that," I mention, voice low. Thinking of Mom still locked in that hospital always makes my thoughts choke.

"Hey! Maybe we kinfolk! Where your people from again? I don't think you ever told me."

"My mother is from the Caribbean, Grenada. But I grew up in Omaha, Nebraska, till our house was burned by the Klan, and then we moved to Lansing, Michigan. You?"

Alfred's smile fades a bit.

"Tulsa, Oklahoma. Born and raised in this little town called Greenwood. Ever heard of it?"

"No. Can't say I have."

Alfred tenses, his mood shifting.

"It was . . . real nice. Nicest place for a Black family to be, if you ask me. We owned our own little section of this country. Everyone was doing good. Going to school, universities. Had our own doctors, dentists, lawyers, teachers, newspaper, a theater for the picture shows . . . Man, you ask anyone and they'd tell you, me and Daddy owned the nicest grocery in town. And Mama? She always had a fresh-baked cake in the oven."

It sounded like the paradise Papa talked about. A place where Black people governed their own livelihoods.

"With a place that nice, how you end up here?"

Alfred thought real hard before responding. He rinses off his pan and hangs it to dry.

"Everyone left. Well, those who made it out alive."

"Alive? What happened?"

Alfred struggles with his next words.

"They . . . ran through our town, shooting folks . . . dead. Killed my daddy, my baby brother, burned down homes and businesses like it was their job. All them little children crying, running, getting snatched up and killed . . . It was . . . the scariest day of my life, man."

Alfred pauses, blinking, as he stares off into the distance. He didn't have to explain who the "they" was.

"Seems like they were just waiting for anything to set them off."

"So what did?" I ask.

Alfred looks at me. "White lady said this Negro boy winked at her in an elevator, something or other. All I know is, whatever she said, stuck. A mob of them crackers came and took that poor boy. And his pappy and them friends went to go help him. But all them white folk saw was uppity Black folk living better than them. The next thing you know there were mobs and tank trucks killing us from every which way. Even from the sky. Felt like World War I. They bombed us, tore through our homes like a tornado. Burned the entire community to the ground."

Man, crackers are sick. They just always terrorizing somebody, and we the ones that end up behind bars.

"We were just Black folks, doing good, being happy, minding our own business, taking care of our families, while the white folks were living dirt poor. And instead of us living together, they just wanted us dead!"

Alfred frowns.

"Well . . . it was a lie that any Black boy would so much as look at a white girl and everybody would know about it but—"

"You see how white girls will get you killed," I go off, my blood sizzling, voice rising. "Or worse, get you thrown in prison!"

Sophia's face sharpens into view again and it makes me want to scream. She sold me out quick. After all we'd been through. All our good times together. What made me think that she was the one, when she never once showed me I was the one? The way she cried in that courtroom, those fake tears. She was okay with me rotting in a hellhole. Never once reached out or sent word to me. Should've never gotten involved with her.

I should've stayed with Laura. All Laura wanted was for us to go to a Black college and get our education, together. Instead, I'm here.

Alfred is quiet for a moment, his mouth in a straight line.

"So, you were with a white woman, huh?"

Something about his tone makes my skin prickle. It wasn't an observation, but more like a judgment.

I look up, and the entire kitchen is staring at me. Shorty's eyes wide, Ozzy setting down his crates slow, Alfred's face unreadable.

"I . . . I gotta get to debate."

He nods, eyebrows raised as I excuse myself and head to the library.

Later, at dinner, whispers hit my back. Alfred sits with a few white inmates, talking in hushed tones. Shorty, Ozzy, and I sit at a long table alone in the canteen.

"Think you've made some of them a little mad," Ozzy jokes.

"Don't sweat it, homeboy," Shorty says, shrugging it off. "They ain't nothing to lose sleep over."

"I'm cool," I say even though my back feels tense.

The same white men that were congratulating me on my debate wins are icy cold upon greeting tonight, until all talk just stops and there is nothing left but silence.

In my moment of vulnerability, I let my guard down. If I had paid enough attention, I would have seen all the ways Alfred had been brainwashed by this place. The way he was proud of being a prisoner here, overly friendly with the guards and the white inmates. The way they made it seem like he had control, that he was one of them, when he was nothing but an informant, a snitch, even after everything he had been through in Tulsa. No matter how well-meaning this place is, it's still a prison run by white men.

Should have taken the time to educate him on history, remind him who the real enemies are, show him the light. Help him be a guide for other Negroes, just looking to be free.

I wrote to the Honorable Elijah Muhammad about this, asking him why Black men refuse to see the light. He encouraged me to let Allah use me to be a tool of His teaching. To open the door and allow Allah to guide me.

Dearest Brother,

Your last letter made me so proud of you. It is so good to hear that you are corresponding with the Honorable Elijah Muhammad.

Also, to answer your questions, yes, in many ways Mom laid the foundation for us to follow Islam long before we met the Messenger, so it must be in divine order.

They pretended Mom was crazy for refusing to give her children pig meat and she suffered unimaginable consequences. Mom has always been a true and faithful servant of God. And Papa a true and faithful minister of God. Everything that happened resulted from a desire to destroy our family. Destroying our family killed Papa's message like it did Mr. Garvey. But he had millions of followers worldwide. They will never destroy the truth. Allah will protect us, Malcolm.

We pray for you daily and cannot wait until you are with us again.

Your Brother,
Philbert

My family writes letters almost daily now. With each letter I learn something new about Islam. I hold on to their guidance with two hands, finding facts in my reading that support Mr. Muhammad's teachings. I don't want to just follow, I want to fully understand and be well versed in my faith. I want to be a scholar of Islam. Much like debating, if you know all the facts with unwavering certainty, no one can refute you. Mr. Muhammad said that Allah is always on the side of the righteous, on the side of one who's true and pure.

I keep focused and do whatever tasks necessary without protest, all in order to return to my studies. As a child, I had so many unanswered questions: Why did they burn our home? Why do they call us niggers? Why are we not equal? Why do they call Black men boys? On and on. I wanted to ask Papa but he was gone. I wanted to ask Mom but she was gone, too. I wanted to ask Wilfred, Hilda, or Philbert, but they sent me away for stealing a chicken. I wanted to ask Mr. Ostrowski, but he said I was nothing but a nigger.

Now I am finding answers to all of my questions through the words of Islam. The words invigorate my soul, better than any drug could.

"Lights-out!"

At 10:00 p.m. on the dot, the dormitory lights shut down, leaving only a faint orange glow from the hall light.

A night patrolman passes my cell, his footsteps heavy. Once he's far off, I leap to my feet, slipping the book from under my mattress and curling up reading.

You have to angle the book in such a way that the dim light can hit the page on the exact spot you want to read. It's tricky to squint in such darkness until you can make out the words.

*Findings in Genetics*
*Negro History*
*Uncle Tom's Cabin*
The Story of Civilization
*The Collected Works of Mahatma Gandhi*
*Days of Our Years*
*The Loom of Language*

I feel reborn, like a new man in fresh skin, bursting with knowledge. I'm eager to share this knowledge with everyone I know and care about.

So I start writing letters.

They are simple at first, but then they grow into long essays, full of everything I've been learning through books and my family. Sometimes it takes me several pages just to say everything I am thinking.

I send a letter to Sammy the Pimp, West Indian Archie, Bumpy Johnson, and at least a dozen other known hustlers in

Harlem and Boston. Unsure of their exact addresses, I send the letters to bars and clubs they frequented. I know them all.

I write to them about Black history that has been whitewashed, Allah, Islam, and Mr. Muhammad. I inform them of our identity, our true identity as Black men, our history that has been whitewashed, that we are the very backbone of our nation.

No reply. I keep going . . .

The mayor of Boston. The governor of Massachusetts. President Truman.

I tell them how, per my studies, the white man is solely responsible for the Black man's condition and that this crisis must be addressed and reprimanded as such.

No reply.

I'm doing so much writing, I think to try my hand at a little poetry. There's something about making a string of words say all the things I can't. I write a special poem in dedication to the man who taught me how to pray.

## MUSIC

*Music is not created*
*It is always here*

*Surrounding us*
*Like an infinite particle that constitutes life,*
   *it cannot be seen but can only be felt*
*Like Allah,*
*like life.*
*No 'tis not created, but like the never dying*
   *soul, permeates the air with its presence*
*Ever waiting for its Master*
*The Lordly Musician*
*The Wielder of the souls*
*To come and give it an earthly body*
*Making it into a song.*
*Music without the Musician is like life*
   *without Allah*
*Both in desperate need of a home,*
*a body*
*The completed song*
*and its Creator*

"What's this word?" Ozzy asks, holding the book up to his face.

At our table in the library, I lean over to examine the word he underlines with his finger.

"'Dif-fi-cult.' Got to try sounding it out just as we practiced."

Ozzy fidgets, pulling the book closer, his eyes narrowing to see.

"It's all right, brother," I say, patting him on the back. "You take all the time you need."

After one of the last debates, Ozzy asked if I could teach him how to read. Never thought I'd be much of a teacher but the more I learn, the more I want others to learn as well. Plus, it's an act of service, to help my brother.

"This may have been a little easier when I was younger," Ozzy admits. "Didn't do much schooling, left that to my brother. I went ahead and started working at fourteen." He laughs. "Tell me again what Big Lee's looking like now."

I grin. "Well, he's big. But you still got a few inches on him. Everyone calls him a gentle giant, especially with that voice of his."

"Glad he still singing for the Lord," Ozzy says, beaming with pride. "Been in choir since he was a boy."

Talking about Big Lee makes me think of all the brothers back in the shop at Charlestown. About Bembry and his wise words. About Chucky. Feels like I abandoned them, leaving for greener pastures.

I glance across the table at Shorty, who's studying up on Plato for our weekly book discussion. If I was able to teach Shorty what I knew about Islam, maybe I can teach others.

"This is gonna sound a little . . . wild," I start, unable to believe the words slipping from my inner thoughts.

"Oh boy," Shorty chuckles, marking his page. "Let's hear it."

"I need to go back to Charlestown."

Shorty raises an eyebrow, leaning in. "Uh, you feeling all right, homeboy? You hit your head or something? Why would you ever want to go back to that hell?"

"I just keep thinking of all the brothers there, how much they're suffering because they don't know all this we've been learning, man. If only they had access to this knowledge. I can teach them about their real history . . . Think about it."

Ozzy shakes his head. "You can't sacrifice yourself like that. That place ain't fit for a dog."

"The Honorable Elijah Muhammad would."

"He'd really do that?" Ozzy asks, intrigued.

"Do you know he takes the time to respond to every single brother who reaches out to him? Look how he turned my life around. Sent his own money to a complete stranger. And here I am—anew. When's the last time you've seen a minister do that?"

Ozzy seems overwhelmed at the thought. I'm ready to answer all their looming questions.

"What's going on, brothers!" Akil comes in just then. His face is sweaty but his lips seem dry. He may be coming down with something. "And, what you doing down here, Ozzy?"

Ozzy huffs. "Can't a man read in peace? And what did I hear about you missing work duty yesterday."

"Yeah, where you been, homeboy?" Shorty asks. "You missed class this morning."

"And ain't I lucky," Akil jokes. "Our dorm was sent down to the infirmary yesterday for testing."

"Testing? What kind of testing?"

"I don't know. They just gave us this shot to see if it works."

An alarm goes off in my head. I close my book, giving him my full attention.

"Oh yeah, they mentioned something about that," Ozzy says. "They sending our dorm down this afternoon. Skipping work duty, too."

"But a shot for *what*?" I'm anxious now.

Akil twist his lips, struggling with the name.

"Tie-flood or something. Not too sure. They said they just testing things out like a vaccine, but we shouldn't feel nothing."

"Sounds like they're . . . experimenting," I say, glancing at Shorty. He immediately follows my drift. Something is up.

"So how you feeling?" Shorty asks.

Akil shrugged. "To tell you the truth, not so good. Might head back down to the nurse. I was just stopping by to return some books."

Ozzy sighs and begins to stand.

"Well, I better head down and get my shot, too, I guess. Don't want to be feeling sick all night."

My arm shoots out to grab his.

"No, Ozzy. You're not going anywhere, brother."

Frankie grumbles under his breath. "Where this red nigger get off, thinking he better than everybody?"

Alfred stays quiet, his eyes down. He doesn't talk to me anymore. He almost seems frightened.

"Ain't no nigger gonna run around here thinking he's better than me," Frankie mumbles.

I ignore the ignorance. Allah, my books, and letters are my priority. This new zest for life feels foreign and yet sacred. Something I don't want to give up. Never want to go back to that dark place again. I'm ready to stand on the sun, in my truth, serving Allah and His righteousness. I'm ready to free my people from Jim Crow's leash. I'm ready to wake my people up.

Toward the end of our shift, Alfred moves closer, angling himself in a way that makes it seem like he isn't talking to me.

"Thought you'd be down getting your shot today," he mumbles as he dumps another pile of trays into the sink.

"Not taking it," I grunt.

"Why not?"

I consider ignoring him, but think of what Mom once told me—*You don't want to drown your seeds, you never know what may grow.*

"That typhoid shot is dangerous," I warn. "Brother Akil still isn't all the way right. Why are we entrusting this place, these white men, with our health when they've never given us reason to trust them at all? Ask yourself this question, Alfred: Why aren't they injecting themselves with a potential 'cure' to see if it works? Why must we be their test subjects?"

Alfred hesitates then finally says, "They ain't been nothing but good to you. Seeing where you came from, why can't you show them some respect?"

I look him square in the eye.

"Brother, you might be fine with accepting scraps as gold. But I never will be."

My stomach ties itself in knots so tight I can barely stand still. We watch the judges tally our scores, but they seem to be debating one another for so long I almost think we should switch places onstage.

The boys from Clark University had obviously heard about our team's record, nearly undefeated, and they came over-prepared for today's topic: Should European Immigration to America Be Unlimited?

One of the white boys even tried to copy my cadence, so I winked at him. He was rather good. But it was discomforting, hearing him parrot me. Watching a white man steal from you in plain sight is a theme in every Black man's life.

We had read up on them in a recent profile the school had in *Life* magazine. Incredible campus, smiling faces, with an "unbeatable debate team."

But still, something feels off.

"Chill, homeboy," Shorty whispers next to me. "We got this."

"Yeah, I know," I mumble.

The room is filled with tense whispers. Offstage, Winslow is quietly arguing with Nash and O'Connell. Twice they look over their shoulders, directly at me.

Something is wrong.


"But it doesn't make sense," Shorty shouts the next day as our team gathers for a post-debate recap. "We had them! You know we did."

Nash and O'Connell sit at the front of the classroom, looking just as defeated as we are. The team is outraged by the loss.

"Fellas, I know. It's . . . complicated. For many reasons."

"Unfortunately, you fellas have gained quite a reputation

for yourselves," O'Connell says, then looks directly at me. "Some think you're too articulate, too outspoken. It comes across as arrogant. Shows a lack of discernment about knowing your . . . place."

This isn't about the debate at all. This is about me.

Nash tries to reason with me. "Malcolm, take this from me, a defeat, like this one, will only set you up for greater victories."

With a sharp nod, I walk out the classroom, Nash calling after me. I am done with Norfolk's debate team. If there's no winning for a Black man even when he's right, then why am I wasting my time representing the very people who hold me back?

"So what is this I hear about you refusing to take the vaccine test?" Winslow sits behind his desk, fingers webbed together, a sharpness in his voice. He hasn't even spared a smile.

"Malcolm, I thought we had an understanding," he says. "We're here to help you. But you have to help us in return."

"By sacrificing my health?" I ask.

"Malcolm, this isn't just about you. You've compelled others to follow your lead and refuse the shot. We both know you're very persuasive. We've seen it in your debates. Everyone has."

This doesn't seem like a compliment. Winslow is losing his patience.

"Compel. From the Latin words *com* and *pellere*, means to urge, by force or pressure. I simply asked a few questions: What is the typhoid shot for and why do we need to take it? If the answer is uncomplicated and of reasonable intentions, a reasonable answer should be available."

Winslow slams a palm down on the table.

"This is not one of your debates!" he shouts. "I don't have to answer your questions. You answer mine! You're the prisoner here!"

His nostrils flare, face red and dampening. Leaning back in my chair, I hold in a smirk.

"Believe me, I never assumed I was simply a guest. But this body still belongs to me, no matter where it's housed."

Winslow blinks, mouth gaping. Slowly, he composes himself, sitting upright in his seat, tapping his desk as he speaks.

"Look, I believe you have promise, and I'd like to see you a reformed man walking out of here. But prisoners who don't comply with direct orders will be transferred out of Norfolk, specifically back to Charlestown. Is that what you want?"

My mouth dries and I glance out the window behind him. At the gardens, the fresh air, the trees, the men playing baseball. A facade of paradise. Beside Winslow's hand is the folder with that pile of pictures. Brothers in suits walking out of here, free. Overwhelmed by the reprieve of this place, I thought I would be one of them someday.

But if I'm called to drive people to the light, I need to meet them in the dark.

"Did you know that there are five religions accepted in this facility, but not one of them is Islam? Are you worried it may give people too many ideas?"

Winslow shakes his head, grabbing a folder. "And then there are these letters. They are preposterous," Winslow fumes, shaking a stack of notes in his hand. I recognize my handwriting on the paper that Ella had sent me. He snatches one from the pile, a letter originally sent to President Truman, and rips it open.

I fold my hands in front of me, remaining unshaken.

"I respectfully disagree, sir," I say, sitting across from him.

When I did not receive replies, I assumed some censorship had occurred. For a brief insane moment, I really thought that I was a free man in here. Thought I had the rights and privileges to free speech, to send mail, like any other man in this country.

But I have discovered quickly that in no way would a white bigot allow Black people to call out their immorality until they themselves are ready for change. They would rather die than see their own reflection.

Winslow shakes his head again, taking off his glasses to rub his eyes.

"After all the progress you've made here . . . school, debate team, the victories . . . this is the hill you choose to die on? Do you have any idea who you're writing to? All this stuff about white people being the devil, when you're lucky to be alive! We've taken good care of you here. What more could you ask for?"

Something occurs to me that I've always known but haven't fully processed: I'll never just be a man, even outside these walls. I will always be a *Black* man. My desire for equality is a burden and an insult in white eyes. So they lock us up, mute our voices.

But what they have in body, they cannot take in spirit.

"It's my religious right," I say simply.

"You understand that I can't allow you to stay here if you don't obey."

I know what is about to happen and the thought crystallizes in my soul. They're sending me back to Charlestown. I should be scared. But I'm not.

What man can tip you over when you're so deeply rooted?

# CHAPTER 14

*You're not supposed to be so blind with patriotism that you can't face reality. Wrong is wrong, no matter who does it or who says it.*

—MALCOLM X

"Y'all ready?"

The group of white kids formed a semicircle around me like a half moon in a large field behind our home.

"I thought we were gonna play baseball," Young Jimmy said, with bat in hand. "You always break us up into teams. What are we doing now?"

Philbert and Reginald hung back by the wooden shed near the edge of our property, watching me direct our neighbors.

"Nah, I have a better game than baseball," I said. "I have a game where some of you guys can pretend to be rich lords and ladies or princesses."

The girls perked up. "What does that mean?"

"Yeah, nigger. What you getting at? Ain't nothing better than baseball!"

I smirked. "The game is called Robin Hood."

"What's that?"

The kids inched closer. Some of them had never heard the story before. We may have been the only Black kids in our neighborhood, but we for sure had more education than most of those white kids. More property, too. That's why they always came to play at our house.

By the time I finished explaining the game, the white kids were excited. As they broke into groups and scurried off to claim their imaginary land and castles, I tried my hardest to keep a smile off my face.

"Told you it would work!" I said to Philbert.

Philbert laughed. "Man, you sure can talk your way out of a paper bag."

I chuckled and turned to Reginald. "You're gonna be in my gang."

"Gang for what? What are we doing?"

"We're gonna steal all their gold and money!"

Reginald frowns. "What? We're gonna steal from them? You're wild, they'll kill us!"

"No, Reginald! I'm Robin Hood and those kids are the ones whose money we're gonna take. Got it?"

"It's pretend," Philbert added, rubbing Reginald's little head.

Reginald bit his nails. "But . . . stealing is wrong."

"Not when you're taking from the rich to give to the poor!"

"It's wrong either way," he shoots back.

"Man, you're just being a baby." I waved him off. "You don't get it."

"You're a kid, too, and you don't get it either."

"But they're white. You know how much they take from us! Don't you listen to Mom when she reads her papers and Papa's letters?"

"Still not right," Reginald shouted.

Philbert straightened, eyes toggling between us. "Now hang on, I—"

"Reginald, it's just a game!"

Reginald looked me in the eyes. Even as a tiny child, he had an old soul. His fists tightened before he turned away with a huff. "I'm not playing with you anymore. It's not funny. We shouldn't be stealing from them. I'm telling Mom!"

"We're not really stealing! We're taking, but then we're giving it to the folks who really need it. Don't you want to help people?"

"Wrong is wrong," he spat before storming off into the woods.


The smell greets me first. The buckets filled with shit, piss, and vomit. In the fifteen months I was away, I learn, not much has changed in Charlestown. The guards are tighter, stricter, abusing their power like sullen children.

Norfolk evicted anyone who refused the shot, including Shorty and Ozzy. The look on their faces as we go through intake immediately reminds me of my first day in Charlestown. Panic and fear wrapped in shock. There is no way to prepare them. They have to experience it for themselves.

But with my newfound wisdom, I feel invincible, shielded. Nothing can break me.

Now that I've returned with my purpose, these walls cannot contain me. Their water hoses feel like dripping faucets. Their shouts fall on deaf ears. I've soared over them higher than they realize.

*5HK-112. 5HK-113. 5HK-114. 5HK-115.*

My old post in the shop is waiting for me. Next to Bembry. I can hardly contain my excitement upon seeing him; he hasn't changed a day. I give him a debriefing on the Norfolk library, all the books I read, debates I conquered, articles I wrote for *The Colony* paper, and my letters with the Honorable Elijah Muhammad. He nods, but seems indifferent. Unimpressed. I thought he, above everyone, would be proud of my turnaround.

On break, Bembry waits until the men step out to stretch their legs before leaning across the conveyor belt.

"How much do you know about this Nation of Islam?"

The familiar feeling of distrust slips under my skin. I clear my throat. "Why do you ask?"

He shrugs. "Something don't sit right with me about them."

"Helping Black men free themselves of self-hate . . . doesn't sit right with you?"

His eyes narrow, face flushing red. "I've been around for a long while, Malcolm," he starts, his raspy voice low. "Studied what I could from who I could. I'm not one to tell another man what to do with his life or which God to serve. But the idea that a man, a human just like you and me, can take a religion that outdates us all and twist it to his own predilection, seems wrong. And dangerous. To call himself a messenger, that he has the ear of God . . . That sounds a bit suspicious to me."

"How is it any different from any other sect of Christianity? The Bible, a story handed down for eons, has been translated so many times, no one knows its true origins. And we Black people were forced to practice Christianity, forced to worship the God of our captors."

Bembry sighs like a disappointed father.

"When a man sees himself as a prophet, he can do no wrong. But no man is perfect. Everyone has flaws and it seems like he's preying on the wounded. You'll see soon enough."

I continue to school Bembry on the different sects of

Christianity, even as the other brothers rejoin us. They whisper among themselves, watching our interaction. He's challenging Mr. Muhammad. The man who saved my life and showed me the light. The man who is much like my father. My heart cracks. Could Bembry be brainwashed like the other lost Negroes in this prison?

"There is only one God. Allah is the Arabic word for God. We pray to the same God as Christians and Jews. It's not too late for you, Bembry. You should write to Mr. Muhammad and see for yourself."

Bembry stares at me. I have a full beard now and broad shoulders. I'm no longer the scared little boy, lashing out, that I was when I first came to Charlestown.

I'm more a man now than ever.

He tips his chin up, then returns to his work in silence. I do the same, standing taller than before.


With no ventilation, the walls of the visitors' center are saturated with mold sliding down from the ceiling. Children cough, old women wave church fans, some women keep tissues over their noses in order not to inhale the toxic smell. Charlestown tries to punish our loved ones as much as they punish us.

"As-Salaam-Alaikum," I say as I approach the table where my brother sits. I've been practicing the Arabic greeting, hoping my pronunciation would impress my family when they finally came to see me here again. The few Muslim inmates here have taken to me like a long-lost brother. And in many ways, I was lost.

Reginald nods, but he doesn't respond back in the standard greeting of Wa-Alaikum As-Salaam. I'm not offended, but I'm alarmed nonetheless. He doesn't seem like himself. Clothes disheveled, hair frazzled, knee tapping as if he's sending a telegram. Only time I've seen someone like this, is if they were coming off a high.

"Brother, what's wrong?" I ask directly.

He looks over his shoulder, eyes bouncing between faces until he looks directly at me.

"Did you get my letter?" he asks, his voice shaky, eyes glazed over.

"Uh, yes. But I could barely read it. Doctor said I've developed some kind of astigmatism, from all the reading I did at Norfolk. Getting glasses this week."

"Really," he says, voice trailing off. He rubs his hands together. "Did Papa wear glasses, too? I can't remember."

The mention of Papa makes my stomach clench. Reginald's doing that thing again, bringing up anything and everything before reaching the point because he knows I'll give it to him straight. He moves about in his chair as if fire ants were crawling up his legs. He's hurt.

"Yes, Papa wore glasses. Reginald, what's going on?"

Reginald pales, looking left then right. There are quite a few other inmates in the visitors' center with us. "I have to tell you something. But I want you to use your own discernment. Don't do anything rash on account of me."

My hands start to sweat. "Okay, man, I'm listening."

"I hate to tell you this, brother. Not after I was the one who . . . brought you in. But . . . we've been led astray."

"What do you mean?"

Tears well in his eyes. He's shaking. "Elijah Muhammad. He is not what he professes."

I lean forward, my back a steel rod.

"Reginald, what's going on? You high?"

"No, Malcolm! I know what I'm saying. I've been . . . released, suspended. From the Nation."

"Suspended! Why?"

"They said I was having relations, with a secretary, from the New York Temple."

"But that's not true, right?"

"You know I practice moral restraint. Always have." Reginald shakes his head. "Listen, Allah knows our heart and He knows our deeds. What matters is what was told to Mr. Muhammad. But he's made an example of me. He has used many of us as pawns. We're disposable. He has his own agenda, his own desires. This isn't true Islam."

"How can you say that?" Islam means more to me than anything in my entire life. It's all I have. It's Papa and Mom.

It's our family. Our ancestors. It's hope for a future to all Negroes. It's reclaiming our past, our roots, an ability to serve, I mean really serve God, Allah. Like Papa. And here is my brother, my blood brother, my best friend in the whole wide world, speaking ill of the Messenger and this sacred religion?

"It's true brother. It's true."

"I will write to him," I offer. "Stand as a witness and provide testimony of your integrity and honor. Philbert and Wilfred, they will do the same."

"Philbert and Wilfred are forbidden from speaking to me. Their own brother. Tell me, what kind of religious man would punish someone this way?"

"There must have been some misunderstanding," I plead.

"There are many things you don't know, Malcolm. Many things no one knows. But once you're free, you will see with your own eyes. You cannot trust everyone you meet in the Nation. Truth, brother. Truth always comes to the light."

Reginald led me to Islam, and now he's abandoning me in it.

My heart twists, like the wringing of a wet cloth. I stay up all night tossing and turning over Reginald's words.

*"We've been led astray."*

The word *astray* means to be led away from the correct path or direction, into error or morally questionable behavior. I can't imagine anything Mr. Muhammad has done that would warrant such a term.

I'm worried about my brother. But my concern is fogged with what I know about Islam. I need to help my brother understand better, that's all. Mr. Muhammad awakened something dormant inside of me. Without his teaching, I wouldn't be mentally free. I can never repay him for helping me find the light. Islam is my identity. It has eliminated my pain and self-destruction. Islam fuels my purpose, my reason for living.

How can what Reginald is saying be true?

I write to Mr. Muhammad, begging for mercy for my kid brother. Asking simple questions, not to accuse him of any wrongdoing, but for clarity. Is there something I don't know?

His reply halts all my disbeliefs.

As-Salaam-Alaikum

In the Holy Name of Almighty Allah, the Beneficent, the Most Merciful Saviour, Our Deliverer, Master of the Day of Judgment. To Allah alone do I submit and seek refuge.

Dear Brother Malcolm,

I trust your letter about Brother Reginald and understand your concern. However, you make me question your faith and your belief in Allah. If you once believed in the truth and now you are begging to doubt the truth, you didn't believe the truth in the first place. Before a man is exalted to greatness, he is put to the test with hardships and trials. Sometimes those trials come in the form of choosing between family and what is right.

Your Brother,
Elijah Muhammad
Messenger of Allah

"You ain't hear of Tulsa? Man, I thought everybody knew about what happened."

In the common room, brothers ask about Norfolk and all the inmates there. They are in awe of the library, the assembly hall, the canteen, the orchestra, choir, and debate teams. Stuff we couldn't dream of having at Charlestown.

"Yeah, I heard of Greenwood. Burnt down some nice homes and businesses all owned by Negroes," Big Lee says.

"So you met someone from there," Bembry says, slamming down a domino. "Live through all that only to end up in prison? Man. If I was him, I would be deep in the woods, never to be seen again."

Norm shakes his head. "I heard about it, but it was a Negro

who started all that. Going down to the courthouse with a gun, scaring white folks. They had to teach 'em a lesson, and they say he done touch a white woman, too."

I take a deep breath. I think about what Mr. Muhammad once said. About being gentle with our brothers who are misinformed. Who are not aware of facts. Norm isn't a bad man. He's a confused man, a brainwashed man. All he needs is reeducating from someone on his level.

"Well, brother, if you believe that, that means you believe the white man's lies. We can't rely on someone who despises us to control our destiny. And that's what their lies do. We need to control our own futures. The only way we can do that is by learning truths and dispelling myths."

"What truths?"

"Brother, we have been miseducated in an attempt to erase all traces of our true selves. We have a history that predates the Roman Empire. That predates Columbus. Predates slavery. Do you know why they don't teach this in schools? Because they are trying rewrite the past. Imagine if you had a nickel in your hand and I told you it was a penny. Boy, you'd fight me tooth and nail until I acknowledged the truth. So why are Black people not fighting back when the white man insists we're worthless? When we *know* that kid in Tulsa didn't touch that white woman."

I look to Big Lee, sitting next to Ozzy. "Big Lee, you ever heard of the Second Amendment?"

Big Lee glances at Norm, then Bembry, then back to me. He slowly shakes his head. "No . . ."

"It states all citizens have the right to defend themselves. We are citizens. Lee, we have just as much right as any other human being in this country to defend ourselves. So how is it that white people were allowed to attack the citizens of Greenwood, but those Negroes were punished for defending themselves? I'll tell you why. The rules that govern this country were not written for our benefit, but for our persecution. To keep us under someone's boot as long as humanly possible.

"This double standard exists in our economy, too. We have been conditioned to believe that whoever can make the most money is the most valuable. But from the start of the white man's arrival in this country, they have stripped us of our land, our traditions, our culture, and freedoms. How are we to prosper? They might have abolished slavery, but they find new ways to maintain this system of capitalism and oppression, invent new ways to keep us divided and distracted so we only see ourselves as inferior."

Slowly, a crowd grows around me. Instead of debating a point, I'm simply stating and articulating one, in a way that my people can digest. Most have never heard any of what I'm sharing with them. Most had no idea we had more history than slavery. I don't just speak their language, I awaken something already deep inside their souls.

In the corner, by his cell, I see Mack leaning against the wall, smiling proudly.

Chucky was released from the hole the day I returned.

He walks with a limp. His eyes constantly shifting. A young Black man with hair white as snow.

I slide my tray next to him and he flinches, wincing up at me as if I am the sun.

"Chucky," I say in a calm voice.

He gives a half smile. "Oh. Hey," he mumbles and his shoulder twitches. "Um, you see Lucille?"

"Lucille?"

"Yeah . . . she was down in the . . . in the place with me. Now I can't find her. I got to get her . . . to get her home."

I take a deep breath, calculating my words.

"There was no one down there with you, brother. No one."

Chucky is contemplative, playing with his food, before a fit of laughter bursts from his lips.

The sight of a broken Chucky sends shock waves through Charlestown. He was kept in the hole the longest of any prisoner we know. A record fifteen months in solitary confinement. That kinda time can cause you to play with your breath and create images with darkness. Chucky spent less time overseas fighting in the war. I tell him he is a descendant of refined and industrious kings who lived under the sun and beside beautiful oceans, who wore clothes of silk and slippers of gold. I whisper to him, "You are one of God's favorite kings, brother. You are one of God's favorites."

More brothers come to talk to me, asking me questions about history and about the Honorable Elijah Muhammad.

I speak with great care to every single inmate who comes to me. I do not try to scare them with the truth, but let it soak in and build them up. To give them some dignity that had long been dormant in their souls. It took years for me to wake up; it is only right I give them such grace.

We are all brothers here.

We are not prison numbers or possessions. We are not labor to build someone else's wealth. We are men. We are Gods. We are Africans. And, we are Americans.

# CHAPTER 15

*To have once been a criminal is no disgrace. To remain a criminal is the disgrace.*

—MALCOLM X

*My parole has been approved*, I write to Mr. Muhammad. *I'm coming home.*

I sign my letter:

Malcolm X

"Little" was not my last name. It was a slaveholder's name. It was the name of my foreparents' kidnapper.

To be reborn, you must free yourself of your chains.

I stand in the warden's office in a cheap brown suit issued by the state. It's hot, itchy, and made of wool; my arms are too long for the sleeves, legs too long for the pants. My socks are showing.

The warden reviews my files with a skeptical eye. He hasn't aged well over the last few years. Outside his window, across the yard, the first walls of the new unit have been constructed. I think of Shorty. He was also up for parole but had trouble finding a sponsor. Maybe when he's free, I'll see him again.

"You're a part of that Nation of Islam, right? I see in your files you've been exchanging letters with an Elijah Muhammad."

I keep quiet, even though the sound of the Messenger's name in the warden's mouth makes my stomach churn. I'm anxious to finish with these final proceedings. As Mr. Muhammad has always guided, we must practice patience.

"I don't know what it is about you niggers that make you so damn dumb."

He slams the file, handing it over to the guard behind me. "Don't need to put this far. This one will be back."

I stand tall, keeping quiet. I am worthy. I am born from many kings.

Outside, the air is sweet. Crisp. Fresh. The August sun is like the greatest blessing. It beams down on me as I walk a few feet from the gate, my chin held high until I drop to my knees, snatch off my glasses, and pray to Allah. Everything outside seems to be bursting with color. I breathe in as much fresh air as my lungs can hold.

I'm free.

I stand up, and continue to walk. I don't look back. I never look back.

But I'll never forget the brothers I'm leaving behind. We are one and the same, always.

"Welcome home, Malcolm."

Ella's house is just as I remember, the aroma from the kitchen an instant hug.

"Welcome home, brother," Hilda says, hugging me.

"I've made all your favorites, with all the trimmings," Ella says nervously. My nephew Rodnell surprises us from the kitchen. He is now almost as tall as me and is a tennis pro. "Been working at it all day. We have fish, chicken, beef, macaroni and cheese, mashed potatoes, collards, string beans, yams—all of your favorites, Malcolm. Even apple pie and strawberry ice cream."

"Sounds wonderful, Ella. Thank you."

Up on the third floor, my room is just as I left it. All my papers, the book I was writing, just where I left them.

Warm water. I never knew something so simple and pure could feel like a luxury. I let the tub fill with piping hot water, dip my toes in before submerging my entire self. I hug my knees to my chest and sit in silence, letting the water cool.

I drain the tub and fill it again. Using a washcloth and soap, I begin to scrub. I scrub until the soapy water splashes on the tile. I scrub until tears brim and I can no longer hear the screams and bars echoing in my ears. I scrub and scrub, ready to peel back my skin anew, shed who I was, wash away the stench.

My body was in prison but I kept my mind intact.

Hilda throws the old suit in the garbage, laying a new charcoal-gray suit and crisp white shirt and tie on the bed for me. "Bus leaves tomorrow at five a.m. We're going home, Malcolm. Okay?"

Tears well in her eyes now. She can no longer contain her stoic self. It must've been painful for my dear sister. To see Papa killed. Mom taken. Our family separated. Our land stolen. The rug pulled completely from under her feet.

I hold her close to my chest, her tears soaking my shirt, and whisper, "It's okay, Hilda. I got you. It's okay."

I step off the bus onto Michigan soil for the first time in over eight years. I help Hilda off and breathe in the cool air. I adjust my thick-rimmed glasses. I'll need a new pair.

My eyes wander about Detroit and its busy streets, the

unfamiliar cars and businesses. Caged like an animal for years, and yet I can still sense the hum of a city pulsing in my veins.

Wilfred, his wife, and Philbert are at the bus depot to greet us. They look older, mature, and refined.

"As-Salaam-Alaikum," Wilfred says.

"Welcome home," Philbert says, grabbing our bags.


At Wilfred's home, Hilda helps his wife cook a feast. After all the food I ate at Ella's, I still have space to spare. The family gathers at the table and we offer a prayer of thanks to Allah. I'm the first to tear into Hilda's warm sweet bread, and I savor it. It's just how I remember.

"It will be a fresh start here for you. A new beginning," Philbert says.

"For all of us," Hilda adds with a loving smile. "I am just so happy to have our brother back. Our family is almost complete again."

"Michigan is the best place for you," Wilfred says. "You understand Elijah Muhammad's teachings, through our correspondences. But you still have more to learn. Come to Temple with us. You can join and build upon your foundation with practice."

My brothers are official members of the Detroit Temple. Soon, I will be, too.

"I already have a job lined up for you at one of the stores."

I look around the table at my siblings. So much has changed and yet so much stayed the same. We are in a new house, in a new city, and have seen what life has offered us, no longer in Lansing.

And yet, something is missing. Or someone.

After dinner, I pace around the halls, happy to have space for my long limbs but my mind is heavy with thought, enough to feel stifled, constricted.

"Something troubling you?"

From his seat in the living room, Wilfred peers over his newspaper.

"Have you heard from Reginald?"

Wilfred's jaw tenses. "No. I have not."

"Shouldn't we look for him?"

"It would be against the rules of Islam," he says in a hard voice that reminds me of Papa. "He was suspended."

"If it wasn't for Reginald, I would not be here today. He is our brother, our blood brother. That should have some precedence."

His face holds several expressions before he sighs.

"You must be reasonable."

"Reasonable?" I snap. "Papa would never let one of his sons fall."

Wilfred places down his newspaper.

"What you're saying is blasphemy, Malcolm! Everyone here abides by rules. You are under my custody. I expect you to use your good judgment."

At night I can still hear the echoes of the prisons. The screams. The guards' batons. I can almost feel their boots on my neck. I wonder who is in the hole. I ask Allah to protect them and to give them emotional strength and comfort.

The night is chilly, Detroit winds blowing against the windows. I wonder if Reginald is out in such weather, remembering all those evenings we spent in Harlem, gallivanting, and how cold he used to get. He was with me at a time in my life that I needed him most. He saved me from myself. My best friend, my kid brother.

How can I turn my back on him?

Outside the Detroit Temple, I watch men with their old conks stumble by. There is a liquor store on almost every corner, a government seal on every bottle. Like bombs in a minefield, they've been thrown in neighborhoods to derail our progress.

I check the time on my new wristwatch Hilda gave me. I buy a few items before our big trip to Chicago with my first paycheck. I didn't have much, but I knew having these basic things were a necessity:

Eyeglasses, to rid myself of the ones Charlestown gave me.

Wristwatch, so that I'm always on time, like Hilda reminds me to be.

*The Green Book*, for my safety.

Suitcase, to travel wherever Mr. Muhammad needs me most.

I walk inside the temple and to my surprise, it's nearly empty. Only a few followers scattered about.

"Why are all these seats empty? I pass dozens of brothers on the streets. Drinking, cursing, smoking, broken."

Wilfred calmly leaves pamphlets on each seat.

"Allah will bring more followers to His word."

"What if Allah meant for us to educate and inspire our brothers to see?"

"What do you mean?"

"Look, I know these brothers. If there's one thing I learned in prison, it's that you have to meet brothers where they are. I am them, I know how to talk to them. We have to bring the gospel to these lost souls. They're everywhere. We have to help them get in these seats. It requires work. I'm up for it."

Wilfred gives me a warm smile and places a stack of flyers in my hand.

"Patience, brother. In due time."

It's hard to have patience when I know in my bones that

everything I've been through has brought me to this moment. Tomorrow is not promised. My people are suffering in darkness with no way out. I may not be able to save my brother, but I can save my people. Give them hope, give them their dignity back, and give them truth.

Wake up. Clean up. Stand up.

"We drive to Chicago tomorrow," Wilfred says. "Are you ready to meet the Messenger?"

I'm . . . nervous, excited. I'm so many things.

But most of all, I'm ready.

# LATER ON

*If you're not ready to die for it, take the word "freedom" out of your
vocabulary.*

—MALCOLM X

*The Black man in the ghettoes, for instance, has to start correcting his
own material, his own moral and spiritual defects, and his own evils.
The Black man needs to start his own program to rid drunkenness,
drug addiction, and prostitution. The Black man in America has to lift
up his own sense of values.*

—MALCOLM X

Sometimes, I think about my first time on a stage. The shining lights, the sweat on my brow, pencil in hand, Shorty in the
orchestra, my fellow inmates cheering. How I wasn't sure if I
was good enough or smart enough. Even when Mr. Muhammad made me chief spokesperson for the Nation, that familiar fear crept up my spine. But I could hear Akil's voice . . .
*follow your passion.* And my passion is to rid my people of

unwarranted pain—to see my people free. You can't separate peace from freedom, because no one can be at peace unless he has his freedom.

*Up, up, you mighty race!*

The room is packed with thousands of brothers and sisters from all over the country. Florida, Alabama, Kentucky. All newly recruited. To think we started with just four temples. Now we're at almost two dozen. Each face holds a memory, of a street corner or a hall from which I collected them like butterflies. Together, we are changing the world for our people. Just as Papa wanted.

"Brothers and sisters, I present to you: Minister Malcolm X!"

There's my cue.

"As-Salaam-Alaikum," I say, giving the familiar greeting, staring into a sea of beautiful brown faces. "Who are you? What is your native tongue? What is the name of your great-great-great-grandfather? Who was his great-grandmother? Who is the God to whom they prayed? Where did they live? What kind of work did they do?

"The white man named us after himself—Jones, Smith, Jackson. He convinced us that our people back home were savages and animals in the jungle. Well, Islam tells the truth. Islam respects righteousness. Men are revered as men. And man protects and respects his woman and children. We honor our bodies with good food, good health, and hygiene. And, we pray to God, Allah, for His guidance, sustenance, and mercy. And it is the Honorable Elijah Muhammad who is Allah's noble messenger. He is our honorable teacher . . ."

Once I'm done, the audience is on its feet, cheering and chanting.

"Allahu Akbar! God is Great! Allahu Akbar!"

My forehead is always a bit damp after a sermon. It reminds me of Papa, how passionately he spoke from the pulpit. I always invite his spirit to take over during our Temple services.

One of the brothers gives me a handkerchief as I step off the stage to a continued thunderous applause. Another gives me a cup of water. Members have already gathered and lined up for quick introductions, words of encouragement, or just a simple handshake. Security gathers tightly around me. We are united. We are family.

A few of the sisters pass out refreshments and information to the newer attendees, including the newspaper I started. An inspiration from my Norfolk days, a legacy from Mom. As I head for the restroom, I feel a tap on my shoulder.

"Brother Minster," Sister Aisha says, smiling. "Wonderful sermon, sir, riveting. As always, you take my breath away."

I keep a respectful space between us. I'm always careful how I engage with the sisters at any temple.

"Thank you, sister. Just remember, all our praise is for Allah and His Honorable Messenger Elijah Muhammad."

"Before you run off, I just wanted to know if you've given much thought to what I asked last week, Brother Minister?"

"I'm sorry, sister, I can't seem to recall."

She gives a bashful smile. "I asked when you were thinking about taking one of these sisters as your wife. A good Muslim man needs a good Muslim wife, sir."

Another question about marriage. It seems to be coming from every angle.

I stiffen but smile. "Sister, at this moment I have too much important work to do. Our people have been asleep for a long time. They need shock treatment, sister. They must be awakened to their humanity before we take action. And that requires a lot of work." I turn to my assistant. "Car. Now, please."

As we make our way toward the door, I avoid the long stares from sisters who wonder the same as Sister Aisha. I could give everyone a dozen reasons why marriage is not in the cards for me right now.

But the real reason . . . Sophia. She laid the foundation of distrust. I often think I can never trust a woman again. I can't risk sabotaging my purpose by entangling my heart.

"Brother Minister! Oh, I'm glad I caught you before you left," Brother Joseph says. He handles the affairs of several of our fully owned businesses. He is one of our most trusted brothers.

"Brother Joseph, how are the children? I trust classes are going well?"

"Yes, yes, all fine, Brother Minister. Classes are going just as you prescribed. But I wanted to introduce you to one of our newest members. She is from your hometown, Detroit."

Her skin glows like fresh brown sugar. She walks over to us with such pride and grace, a beaming light surrounding her.

"This is Sister Betty X. She is a nursing student and she lectures the young sisters on health and hygiene."

For a moment, a foreign sense of peace consumes me and I'm almost lost in her beautiful brown eyes. They shine with gentility and kindness, and I feel a beat in the part of my heart I had long thought was gone.

"Hello, Sister Betty." I say her name like sweet music. "I'm . . . Minister Malcolm X."

She smiles. "Yes, Brother Minster, I know who you are."

*Malcolm and his half sister, Ella (far right), with friends at a park in Boston*

# MORE INFORMATION

## THE NATION OF ISLAM

In 1952, Mr. Muhammad appointed Malcolm, age twenty-seven, as minister and chief spokesman for the Nation of Islam. In just three years, Malcolm was credited for increasing four temples to fifteen temples, and later to fifty temples by 1958. Membership increased from a handful to tens of thousands by the late 1950s and to several hundreds of thousands by the early 1960s. In his role, Malcolm successfully displayed a focused leadership and organizational skills matched by no other.

The Nation of Islam's income ballooned to tens of millions of dollars annually. Malcolm incorporated into the Nation of Islam classes and lectures the principles of self-help, self-determination, and cooperative economics like those Garveyite principles introduced to him by his parents. The Nation of Islam expanded to own bakeries; barbershops; coffee shops; grocery stores; cleaners; a printing plant; retail stores; real estate, including three apartment buildings in Chicago; a fleet of tractor trailers; and farmland in the states of Michigan, Alabama, and Georgia. It is safe to say that the NOI owned the largest Black-owned businesses in the United States during the Jim Crow era.

The children in the NOI attended separate schools owned

and operated by the NOI with a curriculum based on truth and which encouraged self-love and a love for literature. Malcolm also founded the newspaper known today as *Muhammad Speaks*.

Malcolm worked closely with attorneys to guarantee that Muslims were permitted to exercise their First Amendment rights of freedom of religion while in prison. Prior, Islam was not recognized nor were Muslims permitted to practice their religion; but Christians were. The lawsuit provided key legal precedence for prisoners of all Islamic sects seeking accommodations for their religious practices.

## CHARLESTOWN STATE PRISON

The Charlestown State Prison opened its doors in 1805. The prison was located at Lynde's Point, a bulge of land that sits north of downtown Boston across the Charles River. It is only five miles from Malcolm's old haunts in Roxbury and ironically a mere half mile from Bunker Hill Memorial, which commemorates a major battle in the United States' fight for freedom from the British. The prison initially housed thirty-four inmates, but that number grew to include many hundreds over the next century. As the inmates increased, the prison became cramped, and several expansion and reconfiguration projects were introduced in 1828, 1850, and 1867. It was rebuilt in 1878.

Prisoners were expected to work without pay on various tasks such as stonecutting, tin work, wood carving, and cabinetry. After the turn of the century, prisoners also made license plates, much like Malcolm does in this novel. Between work hours, men would return to very simple living quarters, composed of a bed, a bowl for water, and a bucket as a latrine. There was no running water in the cellblocks.

Today, the site of Charlestown State Prison is home to Bunker Hill Community College.

## NORFOLK PRISON COLONY

Founded in 1927, the Norfolk Prison Colony was the first medium security prison of its kind. Its approach was rooted in redemption rather than punishment. The primary goal of the facility was rehabilitation, helping prisoners reintegrate into society with practical skills and knowledge, thereby reducing the rate of repeat offenses and allowing the prisoners to become productive members of their communities. Programming included school courses, work/trade training, and cooperative economics, which encouraged prisoners to take an active role in their own rehabilitation. The facility was designed to feel more like a college campus that closely resembled the outside world, which included having a library, newspaper, jazz orchestra, baseball team, self-sustaining farm, and debate team, which went undefeated for seven straight years.

The progressive reform tactics were met with criticism but had lasting effects on its inhabitants. By the 1980s, most of its programming was eliminated to mimic the strict policies throughout the country that has yet to produce the same positive results.

# TIMELINE

**May 19, 1925:** Malcolm is born to Earl and Louise Little in Omaha, Nebraska. Malcolm has three older siblings to welcome him into the family: Wilfred, Hilda, and Philbert.

**December 1926:** After threats from the Ku Klux Klan, the Littles leave Omaha and move to Milwaukee, Wisconsin.

**August 23, 1927:** Reginald Little is born in Milwaukee.

**1928:** Wesley, the sixth child, is born to the Littles.

**1929:** The Little family moves again, this time to Lansing, Michigan. On August 11, Earl and Louise's youngest child, Yvonne Inez Little, is born. In October, the stock market crashes, launching the financial crisis now known as the Great Depression. The following month, the Littles' family home is burned down by a local white supremacist group called the Black Legion.

**September 28, 1931:** Malcolm's father, Earl Little, is killed. Malcolm is six years old.

**August 31, 1938:** Robert Little, Malcolm's half brother and youngest sibling, is born to Louise Little in Lansing, Michigan.

**December 23, 1938:** Louise Little is diagnosed by the state as mentally ill and sent to the Kalamazoo State Mental Hospital.

**1939:** Malcolm moves to Mason, Michigan, and attends Mason Prep, a nearly all-white school. He does well there, earning straight A's and being elected president of his seventh-grade class. But his teacher discourages him from pursuing his goal of becoming a lawyer. Malcolm drops out of school.

**1940:** Fifteen-year-old Malcolm visits his half sister, Ella Collins, in Roxbury, a predominantly Black community in Boston, Massachusetts. He moves in with her the following winter.

**1942–1945:** Malcolm lives in Harlem, New York, working first for a train company, then at various jobs in and around the nightclub scene. During his time in Harlem, he has a front-row seat to the performances of some of the greatest stars in Black music history.

**1945:** Malcolm returns to Roxbury after some business goes bad in Harlem. His white girlfriend, Sophia, and her friend convince Malcolm and Malcolm "Shorty" Jarvis to rob houses in wealthy white neighborhoods outside of Boston.

**1946:** In January, at the age of twenty, Malcolm tries to have a watch he had stolen from one of those houses fixed and is arrested. He is charged with grand larceny, breaking and entering, possession of stolen property, and firearms possession. He is convicted and, along with Shorty, receives an eight-to-ten-year sentence. In February, Malcolm enters Charlestown State Prison in Boston, Massachusetts. He serves the first two years of his sentence there and at the Massachusetts Reformatory in Concord.

**1948:** In March, at age twenty-two, Malcolm is transferred to Norfolk Prison Colony. During his time there, he joins the debate team and shines as an orator and persuasive speaker.

**March 23, 1950:** Malcolm goes back to Charlestown for the remainder of his sentence.

**1952:** In August, at age twenty-seven, Malcolm is released from Charlestown State Prison.

# MALCOLM X'S READING LIST

*The Collected Works of Mahatma Gandhi*

*David Walker's Appeal to the Coloured Citizens of the World*

*Days of Our Years* by Pierre Van Passen

*The Destruction of Black Civilization* by Chancellor Williams

*Findings in Genetics* by Gregor Mendel

*The Green Book* created by Victor H. Green

The Holy Quran

*How to Win Friends and Influence People* by Dale Carnegie

*The Loom of Language* by Frederick Bodmer

*Macbeth* by William Shakespeare

*Moby-Dick* by Herman Melville

*My Bondage and My Freedom* by Frederick Douglass

*The Outline of History* by H. G. Wells

*Negro History* by Carter G. Woodson

*Romeo and Juliet* by William Shakespeare

*Sex and Race* by J. A. Rogers

*The Souls of Black Folk* by W. E. B. Du Bois

The Story of Civilization, Volumes 1–3, by Will and
Ariel Durant

*Twelve Years a Slave* by Solomon Northup

*Uncle Tom's Cabin* by Harriet Beecher Stowe

# AUTHOR'S NOTE

When young Malcolm found himself incarcerated at the age of twenty, I imagine he felt a number of things—from fear and anger to, eventually, hope. I wrote this book with Tiffany as a way to explore my father's emotional and intellectual experiences during this very formative time in his life.

While Malcolm was imprisoned, the world was changing around him. He was exposed to new ideas through fellow inmates, newspapers, letters from family and mentors, and his personal readings. As he sorted through these differing perspectives, Malcolm found his true identity. From his studies, he earned a spot with the Norfolk Prison Colony Debating Society, with whom he debated against some of the brightest students from Yale, Harvard, MIT, and other Boston-area universities. His critical-thinking skills and persuasive arguments served him well after prison and paved the way for him to become one of America's greatest leaders and thinkers.

In writing this book, we took some creative liberties that may not align perfectly with research on Malcolm's life during this time—but we felt these illuminated his clarity of purpose and zeal for equality. For instance, there is evidence that Malcolm rejected the typhoid shot at Norfolk Prison because it was against his beliefs as a converting Muslim, not because he thought the guards were experimenting on prisoners. However, there is a long history of unethical scientific testing being conducted on African Americans, especially those who were incarcerated. For example, between 1932 and 1972, researchers at the Tuskegee Institute intentionally neglected to treat hundreds of Black people with syphilis—without their knowledge and under the guise of free health care—in order to study the disease. This systemic abuse of power aligns closely with the abuses Malcolm was identifying in the prison system and society at large at the time.

There is also reason to believe that Maurice Winslow, the warden at Norfolk Prison during Malcolm's time there, was more sympathetic to Malcolm's perspective and pursuits than we depicted in this story. Winslow's personal diaries speak to a frustration with his superiors' management of Malcolm's case, particularly in returning him to Charlestown. Winslow felt forced to enact the transfer after Malcolm disobeyed certain Norfolk rules. While Winslow is clearly more kind to Malcolm than other wardens and guards in our book, we were also interested in interrogating the power dynamic inherent in any warden-prisoner relationship.

Lastly, my uncle Wilfred said that Malcolm was an avid reader (we have provided for you a suggested booklist), but it was this book in particular that helped my father win his parole: *How to Win Friends and Influence People* by Dale Carnegie.

I remain awed by young Malcolm's brilliance and resilience during his time in prison. Despite his lack of formal education, Malcolm was confident in his intellectual prowess and used his voice for the betterment of others. He knew he was the equal of any man. And so are you.

# ACKNOWLEDGMENTS

### Ilyasah Shabazz

First and foremost, I give my undying gratitude to God the Almighty!

Also, my super-duper gratitude to the people who aided me in the process of bringing this story to life. I am, of course, grateful for the strength and support of my family, who share my commitment to imparting, safeguarding, and preserving Malcolm's legacy to future generations. Again, to my most endearing mother, for keeping my father's presence alive in our home. To my five sisters—Attallah, Qubilah, Gamilah Lumumba, Malikah, and Malaak—as well as my nephews and niece—Malcolm, Malik, and Bettih-Bahiyah—with eternal love.

To my paternal grandparents, Reverend Earl and Louise Langdon Norton-Little. Thank you for shining your light.

To all my father's siblings, who endured unfathomable trials and triumphed. All of the remaining "Littles" who shared the many family stories of accuracy, including my father's eldest sister, my beloved aunt Hilda Little. She sacrificed her life for her parents, Earl and Louise, and her seven siblings and other relatives, including my cousins Steve, Deborah, Shawn, Sheryl, Doneesha, Shalishah, and just the whole beautiful Little clan. I especially want to mention Ilyasah LeAsah and

Shahara Little-Brown, for sharing the countless laughs, stories, photographs, and love. And to our cousin, the visionary multiplatinum recording artist Nasir bin Olu Dara Jones, aka Nas. We are so proud of all your accomplishments as you continue to keep your eyes on the prize.

Much gratitude to my agent, Jason Anthony, along with the entire gang at the Massie McQuilkin Agency and the Bradford Literary Agency for your work in bringing my coauthor and me together. A special thank-you to our senior editor, the phenomenal Grace Kendall, for shining her editorial skills on this literary journey. And a most important kudos to my coauthor, Tiffany D. Jackson, for whom I am eternally grateful for her patience, brilliance, and promise to share a more accurate and dynamic novel of my father's young story to inspire future generations. You are beautiful both inside and out.

I would also like to acknowledge Imam Omar Suleiman; my lifelong sister Lisa Simone; my goddaughter Nadia Gourzong; my dear sister and goddaughter Inga Marchand, aka Foxy Brown; and baby C'yani; the Delta Sigma Thetas; The Links, Incorporated; and all my inspirational and brilliant comrades—Sister Aisha al-Adawiya, Mary D. Redd, Sharisse Stancil-Ashford, Karl Evanzz, Spike Lee, Danielle Philogene, Lisa Curvin, Bernice A. King and her family, Julio Peterson, Mikkel Tzamtzis, Kamal Koraitem, Omar A. Ali, Wassim Malak, A. J. Calloway, Ron Baldwin, Adrian Talbot, Michael Latt and Common, Jermaine Johnson, Molly Madden, Will

Mega (Hiram Ashantee), Ray and Zoraya Hamlin, Carmelia Taylor, Danielle Henry, Joan Balkcom, Jennifer Smith, Tony Phillips, Lisa Simonsen, Lisa E. Davis, Lauren Walsh, Yvonne Wolf, Rafael Monserrate, Patrick Parr, Paul Eckstein—and you, the reader.

Thank you, and God bless!


## Tiffany D. Jackson


First, I want to thank Ilyasah Shabazz for allowing me to be a part of your journey. I have learned so much from your grace, plethora of knowledge, and stunning resilience. Above all, thank you for caring for my well-being in the midst of this chaotic world. It has been an absolute honor.

To the brilliant Grace Kendall, thank you for considering me for this project. You are a light in this dark publishing world.

And to Brother Malcolm . . . you were right. About everything.

# ABOUT THE AUTHORS

**ILYASAH SHABAZZ,** third daughter of Malcolm X and Dr. Betty Shabazz, is an educator, activist, motivational speaker, and author of multiple award-winning publications, including her latest books, *Betty Before X* and *X: A Novel.* She is also an active advocacy worker and an adjunct professor at John Jay College of Criminal Justice in New York City.

**ilyasahshabazz.com**

**TIFFANY D. JACKSON** is the *New York Times*–bestselling author of YA novels, including the Coretta Scott King/John Steptoe New Talent Award–winning *Monday's Not Coming*, the NAACP Image Award–nominated *Allegedly*, *Let Me Hear a Rhyme*, and *Grown*. She received her bachelor of arts in film from Howard University, her master of arts in media studies from the New School, and has over a decade of TV/film experience.

**writeinbk.com**